GW00949730

K.M. Daly lives in the UK. She describes herself as a person of small interest.

it's

You

it really is

K.M. Daly

The Man from Amsterdam

AUSTIN MACAULEY PUBLISHERS™

LONDON • CAMBRIDGE • NEW YORK • SHARJAH

A CIP catalogue record for this title is available from the British Library.

ISBN 9781788232616 (Paperback)
ISBN 9781788232623 (Hardback)
ISBN 9781788232630 (E-Book)

www.austinmacauley.com

First Published (2018)
Austin Macauley Publishers Ltd.
25 Canada Square
Canary Wharf
London
E14 5LQ

Acknowledgements

Biker Girl

Fatty

&

The Divine Infant of Prague

not necessarily
in that order

'…I will remove from you your heart of stone and give you a heart of flesh.'

Ezekiel 36 v 24-26

Book One

1.1

'Coo-eeee.'

It was dawn and down on the towpath Severin Brille walked the walk of a happy man. 'Coo-ee-eeee.' When he got to the bridge he stopped and looked around. He wanted this moment to last forever. Then he turned and walked under. He couldn't have been happier.

It was April. This mist was up, the light was patchy and the first skiff passed without stopping. A second one passed. The third stopped.

The police arrived just after 7.00 a.m. The cordons and tent went up, the sheeting went down and the road got closed.

Severin Brille was still warm when they cut him down. Dead.

****

Cordelia Brille aka Butters, took it bad. She sat at the back of the gallery for three days drinking and thinking. Across her desk were twelve monthly reports on Severin Brille - where he went, who he saw, what he did - all of that and still dead.

Severin Brille's other sister - Shirley-Anne Amis - took it better. She closed her eyes and said nothing. It was her way.

The Brilles were old slaving money and for nearly two hundred years the sun didn't set but when it did it was quick and by the 20th century all that was left was a small Family Trust, a house by the sea and a real fear of being poor. Butters knew that fear now and after three days of gin, it was dark.

Her gallery was on the slide. The flat in Monaco was gone, so was the yacht. It was looking bad. Then about eighteen months ago, a man called Alan Tree recovered a stolen Stradivarius belonging to one of her friendly rivals and in short shrift it started to look up. Butters engaged Tree to keep her younger brother - Severin Brille - alive. Not well, not happy, not safe, just alive and alive only up to his 50th birthday. After that, her money worries would be over. It seemed so simple.

To have come so close.

Close to a fortune.

The fortune in question was the Brille Family Trust set up by Frederick Brille, a man afraid of water.

Early in life Frederick Augustus Brille contracted pneumonia and nearly died. He had no memory of this although it left him with a strong need to run from the sea and an even stronger need to dominate it. At the age of twenty-eight, he took over the management of the family shipping business and within ten years turned a small carrier of wool and chattels to a big carrier of guns. Guns and people. Golden times. His success was all the more remarkable because it was achieved from behind a desk in Leadenhall. From here he bought factory ships, designed new ones and counted money. He never went to the docks. He had no idea what his ships did - what they really did. He thought it didn't matter.

Brille was riding high when he got caught in a spring downpour. One of those things you don't see coming. With no carriage in sight he ran to the nearest open door and this is how he ended up sitting down in the House of Commons just as a tired man stood up.

12

The tired man was William Wilberforce, MP, and he was about to make one of those speeches. Pictures were circulated in the House. Pictures of people - what was left of them - and ships. Brille ships.

A week later Brille walked barefoot into the street with the look of fever. He threw himself into the Thames, but was rescued. He stood in the rain. He stopped eating. He lay naked in the gutter and waited for death. Fearing contagion, the family left him alone, which was a good thing because death didn't take him, a passing Quaker did.

Warmed, dried and dragged back to his senses, Frederick Brille yielded himself up to remorse and restitution. With the help of his Quaker friend - a lawyer - Brille put his entire personal wealth into a Trust Fund. He then set sail for Africa to devote the rest of his life to lepers. However, the ship carrying him also carried more than its safe capacity in irons and it sank in a small storm somewhere south of Portsmouth - all hands lost, including Brille.

Brille was gone but not forgotten back in London where the occasion of his death brought to light, exactly how far out of the family reach he put his wealth.

Frederick Augustus Brille left a fortune in trust for the first entire generation of Brilles to reach twelve noon on the day of their 50th birthday without being either bankrupt or in gaol. A simple thing - and if it had been intended as a guide to good living, it failed as each generation fought it and each other to get at the money. No generation succeeded and The Trust - as it came to be known - grew.

The great G.F. Brille - mother to Butters, Shirley-Anne and Severin - came nearest. An only child, it seemed inconceivable that The Trust would not be hers, the way everything in life was hers. On the eve of her 50th birthday she hosted a magnificent party at her townhouse in Belgravia. Entertainments and carnival floats lit up the street. At dawn the merriment increased, with all eyes on the clock. At half-past eleven G.F. Brille retired to her study on the top floor, to wait the final thirty minutes alone. She tied her lucky silk scarf around her neck and sat like a statue.

Severin, then four years old - wandered out of the nursery wing at the back of the house to the large window at the front, to get a look at the carnival below. Excited and fearful in equal measure, he crawled under a table and stayed there, watching.

G.F. Brille remained in her study across the hall, motionless until three minutes to noon then, momentarily distracted by hunger, she reached to a tray of sandwiches and slipped on a slice of cucumber. She fell backwards and her scarf caught on a wall mounted figurine. As she tried to free herself the knot tightened.

In her final minutes of life a breeze - a breath - brushed her face. She reached out to be rescued but the suddenness of it wrenched the knot and something in her neck clicked. Her body was discovered that evening by one of the maids.

Severin saw it all through the eyes of a four-year-old. He told himself that mother flew away and the big party was her saying goodbye because that's what grownups do - they come and they go and they make a lot of noise. But as he grew older, these imaginings dimmed and he wasn't sure what really happened. He thought he saw Shirley-Anne walking slowing from mother's study - like on tip toe. Was it a dream? He saw mother waving and Shirley-Anne closing a door - did that happen? Why couldn't he forget?

At age nine Severin invented a game. He collected small porcelain figures from Christmas Crackers and he moved them about on a coloured board. In the game, these were small people living on the edge of a storm and Severin came to their rescue. There was a rolling of dice, too. Shirley-Anne liked it and played it - they played it for years, although neither knew why.

Time passed.

Severin lost himself in work and made money and for most of the time he thought he was happy. Shirley-Anne lost herself in mother's footsteps and thought she was happy, too. But something inside stayed restless. Severin stopped making money and started rescuing people and for a while that brought calm. When the restlessness came back, he started giving things away. First, his money, then his marriage, his family, his home - all brought calm but never for long. By the time Butters made contact with him, Severin was a shell.

Butters sent him a birthday card. She wanted to meet and tea at The Ritz on the occasion of Severin's 49th birthday, seemed right. She had wonderful news.

Severin turned up as requested. He brought the box with the game to show Shirley-Anne, although he didn't know why. Tea didn't go well. Yes, he'd heard the bit about the money and yes it sounded like good news, except that it wasn't. Not to Severin. He left the Ritz like a man condemned. He didn't want the money. It didn't occur to him that there might have been a whole other reason for his gloom. Shirley-Anne.

Over the next two weeks, Severin sank.

He lay on his bed in a dark place and then - as can happen - his mood suddenly lifted. Flash. Give it up. It worked before, didn't it? He didn't have to keep this money. He'd give it to Shirley-Anne. She was ailing and needy, wasn't she? He could save her, couldn't he? Yes. So, Severin hit on a plan of rescue and all those bad feelings went away. Again.

Meanwhile, Butters faced the uncomfortable truth that Severin and Shirley-Anne would be of no help, whatsoever. If The Trust was to be gained, it would be down to her and to this end, she engaged the services of Alan Tree. Tree's brief was simple: watch Severin and Shirley-Anne and alert Butters before their odd ways got them arrested or killed.

Simple enough except unknown to Butters, Severin was already a person of interest to the police.

Tree's first report was encouraging. Shirley-Anne and Severin looked like quiet people. Law abiding. They had few friends. Severin left his job as a money trader in the City to work as a volunteer in a soup kitchen. He lived alone in a boarding house near Camden Lock, took long walks down by the canal and led a blameless life. Shirley-Anne was a prisoner visitor and a vegan.

What Tree didn't see was that Severin's former employers - City Bank National - suspected him of fraudulent trading and that the police were taking an interest. Nor did Tree see Shirley-Anne below the surface. She was suffocating. She walked at night without purpose and sometimes - when she thought she was alone - she screamed.

As the months went by, Severin broadcast his good fortune to the Soup Kitchen. It got him noticed. Strangers befriended him - nothing very serious, nothing very long - until in September a new man arrived and he kept close. This man was Steven Witt.

Tree saw nothing to worry about in Severin's open ways, but Butters did and with each monthly report her anxiety grew. She doubled Tree's salary and sharpened his brief. Concentrate on Severin. How did he end up with the homeless? Why did he walk out of his job - his marriage, his life? Was he depressed? Suicides in the money markets were common - was he heading that way?

So Tree followed Severin from September to the following April, when he died and it was during this time that he saw him meet up with Shirley-Anne. Their meetings were short and it looked like Shirley-Anne was giving him money. They argued and at their final meeting, Shirley-Anne knocked him to the ground and drew a knife. It looked like she was going to kill him and then - it all changed. She helped Severin to his feet. She gave him the knife. They spoke - not long - and before they parted, they kissed.

A week later, Severin was dead.

All of this was in Alan Tree's last reports but not read by Butters. Sitting alone in the back of the gallery three days after Severin's death, she mourned her stupidity and fed Tree's final report into the shredder, still unread. Where could she go now, for money?

Another day of drinking came and went and then it dawned. Mother.

The Trust was gone but mother remained - split two ways between herself and Shirley-Anne, about 5 million each - not much, true - but, something.

G.F Brille. Mad, bad and marketable. Her works grew in value with each year, although most were in private collections and rarely came on the market. But one was within reach - a Self Portrait considered by many to be G.F. Brille's finest work. Over the years, several collectors made offers in excess of its value and all declined, politely but firmly by its present owner. Shirley-Anne Amis, the hermit of Holland Park.

Shirley-Anne - the cripple - was sitting on a fortune.

Butters closed the gallery and took a taxi home. Two days later and sober she called Shirley-Anne but there was no answer. She imagined her distraught. She imagined her locked in her room, alone and confused and Butters was right - Shirley-Anne was alone and locked in her room and she was confused but not because of Severin. She was staring in disbelief at a handwritten note from an old friend, Harry Steiner. He wanted to let her know, he said, that one of her early paintings had just sold at auction for 250,000 pounds. What he didn't say, was that the picture was rubbish and that no sane person would buy it.

But someone did.

1.2

DS Rainbow did money not bodies, but Severin Brille's unexplained death was handed to him on the spurious grounds that he'd been following him when he was alive, so why stop now? He was also put on temporary secondment down at Holland Park where the last few years had thrown up 4 other unexplained deaths linked to the money markets and the quiet hope was that he would take these on as well. It was all about targets. Rainbow didn't agree. It didn't matter. He was given a desk of his own in Ladbroke Grove nick and Severin Brille came with it.

Severin Brille's departure from City Bank National was sudden and it coincided with some high-end losses but after a year of surveillance, Rainbow found no evidence of crime. Yes, Brille made impulsive buys and yes, he made a lot and lost a lot, the way traders do and his personal life was a shambles but did this make him a suicide?

Money suicides were usually violent and messy. It was the bit Rainbow never got used to - the end - the struggle - and there is always a struggle. But with Severin Brille, there was no mess. No struggle. The sand was smooth. Brille's neck was not broken, so he died slow. He certainly kicked and kicked hard, but that sand said something different - like, it doesn't matter. Like, you can kick all you like and it doesn't matter - it never mattered. Someone did that.

At exactly the same time that DS Rainbow was lining up pencils on his new desk and trying not to think, in another part of London, another man was looking at seagulls and trying not to think. This was Steven Witt.

Witt was living in the shell of a Ford Transit down on Canary Wharf. He'd been here since Christmas, shaking. Up to last December Witt was part of a victimless crime - to relieve a rich man of money he didn't want. Witt's job was to befriend the target and for a few months last autumn, that is precisely what he did. The target in question was Severin Brille, an eccentric. Witt met up with him down in the Soho Soup Kitchen, they talked, took walks together down by the canal and the job turned into a friendship. Witt knew what was going to happen and now that he knew Severin as a man, he wanted to save him. He tried to warn Brille but Brille wouldn't listen. He had a plan, he said. Witt tried. But Severin wouldn't budge - you don't understand, he said. But Witt did. Severin was walking into his death and Witt couldn't stop him, so he ran.

Now Steven Witt was a dead man living in a van. At first, he thought if he could get lost in a city - somewhere up north - time would pass, he'd be forgotten and it would all turn out fine. As plans go it wasn't much and it could have worked, except for Brille. Brille weighed on Witt's mind. He got as far as a white Transit on Canary Wharf and then stopped. He told himself he'd try one last time to warn Brille - he knew his habits, he'd wait by the canal, he'd tell him he trusted the wrong people. Brille would see sense. Of course he would.

And Witt was good to his word, at first. He did go back and wait and he did speak to Brille but Brille was deaf. Nothing moved him. Now Witt sat in a cold van torn between wanting to run and wanting to stay.

A bleak light distracted him now. Someone tapping on the windscreen. Without thinking, he clicked the door open. Thirty seconds later Witt was rolling about in the back of another van with a sac over his head.

The ride back to Danbury Street, Islington, was uneventful. Two hours later when he was washed, shaved and back, Vic poured tea like nothing happened.

'We baked a cake-' Vic cupped the teapot in his hands and smiled '- chocolate. Your favourite. Butter cream.'

Steven took a slice obediently. It tasted of putty.

'Anyway. Looking good - all that fresh air.' Vic said nothing about Steven running away. What he did say - and at some length - was that 'Steve' was missed. 'Another slice?'

Danbury Street was a well-run business. Trading was brisk - mostly in Class A's - and no one lasted long, but it was no word of a lie when Vic said now that Steven was precious to them and that it was nice to have him back. 'Really nice.' Steven chewed morosely. 'Remember this?' Vic opened a drawer. 'See?' He handed Steven a sketchpad; drawings from prison. 'Talent,' said Vic. 'Didn't we say that? We said that - didn't we say that?' The drawer was full. 'We kept them.' Pencils sharpened, erasers cleaned, loose pages clipped and other things which didn't belong to Steven but which looked like the sort of thing he'd like: chalks, crayons, rubber bands, sellotape, paper tissues, nothing sharp. 'See? Now, why would you waste yourself out there on the mud flats when you could be here - at home - doing what you're good at? You could be something - ' he touched Steven's shoulder '- really. I mean it. More tea?'

They didn't tell him Severin was dead.

****

Vic was hard to read. When he left, Steven had no clue what was going to happen next and if it would be quick, so he stayed sitting upright in the chair until warmth and exhaustion pulled him into sleep. He dreamed of snow. It was somewhere high up and he could see birds circling below. In the distance, happy people - gypsies, in circus clothes. They waved. One woman was carrying a bouquet of flowers. She wore flippers, which made her quick in the snow. She was glad he was back, she said. She gave him the flowers. 'It's going to be different now.'

Steven woke with a start. Vic was standing over him with a tray. 'Out like a light. Looked in earlier. Out like a light.' Steven was in pyjamas, his clothes were folded on the chair. 'Well, that's fresh air for you. There's toast.' He told Steven to rest up - take today, tomorrow or longer. 'No hard feelings?' he said, before leaving.

Steven looked at the tray. There was a paper napkin folded, a cup and saucer - he didn't know whether to laugh or cry. Did he really think he could escape? Did he? He tried to go back to the snow but his mind was too awake and churning.

In prison nothing makes sense, so on the day of his release Steven took a ride in a stranger's car like it was normal and three men, one called Vic, took him to a house in Danbury Street. They gave him a bed, a room - his own. Clothes - new. They said this was his home. In return, he did what he was told because in prison that's what you do. He ran errands, did some street dealing, talked and got information. They taught him how to see without being seen, how to remember, how to make a mental map of places. They encouraged him, they trusted him and that is how he met Severin Brille back in September.

At the time, Steven was watching a flat trafficking cannabis and ripe for burglary. It was in a high rise. He was coming down the stairs when something fell heavy against him. A man. Dazed and bleeding. It looked convincing. Brille said he got lost. He was more shaken than hurt. The soup kitchen sent him out on a delivery but he ended up here. It looked like a straightforward mugging. When Steven reported it back in Danbury Street that evening, Vic was moved. 'That man needs looking after. We know him. Works in the Soup Kitchen.' Vic took Steven off the street and told him to keep an eye on that man - be his friend, he said.

So Steven did. Steven was not long out of prison and he had that look - pale, underweight, shifty. He fitted in well at the

Soup Kitchen. In the weeks that followed, Brille adopted him. He saved fresh bread for him. They spoke about this and that and by degrees, Severin confided. It was his way of making Steven feel at home. He told him that he also had troubles but that helping others less fortunate made it easier. Steven cringed. The subject of Brille's impending fortune inevitably came up and in a way that was shameless and stupid, he told Steven about his ailing sister and how he would change her life by giving her this fortune. Steven watched the hungry eyes that followed him.

Steven felt bad but he felt a great deal worse when he realised who this ailing sister was. The co-incidence was stunning. He knew Brille's sister from Belmarsh. She was one of those people who visit strangers in prison and confuse them. At the time, Steven had been beaten and with such accuracy and frequency that he lived in almost complete isolation on the 'Vulnerable Prisoners' wing. Then this gentle person arrived - the visitor. She smelled of flowers and told him to have hope. 'You were something, once -' she said through the glass 'you could be again.'

Autumn turned into a wet winter and Severin Brille took on the look of a hunted man. He walked down by the canal at night and Steven walked with him. By November, Steven knew the stories of Severin's life and the more he heard the sorrier it got. But Steven was in a difficult place. Vic and the others were watching. They knew - the whole world knew - that Severin had to be alive on his 50th birthday and that at least gave Steven time. But each evening, going back to Danbury Street the debriefs got harder and Steven was not a good liar.

It was clear they were keeping Severin alive long enough for him to pass his wealth on and then Steven would lead them to Shirley-Anne. Steven tried to keep Severin and Shirley-Anne apart. It didn't help.

Christmas came, time was running out and Steven started shaking, so he ran. He got as far as Canary Wharf - but it was like he'd left a bit of himself behind. He went back to the canal again and again, to persuade Severin to run but with each meeting Severin got harder to reach and at their last meeting Severin looked like a ghost - he told Steven not to worry. He said soon he would be the happiest man on earth.

Four weeks ago.

****

Three days after Severin's body was discovered DS Rainbow paid Shirley-Anne Amis a visit. Routine. He knew Severin and Shirley-Anne met up. He knew their meetings were short and that she gave him money. Now he wanted to know, why? The visit didn't take long. No, Shirley-Anne couldn't call to mind anything unusual about her late brother - she hardly knew him. They were not a close family. He - dear Severin - had some kind of business proposition - he needed a loan - really, was any of this necessary? Grief does strange things, Rainbow knew this, but there was a woodenness to Shirley-Anne that was odd, like she was reading from a script. Rainbow's attention wandered. He noticed framed photographs on a side table. Happier times. 'This you?'

'Yes. Rowed for Oxford. A long time ago.'

An hour later, Dr Gilmore's car pulled up and parked in the space left by Rainbow. It was the doctor's last call of the day and his driver - Vic - waited as usual, outside. This was Vic's day job - driver to Dr Robin Gilmore, General Physician - he'd been doing it since last April when Dr Gilmore's other driver died tragically in a hit and run. Vic liked his job because it made sense, under the circumstances. He also liked it because it brought him to Paradise - which is something he didn't expect.

No one did.

1.3

Severin was gone and Shirley-Anne was happier than she'd ever been.

Friends were coming back. 'Now is your time' they said. Her estranged sister, Butters, was back. 'Don't bury yourself' she said. 'You have a husband - a life - don't let this go' she said. Now it was all about the mystery picture. Who bought it - and why? Was Shirley-Anne - daughter of the great G.F. Brille - coming into the market again? Was she a money maker? 'This is your chance -,' said Butters. She offered Shirley-Anne gallery space - she'd do it for nothing. 'We're family, after all' she said.

It was three o'clock in the morning and Shirley-Anne listened for Tom coming in. There was thunder in the air. A picture - poor by any standards - sold, and now people wanted her. 'Come back.' It was meant to happen. This. She'd been hiding too long - and why? Really, why? A bright light flashed. Yes, she thought.

Severin was gone. What was there left to be afraid of? It was time to be Out.

Out in the rain. Out in the storm - just plain Out.

Thunder split overhead. The curtain lifted and the first gust of an early summer storm jumped in and rolled down the hall like a mad thing.

****

It did some damage. The storm. It broke a loose pane upstairs outside the office and soaked the carpet, but it also brought Vic to Paradise.

Paradise was Miss Penelope Richmond, secretary to Mrs Shirley-Anne Amis. She wasn't a prostitute or drug addict or mental. She was Miss Penelope Richmond and she walked on air. Tinkle. Vic lived a lot in his mind. He thought about things and this made them real. But his longing for the divine Miss Richmond held him still. On the one hand she was flesh and blood and he wanted to eat her, but - on the other, she was too bright to be true and he wanted to run and hide. So, he ended up doing nothing and it might have stayed but for Severin Brille and DS Rainbow.

After DS Rainbow left Shirley-Anne back in April, Dr Gilmore's visit - also routine - turned into something much longer and just before ten o'clock, a wispy black woman came up from the basement and called Vic in. This was La Petite, the maid, and she had cocoa.

Vic had never been inside the Amis house before. He sat at the pantry table warmed by cocoa and scones and with time passing his natural inclination to meddle drew him to the broken toaster, which he mended. Then the bird cage. He oiled its hinges, smoothed the cuttlefish and changed the water. He was dimly aware of shouting upstairs but his thoughts idled on Penelope Richmond - had she ever sat in this chair - was she still in the house - etc? And this gave him an appearance of such calm that La Petite determined to invite him back into the pantry next time and that is how Severin Brille changed Vic's life.

After that, every Tuesday when the doctor came to visit upstairs, Vic came to visit downstairs and mended stuff. La

Petite was passed her eightieth year and unsteady. Vic's visits made her remember what companionship was like and once it started, it was hard to let go. The fact that she couldn't speak English and Vic couldn't speak Creole didn't matter. It was a high point in the week.

But La Petite's need for companionship did not blind her. There was something not right about Vic. The way he froze when someone came down the stairs, or how his eyes scanned - like he was looking for something. She saw no malice in it and eventually put it down to shyness. In her young life back in Haiti, it was not uncommon for lower servants to go strange when - if ever - they entered the big house, and she assumed this to be the case, now. She did what she could to put him at ease but it was not until the summer storm and the broken window upstairs, that she realised different. Vic was not shy.

The dreamy look on his face said it all. He'd been upstairs mending the window and in La Petite's mind, it could only mean one thing. She was right. To Vic's unutterable joy, he'd laid hands on Paradise. Crouched behind a side table and intent on a seamless join between the glass and the window frame, he didn't see Penelope Richmond come round the corner and she didn't see him. She tripped, he turned and his face collided with her tight bosom and crisp white shirt. The contact was fleeting and innocent but after that, Vic was a lost man.

In the weeks that followed, Vic found jobs to do upstairs and La Petite watched with sinking heart, not because Richmond was becoming an unwelcome distraction, but because she ate people. First it was the Master, then the Mistress and now the same thing was happening to M. Vic.

La Petite went back to her baking distracted and annoyed and one evening, following another argument over nothing with Penelope Richmond, she threw a handful of the mistress' pills into the butter icing. Next day, to her astonishment Richmond tasted it and smiled. She came back an hour later for a slice of the cake - coffee and walnut. It put her in a good mood.

Mon Dieu.

By trial and error, La Petite learned that the Mistress' pills brought out the better side of Richmond - some more than others. The red ones made her giggly. The green and yellow ones made her giddy and there were others that made her fall on the floor like a drunk and if there was one thing the Mistress could not abide, it was a drunk.

Alors. Un sign du ciel.

La Petite had stumbled on a way of getting rid of the bitch. She told herself it was for poor Vic. She told herself one day he would thank her. What she didn't tell herself was that the person she was really trying to protect was herself. La Petite.

July blistered. Richmond waited by the library window for the doctor's visits. She found increasingly improbable odd jobs that needed doing upstairs. There was even a week or two when she found Vic almost attractive. But it would have fizzled out the way everything in Richmond's life fizzled out, were it not for one thing. Richmond had her own plans to leave St James' Gardens and for this she needed a car and a man who was good with his hands.

Richmond told Vic she was in trouble. There was a house by the sea belonging to Mrs Amis and she'd been a fool and lost the keys and now Mrs Amis expected her to produce an inventory of contents and it was all such a mess - she might even lose her job and oh what would become of her? Oh. Oh. Oh. Tinkle.

Richmond talked and Vic melted. "Yes," he said, to everything.

The following Saturday, he drove Richmond to the coast. They stopped off at Mrs Amis' house by the sea - so that Penelope could start making her lists. They had a picnic. The first of many.

Vic glowed. La Petite brooded and Penelope Richmond didn't give a damn.

1.4

August was blowsy and things long repressed started to come up and Tom Amis, master of the house - saw none of it.

On the outside, he and Shirley-Anne were happy. She was an artist - sensitive and good. She lived for others. He was a man's man in advertising. He got the awards, the accounts, the women. He was faithful to Shirley-Anne in his way, except that he lied. He lied to protect her. He lied to protect himself and he lied because he could. The big lie now, was his job. It didn't exist. The agency - McVie & Co - let him go eighteen months earlier over a trifle. He was sure they'd call him back so he said nothing. The deception was innocent enough and amusing at first as he invented clients, campaigns, office gossip - to the delight of Shirley-Anne, who believed every word. But the months passed and the call didn't come and the lie got harder.

On fine days Tom still sat in Hyde Park or walked along the embankment and when it rained, there were the museums and art galleries and in time he planned to bed an assistant in the Reading Room at The British Museum. But the spark was gone. He drank more. He cared less. He spent too much on his favourite prostitute - Denise - and he stole from his wife to pay for it. He lost track of time and then he lost track of himself.

When Severin Brille died back in April, Tom Amis was not in a good place. He surfaced one afternoon in his studio after a binge feeling like half of him was gone. He wasn't an idiot. He knew his lies were out of hand and that if he didn't get a job - a real job with real people - he'd disappear altogether. But there was another more important reason to stop lying. Butters.

Butters was now a constant visitor to St James' Gardens. She reminisced with Shirley-Anne about how happy they'd been as children and how proud mother had been, with Shirley-Anne's childhood paintings. Tom couldn't abide her, nor she him. He knew she blamed him for what friends called Shirley-Anne's 'breakdown' and that hurt. Shirley-Anne was a saint. She came into Tom's life after his first wife - Evelyn - died. She stood by him. He owed her his life and he would never knowingly injure her; that's how he saw it - so, it was hard when people like Butters said different.

But the truth is, Butters was right. Tom was a burden. He meant well but his marriage to Shirley-Anne was blighted by the death of Tom's first wife Evelyn. He didn't see it, but everyone else did. His drinking went dark. He had affairs, got reckless and it looked like he was hurting Shirley-Anne because she was alive and Evelyn, wasn't. That's how people saw it, including Shirley-Anne. Then came the breakdown. It was the last party of the season, down at Sea View. The yachts were in. Everyone was there and a big day turned into a wild night with most guests collapsed or missing before dawn. Recollections were vague, but at some point a friend of Shirley-Anne's - Veronica Lakey - fell to her death. No one saw it and it was only when her body was recovered by fishermen further down the coast that the tragedy came to light. Shirley-Anne was never the same.

Veronica Lakey was gone and Tom had no clue. He was found semi-conscious on the upper terrace of Sea View along with a few others - but unlike anyone else, Tom's face had scratch marks. He came to his senses two days later in a hospital bed with a drip and Shirley-Anne holding his hand. She kissed him and wept and swore his secret was safe with her. She'd seen it all. Tom and dear Veronica were arguing. Tom slipped or something and Veronica tripped or something and then she was gone. No witnesses.

Oh, dear.

Tom believed every word. Shirley-Anne closed down Sea View. She withdrew from public life in order - she said - to save him. It wasn't a good story and Tom was not a stupid man and at another time he would have questioned it closer, but not then. Then, he still thought about Eve and the way she died - the suddenness of it - and he blamed himself. Then, he believed if he had been a better person, done things differently, Eve would still be alive. He killed Eve - not in a conscious, logical way - but by being who he was. A man.

So, it didn't take much to persuade him that he killed Veronica Lakey, too.

All of this - and none of it nice - surfaced again in Tom, when Severin Brille died and Butters came back into Shirley-Anne's life.

Then it got worse.

A polite man in a suit calling himself Raindrop or something, came by. Police. Just a few loose ends. He offered condolences, complimented Shirley-Anne on the almond puffs and asked about Severin. The visit was short but Shirley-Anne didn't take it well.

'Grief,' said Butters.

'He'll be back,' said Tom. 'It's me he wants.'

****

'Plain? Or, stripes?'

Rainbow's visit to St James' Gardens did it. Tom was going to throw himself on God. 'Plain, I think. Sober. Yes, sober -' and this is why he was now bent double in Burlington Arcade talking to himself and looking at shirts.

God - aka Alistair McVie, Chairman of Mc. Vie & Co - was a reasonable man. Tom would put on a tie, tell him he was sorry and God would give him his job back, the police would go away and Tom would go back to being real. It made sense. A set of enamelled cufflinks winked from the display just as something pushed Tom from behind.

'Boo.'

He straightened ready for an argument but stopped - held by two luminous pools. 'Badger?' Tom thought he was dreaming. 'Saw you down there. Took off my glasses - thought - fuck me - that's Badger.'

'Solly?'

Could it be true?

'Solly? - is it really you?'

And yes, it was. Solomon Solomon, Head of Accounts at McVie & Co, and Tom Amis' best friend until the end. He took Tom's hand and shook it warmly.

'Solly? My, God. Solly?' Of all people, Solly? Here? Now? 'Bloody Hell - you'll never believe it, no really, you'll never fucking believe it - I'm on my way to see you - and God - and here you are - turned up out of nowhere like it was meant to be - fucking unbelievable.'

'Yes. Yes. It's me.' He kept shaking Tom's hand. 'Bloody hell. Who'd have thought? Old Badger - here in Burlington Arcarde - must be doing well. How are you, you old dog?'

Tom was swept up. Solomon Solomon and Tom Amis used to be the best of friends. 'So - Solly - really, if you were better looking I'd kiss you.' They walked down Piccadilly towards the river and Tom told of his plan to get back to the agency. He was going to dress the part - new shirts and all - 'and then you turn up.'

'We made a great team,' said Solly.

'Yes. That we did.' Back then, when Tom Amis and Solomon Solomon really were a team, success came easy and everyone was happy. Amis was the creative and Solly was the numbers and the contracts kept coming. Then the slide started and Solly changed from being Account Handler to bag carrier.

He changed from being someone, to being no one. Now they laughed like old friends. Solly asked Tom about his freelance work and Tom offered to buy lunch at Rules.

Rules didn't happen but a long and sobering walk down to Embankment Gardens did. They sat on a bench overlooking the Thames, Tom talked and Solly listened and slowly things seemed less funny and less certain '…thought you of all people would be glad to see me back. I mean, I know it's a cut-throat business, young blood and all that but -'

'Just thinking of you,' said Solly, throwing crusts at the pigeons.

'Thing is - I'm a bit stretched.'

'Broke?'

'Yes.'

'Welcome to the club.'

Tom said he was tired of being freelance. People didn't pay their bills. He was short of cash. He wanted steady work. It was plausible enough and Solly was a good listener. Tom needed this chance, he said. He would bring in new work, turn things around. 'Remember the old days?'

'Makes no difference,' said Solly. 'God won't take you back. Believe me.'

'How do you know?'

'Oh, please.'

'I'm better now. Sober as a judge. I'd do it on commission - no outlay - I'm one of the best -'

Solly shook his head.

'If I could just meet him -'

'Don't -' Solly snapped '- don't even come into the building. You'll burn whatever chance you have. Trust me.' Solly told stories. Things had changed. The Bubex account walked last year. Tex Mex, followed. God lost the Ferrari on the horses and now he was talking to the Russians. 'Fuckers -,' said Solly '- can't move for fur and huskies.' Solly wasn't telling Tom anything he wanted to hear but it was OK; more than OK - and when the afternoon ebbed and the rush hour started, they were still on the bench and it was still, OK. Tom didn't go back to the agency and he didn't speak to God. Instead, he found Solly and Solly would help.

'But on one condition.'

'Anything.'

'I need to know everything. What you do, who you see, where you go - this time no fuck up.'

****

As Tom and Solly watched the sun set over Waterloo Bridge, Vic watched it set over Chelsea.

'- you're like a girl in love,' said Gilmore, in the back of the car. It stung.

'- and that's the second fucking red light -'

'- No, sir - orange, sir - I was committed.'

They were driving over Battersea Bridge on their way to a Private View in Chelsea Harbour. A last minute invitation which neither wanted. Shirley-Anne's mystery painting - *'Poppies in a Jar'*- had surfaced and was being shown at this special view. She insisted Gilmore attend.

Vic didn't want this either, because he hoped and feared Penelope Richmond would be there and he would die.

Things between him and Richmond had changed.

Up to a few weeks ago, she was all over him and then - poof - gone. No word, no explanation, nothing. He still stopped by on his days off but she was never there. He left her a note but she didn't answer. What did he do?

'Ah -' they pulled into a private cul-de-sac '- you know what to do?'

'Yes, sir.'

Gilmore left Vic to park the car and wait. Alone and tormented, Vic tried again to take apart this thing with Richmond but it wasn't a broken hinge or a faulty cable and the more he pulled at it the worse it got. Something had gone wrong - but what? All the signs were good - she threw herself on him - she waited by the window and smiled and waved and called him up and said he was clever and she loved it down by the sea and then nothing.

Cars - big ones - were arriving. Drivers stood in groups to admire the tight parking. Smoking and laughing, they knew each other and beckoned to Vic to join in. Vic waved back but didn't move. Last week he thought he saw Richmond in Holland Park Avenue. He followed her and he hated himself for it. It was starting to rain. She was on the other side of the road and he had an umbrella in the car. But just as the downpour came, she dipped under another umbrella. Who's umbrella? Who?

A sharp tap on the windscreen snapped him back to the moment. Waiters with trays were coming down the street. There were sandwiches and pastries and the mood was good. Everyone was busy. Now was the time.

Vic left the car and walked.

1.5

Chelm House was at the end of a gated cul-de-sac. Stragglers were still going in and Vic had no problem getting past security.

'Drink, sir?'

'Coat?'

Invisible hands gave him a glass and a catalogue and guided him in. Back in familiar territory, his mind eased. He took the central staircase checking for CCTV cameras, panic buttons, fire exits and easy exits. A couple noticed him lifting the corner of a picture. They smiled and moved on. He lifted it again. No alarms, no sensors, no sprinklers - too good to be true.

On the top floor he poured his drink into a vase and concluded wrongly, that the place was unprotected. What he didn't see were the multiple pin size cameras following everything, including him. Below, two women got out of a taxi. One, dressed in a grey dress like a gymslip raised her hand, slow. Her companion - a tall thin woman, in yellow - waved strong and clear. Harry Steiner - host of the Private View - watched them approach from the top of the steps, arms open like a welcoming Caesar. 'Darling, Shirley-Anne. Welcome to Chelm. Oh, darling, darling - welcome -'

The smaller woman stalled. 'Mr Steiner? Harry?' She coughed. 'Is that you?'

'Mr Steiner?' He boomed. Two men in black appeared from nowhere.

'Will you listen to her -?' Steiner's humour was warm '- come in. Come in. The gang's all here - dying to meet -'

A marble lobby opened up and other hands, gentle and precise, took their coats and bags. 'Yes. Oh, stupid me - Harry. Sorry. Sorry. You know Miss Richmond? Penelope. My assistant. Oh -?' Shirley-Anne let herself be carried by an invisible current down the corridor and only when a heavy door clicked behind her and a forgotten quietness returned, did it start to feel real. She was back.

'Shirley-Anne. Shirley-Anne, let me look at you. How long has it been?'

Time sighed. 'I can hardly believe it. Here -' they were in Steiner's library '- sit - tell me all - really, where have the years gone?'

'Don't ask - and please don't tell me, I haven't changed. I'm a wreck. I know it, the world knows it - well, the few that remember.' This was easier than she thought.

'Ah, time has no mercy for any of us - but you do look marvellous Shirley-Anne, you do. Drink?'

She sat stiff backed, her hands like tame doves on her lap. 'No. Thanks, but no.'

Steiner poured a large single malt and raised his glass - 'to you.' The French windows were ajar and the buzz and the music from the courtyard below, came in. 'Yes. Well. Here I am. Here we are. You met my assistant, Penelope Richmond? Oh - I've said that.'

Steiner jolted 'that lady? That was Ms Richmond and I whisked you away? Oh - I'll get someone to fetch her' Steiner raised a hand and the library door opened silently.

'No. No, I'm fine.'

'Sure?'

'Yes. Fine. Why wouldn't I be? Loves a party - these young things.'

Steiner smiled and nodded and the door closed again. 'Very well. No doubt we'll catch up -' he looked down into the courtyard and smiled. Small groups eddied, trays of drinks and canapés floated. 'After all, it's her show really.'

'Yes - but Harry I had no idea, you must believe me -' it was an embarrassing fact that this meeting, this Private View, this whole evening, came from a chance phone call four months earlier. Penelope Richmond - announcing herself as Publicist for Shirley-Anne Brille, Artist - contacted Harry Steiner to tell him that Shirley-Anne was coming back into the market and that now would be a good time to buy in. Steiner warmed to the girl's naivety. It was like getting a daisy from a child and perhaps he was also a little flattered. Like everyone else, he knew about the spectacular sale of *'Poppies in a Jar.'* But unlike anyone else, he also knew the buyer. He was.

Shirley-Anne's decision to attend this evening had been a last minute thing. She dithered - half wanting, half fearing - then on impulse, she sent round two works for sale. She said it wasn't an easy thing to do - she still couldn't believe anyone would want them - but Steiner was persuasive. He said he'd acquired the recent - now famous - painting *'Poppies in a Jar;'* he was showing it on behalf of a client and interest was growing. How could Shirley-Anne refuse? All three pictures were now in a room specifically for them at the top of the house. He poured another glass and put it in Shirley-Anne's hand. 'Your favourite.' She drank without thinking.

Steiner talked about the art market - slippery with new money from Russia and China. There were fortunes, he said, waiting. He was an amusing storyteller and for nearly an hour, he told of trials and tribulations and occasional flutters of good fortune and Shirley-Anne - now a little tipsy - laughed until she cried. Then, she really cried. When silence fell, it was hard. How could she go on pretending? She was not part of this world anymore. She'd fallen from grace, she knew that - and in this world, when you fall there is no way back. She knew that, too.

So, why was she here? Really, here? 'You know, Harry, I can't apologise enough. All of those people out there. You've gone to such trouble; I hope not on my account -?'

'Don't.' He pressed a finger to her lips. 'We've been over this.' And it was true: they had been over this. 'This' being Harry Steiner's version of why Shirley-Anne was really here and it was simple. The time had come for Shirley-Anne to reclaim her life. He told her what everyone else told her i.e. *'Poppies in a Jar'* was proof positive that the world wanted her back. What he also told her was that he valued his reputation for being the first to spot talent. All true. Steiner's Summer Views were a thing not to be missed. So it made sense for him to court Shirley-Anne and it made sense for her to let him. And besides, they were friends - weren't they? What he didn't say was that there was a whole other reason for his interest in Shirley-Anne.

Steiner and his wife Emily, were part of the old crowd. The 'set'. He had good reason to remember Shirley-Anne's mother because it was she who turned him from selling second hand prints to tourists, to selling real stuff to real people for real money. They met when he let her use his shop doorway, for a day. It gave an unusual view of the street, she said - and other traders had refused.

A month later, he received a cartoon signed G.F. Brille. He never saw her again and years later, after her death, he sold the cartoon. It didn't make much but it did make something. More importantly it taught him to take risks - to go against the tide - and that's when he started to rise. It wasn't long before he got a reputation as a shrewd - some would say, ruthless - dealer.

Penelope Richmond's call did not come as a surprise. He was aware that she had been speaking to Betty Rae, a freelance journalist commissioned by Steiner to promote *'Poppies in a Jar.'* It amused him that Richmond's idea of showing Shirley-Anne's work at his summer Private View was in fact, his own. This evening had been a long time in the planning. It was meant to happen.

Steiner was solid and people trusted him. Now, sharing a drink in the library, he told Shirley-Anne how much he and Emily missed her. They reminisced about the past and about friends now gone. Life is short, he said. It worried him. He offered condolences on Severin and - strangely, just like Butters - he said it was this, this terrible tragedy that prompted him to contact Shirley-Anne, after all these years. To have a life and not use it, he said, was a crime. Let go of the shadows, he said - and Butters said that too. So here they were in the library with whoops and shrieks and music coming in. He was offering her a way back and it was tempting. 'But truly - I had no idea what Penelope was up to - you must believe that. I would never throw myself -'

Steiner refilled her glass and nodded. 'First night nerves.' He was slow and fatherly. 'One more - doctor's orders.'

'Well, if you say so - I'm not much of a drinker these days.' She sipped and coughed and they laughed.

'If you're a good girl, I'll let you into a little secret.'

'Secrets? Secrets - oh, do tell.'

'When we've done our tour, I'll take you down to the pool house. You can be the first to see. Something we've been chasing for years; Emily gave up all hope, but by a stroke of good luck - can you imagine - no, how could you -?'

'Tell me. Tell me - she doesn't know?'

He tapped his nose. 'Not yet.' The secret - and it really was a secret - was that Steiner had acquired a statue of a young man. Greek, marble and flawless. He'd been chasing it for years and now it was his. He'd driven the previous owner into bankruptcy to get it and that made the acquisition all the sweeter. Harry Steiner was not a man to say 'no' to.

Shirley-Anne gulped the last of her drink.

'There. Now, was that so bad? And this -' he held his hand in the air as if to catch the magic '- will be easy, too.'

'So many people?'

'All for you.'

'It isn't out of pity? I couldn't bear that.'

He laughed again. 'Oh. Oh. Why is it that the real artists are always the ones who doubt?'

'Oh, Harry, do be sensible. You know what I mean. She shouldn't have done this - really, sometimes I wonder what goes through her head.'

'Good for her. Miss Richmond? Penelope? Yes?'

Shirley-Anne nodded, wooden - the drink now taking hold.

'One more for the road? Here. Drink up.' There was a knock at the door and Steiner waved it away. 'Listen, why don't we sneak down to the pool, now? Remember how we used to sit and look up at the stars?'

'Oh, Harry.'

'I'm dying to show you, you have such a good eye - just like Emily - what do you say?' He took her glass '- picked it up in New York. Nearly broke the bank, don't mind saying. We'll pinch some strawberries on the way.' He linked her arm through his - so steady.

'It's OK. I'm OK. Really.'

'Well, of course you are. First night jitters. We're a rough lot, really.'

'No. Anything but.' She breathed in deep. She would do this; it was the least he deserved. 'So? Time to perform?' Coloured lanterns lit the night. Guests clapped. Some waved and blew kisses. Steiner guided Shirley-Anne through friends new and old and in between, he asked about Penelope Richmond. 'A bit of a find, actually.' Shirley-Anne smiled, now opening up. 'Working on a stall in Portobello Market of all places, poor girl. Bric-a-Brac. I was out looking for cheap silver - you know, stuff for the kitchen. Saturday. Raining. She was wet through. Dreadful place, have you been there recently? No? They sell such rubbish. At any rate, there she was - drenched like a rabbit. Well, what could one do? Oh, dear.'

They toasted again, this time on champagne. 'So, shall we do the exhibition? I'm sure your Ms Richmond will find us eventually?'

'Yes, of course. Right as usual. Let's do the pictures.'

'That's my girl.'

****

Down in the basement a litre of olive oil tipped over, a waiter slipped and two trays of canapés fell to the floor. Kitchen security radioed for one man to come down from the top floor. Two came. It took six minutes.

****

Towards the end of the evening, the mood of the party changed. Strangers became friends and promises which would not be made in other places, were made here and kept. Shirley-Anne and Steiner were back at the fountain, Steiner vetting each contact - none too long, or too serious. As the party edged towards the south wing and the buffet, Steiner left Shirley-Anne with a group from the old days. She seemed easy, now.

A woman dressed in black stepped out of this group. She introduced herself as Betty Rae - a writer, she said. She was researching a book on G.F. Brille and wanted to interview Shirley-Anne. At any other time, Shirley-Anne would have shied away, but not tonight. Tonight was hers. The two women sat talking for nearly an hour. Afterwards, Shirley-Anne remained by the fountain pleasantly inebriated. Through half closed eyes, she watched Steiner hold court and in the half-light and without her glasses she could make anything out of anything. She was glad to be here. Glad she let this happen.

1.6

As Shirley-Anne raised another glass with friends in Chelsea, Tom fell on his face in St James Gardens. 'Bit of a turn,' he said to the floor. 'Bad day - lost my keys - oh, fuck.'

'Oh, Thomas,' said the floor 'will you never learn?'

After Solly, Tom stopped off at The Castle in Holland Park Avenue for a quick one - but now on the stairs, a familiar heaviness began to pull. He stopped on the landing outside Shirley-Anne's room and let his head fall on the wall. This is where he said sorry. Sorry he cheated. Sorry he broke things. Sorry for everything. A small carriage clock pinged from inside the wardrobe; on nights when she couldn't sleep, she put it there and forgot. 'She'll be alright,' he said to the clock, but the ping said different. The wardrobe and the portrait above the fireplace said different.

'No. Really. Nice people. Loves a party. I was going to go - anyway, too late now and besides - she can do things. She's not helpless.' A white card on the dressing table called him over - he knew that writing.

'Bitch.'

He knew that writing and it knew him. The card was an invitation for tonight from Harry Steiner and that writing was Penelope's. Across the hall, the office phone rang and his heart jumped - Penelope again, leaving a message. He strained to listen.

Oh. If only.

He took the last flight up on tip toe. This was the attic where Tom lived with Billy. Billy was an elderly marmalade and a comfort. He spent most days asleep on top of the record player - his food untouched. Tom poured a gin and sat down beside Billy, the way he did. It would come right, he told him. It would all come right. 'Solly's right. Stupid idea. God would never take me back - not, without Solly.' Billy felt Tom's hand and started to purr.

He poured another and let the burn spread. 'Let go,' said the burn. 'It doesn't matter. You are what you are and it doesn't matter. She's there and you're here and it doesn't matter. It never mattered.' Billy stretched a paw. 'She's got friends' he said. 'She doesn't need me.'

'She never needed you,' said Billy.

****

'Ssssh. Bon Ange.'

Downstairs, in the pantry, Harold bobbed and pulled at a bit of wire. 'Sssh' he squawked back. Harold was a parrot of indeterminate age and origin with a liking for picking at things. The object of his interest now was a bit of wire pulled from a box of odds and ends under the sink belonging to charmant M. Vic.

La Petite, in her nightdress, hooked him on to her finger and went back to her room adjacent to the pantry. This was slightly bigger than the linen cupboard with a narrow metal-framed bed against the wall, a small chest of drawers and a shelf which served as an altar and a perch. There was also a cage for Harold but his shrieks were without mercy so he and La Petite reached an accommodation. He would settle on the shelf and shut up, if she let him be. That's where she put him now.

Harold ruffled his feathers and took his place between Bambi and a plaster statue of St Expedite. The shelf was a mix of Voodoo and Catholic, revered equally in times of trouble. Currently, the Catholics were riding high due principally to the fact that the rowing upstairs between the Mistress and the Doctor, stopped on the day she took St Expedite out of the sock drawer for an airing. St Expedite was unsteady, lightweight and chipped, but since his re-instatement, things upstairs had calmed and that had to mean something.

La Petite lit the evening candle and gave thanks and Harold held his peace.

****

Back at Chelm House, a doll like woman walked between rooms, sticking red dots on works sold. Steiner met her on the first landing, pleased to see some good sales. Shirley-Anne's works upstairs were attracting attention. The low leather seats and the tranquillity of the upper house drew people in. Individuals and small groups contemplated *'Poppies in a Jar'* and from the comfort of soft chairs and mild inebriation, it started to look like something. Betty Rae was a big part of this. She'd got a small piece about *'Poppies in a Jar'* into the broadsheets and within hours it was on-line.

Rae came back to Shirley-Anne at the fountain with two glasses of champagne. Shirley-Anne warmed to her and the words - 'gifted recluse - visionary - troubled soul' were aired with no sense of irony or resistance. 'Poppies in a Jar' said Rae, was a story waiting to be told and Shirley-Anne was loving it.

Steiner was also in good form. By mid-evening, two Hedge Fund scouts made offers on *'Poppies in a Jar.'* He declined both. He was pushing the price up - it was what he did.

Meanwhile, Vic learned the layout of the house. He knew where to start a fire, how long it would take security to move from the top to the ground and back again and when the circuits

44

changed. He also found Penelope Richmond. His first sighting was in a corner and she wasn't alone. There was a skinny woman with her and had Vic not had other things on his mind, he might have noticed that the legs belonging to the skinny woman were the same legs he'd seen under the umbrella in Holland Park Avenue. But now as then, the sighting of the divine Penelope threw him.

An hour later, he found her again - glowing like an ember - in the courtyard below and now much calmer, he approached - tentative - and she waved.

'I am yours.'

The music swelled and a line of waiters with trays airborne, cut in. Richmond waved higher and Vic waved back. He saw the tips of her fingers calling him over. What he didn't see was Robin Gilmore behind him.

By the time the waiters had gone, so had Gilmore and so had Vic.

The evening was changing again. Small groups settled around the tables, others walked back to the house. The singing got louder and a few of the younger guests started an impromptu cabaret. The security men widened their circuits. The mood was turning to money.

Steiner found Shirley-Anne in the pool house sitting on a stone bench, her eyes closed. 'It's started,' he said.

'Oh, darling? I was miles away. Reservations already?'

'Yes. Good crowd. Keen. A couple gone - good prices.' He smiled and looked around. 'Tom here?'

'No. Just me.' She laughed. 'I stole away for a quiet moment - can you forgive me?' She sighed, content. 'It's beautiful in here, just beautiful.' Light played on the ceiling. Around the pool stood statues - some complete, others busts on plinths - and in the soft and moving light they looked alive. 'My God, Harry - they're wonderful. How on earth did you find them all - more to the point, afford them?'

'Don't ask. Small fortune. Sensible people keep their money in banks - this is where I keep mine.' The pool house was always something. Shirley-Anne remembered when it was built and it had gone through many changes since then, each grander and more despairing than the last - but this was something. Marble. Flawless ivory. Smooth. Impenetrable. Steiner was characteristically modest. 'You know what Emily is like when she gets an idea into her head -' he lifted his arms in mock helplessness '- and oh, you haven't seen the half of it, look -' he took Shirley-Anne's hand and walked to the end of the pool, where there was something that looked like a large bird in flight.

'Oh, Harry?'

It was a life size sculpture of a young man running. It bore no shadow of time. Its perfect surface drew Shirley-Anne close and she rubbed her cheek against a leg without thinking.

'Careful.' Steiner pulled her back. The balance, he said - the entire weight of the statue - rested on one point on the foot.

'Oh - what was I thinking?'

'Don't worry. He has that effect on people - well, the few that we've allowed in, that is.'

'He's so life-like; not a chip or a crack - just without blemish.'

Steiner nodded. 'You can see why I wanted to show you. With this, I broke the bank.' His fingertips caressed the figure's outstretched arm. 'To have survived this far without a scratch - unbelievable. Of course, purists dismiss these; not real they say - no flaws - but that was the time; to be ugly was a sin.'

Shirley-Anne smiled. 'It still is.' She turned back to the pool, her voice now thready and sing-song. 'You have such an eye, Harry. How I envy that.' Steiner laughed then hesitated. When he spoke, it was quiet - firm, like he'd made a decision. 'The truth is, Shirley-Anne, it hasn't been easy; the world is changing. Maybe I've put a bit more into this statue than I should -' It wasn't easy knowing that all you have left in the world was there, balanced on a toe. He wasn't as brave as he pretended, he said. 'Oh, will you listen to me? - here, let's get you back to the party.'

But Shirley-Anne put her hand on his chest. She understood. Harry Steiner was a giant. For him to show fear was unknown and yet, here he was, telling her that she was not alone. In that moment, whatever doubts she may have had about trusting him, were gone. 'Thank you, Harry. I know I have feet of clay. Anyway, thank you. It's not everyone who would say how things are - really, are. I'm out there with my begging bowl for all to see; thank you for, well - everything.'

A firework whizzed and the crowd outside clapped. 'The party calls.'

'Yes. Yes, it does.' He offered his arm. Flashes cut through the sky. Cascades burst. As Steiner closed the door to the pool house a man waved to them from the upper balcony. He pointed to Shirley-Anne.

'What? Not one of mine? Oh? God, no?'

'Half a dot. Yes, I think that's what he's saying - half a dot.'

'Surely not?'

'It will be a full one before the evening is done, mark my words.' Steiner was jubilant. He imagined *'Poppies in a Jar'* gone, too. Another chrysanthemum burst overhead. Rockets shot up, squealing. There was more clapping, the music turned to a waltz, couples started to sway. 'I can't believe it. Oh, Harry I hardly dared hope. When you said you'd exhibit me, I honestly didn't think anything would come of it. Can this really be happening? Am I coming back? Truly?'

Steiner lifted a bottle from a passing waiter. Another waiter came over with chilled glasses. Shirley-Anne laughed. 'Oh, really I've had far too much -'

He poured. They toasted. 'To fate.'

Back in the library he rang for coffee. Shirley-Anne couldn't remember a time so - so - magical. 'It's like a dream, Harry. Really, you've no idea how dark it's been - all this time - how alone -' He put a cushion under her head and lifted her feet to the couch. He lit a cheroot for her. They talked of the strangeness of life; how people can drift apart and after a lifetime find themselves together again, like nothing happened. They reminisced. They talked of the future. Steiner had plans for Shirley-Anne. He said he wanted to do a one-man show, a retrospective. She listened and nodded. 'Catch the moment -'

he said '- the market is turning in your favour - it'll be better than printing money - a dream come true.'

She reached up and kissed him on the mouth then giggled into the cushion 'you must think me very sordid.' She could see that no one took her self-imposed exile seriously and here in this room with the fireworks outside and a hunger for money - real money - uncoiling inside her, she was beginning to see why.

There was a knock on the door and whispering. Her eyes still closed, she blew smoke rings dreamily. 'Remember the parties? My God, how we lived. Emily so loved my little place by the sea.'

'That she did, that she did. Still closed up?'

'Yes, well - you know how it is. One gets busy, time passes. Property is such a drain.'

The phone buzzed. Steiner sat quietly, listening. Then - 'It's gone.'

'Oh?' Shirley-Anne sat bolt upright. 'Harry? Truly? Truly? No!' Her eyes dazzled.

'Yes. A full red dot.' He swept her to her feet like a doll. One of the paintings exhibited by Shirley-Anne, had sold. 'My first sale, my first sale, my first sale in a new life. Darling Harry, you miracle worker.'

They waltzed and he twirled her round his finger. His little finger.

****

It wasn't meant to end this way. Steiner stood under an umbrella, watching the fire engine edge out. Rain and smoke ended the evening sooner than planned and guests were leaving. The mood was good and the cabaret crowd were still singing, unaware how near it came to a stampede. But thanks to the quick responses of Steiner's security, a small confusion caused by a stray firework was contained. It took two minutes and would have passed unnoticed had not a neighbour called the fire brigade.

Back in the library, someone put a glass in Shirley-Anne's hand and she drank without thinking. 'Drink this. Pick me up. Where's that no good husband of yours? Have you met Tree? Alan Tree. Friend of mine.'

There was talk of bacon and eggs. A couple nearby were wrapping up and saying their goodbyes. Gilmore shook Steiner's hand and accepted umbrella cover to his car. Steiner meanwhile, poured more drinks and directed a quiet and efficient search of the house.

Beatrice Cordelia Brille - aka Butters - shook hands with the few guests that remained. Her grip, like her voice, was firm. She offered cigars and helped herself to the whiskey. 'B.C. Brille but you can all me Butters.' She drew deep on a cigar and spoke scathingly about her trade. 'Vultures, to a man.' She poured another whiskey and beckoned to a stranger sitting in a corner; his long legs crossed, his eyes pensive. 'Oh, do make an effort -' she called over, in mock reproach '- party's over - come and join the mourners.' Then to Shirley-Anne, 'that's Stringler - lawyer from New York. Snapped up one of mother's in Miami last year - man's a shark.'

Stringler came over and bowed slightly. 'Mrs Amis?' he said. 'You cannot imagine how I have longed for this moment.' He drew her to the end of the library, away from the others. 'I was admiring the pieces upstairs, although it wasn't easy. You have quite a following.'

'Oh, will you listen to him' Butters came up behind, coughing. She smiled and shook Stringler's hand like they knew each other well. But Shirley-Anne heard and saw nothing of this. Stringler's eyes held her. Kind. Accepting. 'I understand from Harry that you've had a sale? Well, why are we not surprised?' He said the art world was tired. It needed a new spirit. They talked about art, ballet, music, literature. Stringler mentioned his collection only when prodded by Butters and even then, he said little. He had a few of Shirley-Anne's mother's works but - with so few on the market - the collection was modest. It was one of his regrets that he hadn't bought more. He said he was glad now, to see that Shirley-

Anne would continue the Brille name. It was a little known fact that G.F. Brille in her final and most successful years, destroyed most of her work. For those who knew, it was explained away as a sensitive nature. Troubled. Artistic. No one knew the real reason and it mattered little, except that it enhanced beyond calculation the few that survived.

'Maybe we might meet again,' said Shirley-Anne. She would have said more but for a flash of yellow outside. 'Oh, will you look?' She tapped on the glass. Richmond below, looked up startled then relieved. She waved. 'She's drenched. I suppose I'd better get her back before she catches pneumonia. These young things. Really, sometimes I wonder why I bother.'

Penelope Richmond was drenched. She'd arranged to meet Betty Reece Rae by the East Gate just as the fire hose opened. Rae was not happy. She'd paid Richmond for information about Shirley-Anne's seaside house and despite several visits, Richmond had come up with nothing. Rae had come to the View tonight not to meet Shirley-Anne - but to get to Richmond. Timing, she said. Timing was everything.

Stringler went with both women to the front door. Shirley-Anne kissed him on the cheek - she didn't know why - perhaps, to show that she really did want to meet him again. Steiner and two men in suits were waiting with umbrellas. 'The star of our little show,' said Steiner 'on your way to another fortune.'

'No, Harry. The old days, are gone. We're older now and wiser. Well, I am.'

Richmond ran to the taxi. Steiner shepherded Shirley-Anne down the front steps, unaware of a tussle behind. 'Well, give my best to Tom - sorry we didn't catch up - maybe, next time - ?' A hand tapped his shoulder, he turned, still talking '- and remember what I said. I meant it. A retrospective - we could include mother - time to come out of the -' a man bent close and grasped Steiner's shoulder. He whispered and Steiner's face hardened.

'What is it, Harry?'

Steiner shot a glance up at the house, then at the street. He lost balance and drips fell into Shirley-Anne's face. 'Harry?'

Steiner handed the umbrella to one of the security men and ran into the house taking the steps two at a time. Shirley-Anne ran after him. 'Harry, Harry. What is it - tell me - tell me - is it Tom - ?' A group of guests came between them. 'Harry. What's happened?' A waiter reached over and pulled her through to the library. Inside, Steiner clipped his phone shut.

'Harry? What is it? Tell me - who's dead?'

He waved his hand, as if brushing away a fly. His voice, light. 'We've closed the upper floor a little ahead of time, that's all. People are leaving anyway, oh here - where are my manners, you mustn't keep the taxi waiting - love to Tom - you really must come by for one of Emily's crab -'

'What is it, Harry? Tell me.' She stood like a petulant child, her heart blistering.

'Slight mishap. Nothing. Go. Go. Your assistant is soaked.'

'What is it?'

'The painting.'

'Yes?'

'The "poppie" painting -'

'Yes? Yes? Yes?'

'It's gone.'

1.7

Next day, Tom woke with a start. He was on the floor. Below in the drawing room, Shirley-Anne clapped her hands and squealed. Already, Steiner and Butters had phoned like last night never happened. Both wanting to front a retrospective for her - and now.

She looked up, radiant. 'Darling -' Tom lurched in '- here, here take a chair. La Petite told us.' The clock in the square struck eight and sunlight cut through the curtains.

'Told you?'

'Migraine? Poor Petite said not to disturb you. Penelope dropped me off - did we wake you?'

'Sorry. No - didn't hear a thing. Migraine? Yes. Bad day. Yesterday.' He said something about a presentation that went on too long and getting stuck in traffic. It was all coming back - the Private View, the good intentions. 'Didn't wait, I hope? I really tried -'.

Shirley-Anne sat on the arm of the chair and stroked his hair. She told him about last night - the welcome, how everyone asked after him, how good it was to be back. She told him one of her exhibits sold for two thousand pounds. She told him

52

about the special place Harry Steiner had given *'Poppies in a Jar'*, the queues waiting to see it, the kind things people said and how easy it all was. What she didn't tell him was the bit about the smoke or the bit at the end when Steiner went strange - because, in truth, it didn't seem real at the time and now that Harry called and made it OK, it was like it never happened.

The smell of scrambled eggs coming up from the pantry was encouraging. 'Let me ring - there's ginger tea, or ginseng?' Shirley-Anne pressed the buzzer. 'I thought we might breakfast on the terrace - that is, if you're up to it? Poor darling, they work you so hard.' He nodded, queasy. If he could last long enough to get at the scrambled eggs - maybe, a little smoked salmon or German ham - he'd take Shirley-Anne's diazepam and codeine and spend the day with The Racing Post. Then came a voice.

'I should go.'

A man's voice.

The maid drew back one of the curtains and a silhouette stepped out.

Shirley-Anne shrieked. 'Steven - dearest. I almost forgot - oh, do come - here he is. Oh, come, come. He won't bite. Thomas, this is Steven. He's been an angel. Steven Witt.' Shirley-Anne drew Steven forward like a reluctant actor. 'There were so many people last night, I almost fainted in the crush and then out of nowhere -' she looked into Steven's eyes '- Steven, what a happy chance - you of all people?'

And it was a happy chance. Shirley-Anne knew Steven from Belmarsh Prison. Then in the smoke and rush last night, he reappeared. Imagine that.

Steven said he'd come to the View because he wanted to meet Shirley-Anne again. Not a word of a lie. He said he never really did thank her, for prison and all that. Also true. What he didn't say, was that he came in the back gate when the party was in full swing and that Vic told him that if he didn't get back into Shirley-Anne's life this time, he would have no life. And as luck would have it - because Vic certainly didn't plan this bit - when Steven caught up with Shirley-Anne, she was ready to be rescued by anyone, even him.

Back now in the drawing room at St James' Gardens, Tom's ears hissed.

'I'm so indebted. Steven saved me - anyway -' Shirley-Anne dropped Steven's hand and walked back to the table in the middle of the room. 'Thomas, can you imagine? Steven has come to show us his work.'

'What?' Tom squinted at the clock. 'Now?'

'Oh Thomas, don't be a tease.'

The man seemed so young. So lost.

'Oh, Christ' thought Tom.

'Really, Mrs Amis I should go - another time -'

'Nonsense.'

'- no, really. I've imposed. I really must be getting along - a lot to do. Nice to have met you, sir.'

Tom got to his feet, unsteady but relieved. They shook hands. 'Thanks. Sorry. Not at my best; another time, maybe.' Scrambled egg and The Racing Post were on his mind.

'Mrs Amis, thank you so much. No, really, thank you. Really, very helpful. I must go. This isn't going to work.'

Despite himself, Tom was struck by this man. Maybe it was the voice, or the way he gave up so easily. This wasn't one of his wife's usual victims. True, he was drawn and pale - and God knows, he had the smell - but there was something. 'Thomas,' said Shirley-Anne 'Steven was telling me -' she put her hand on Steven's arm '- he's very interested in landscapes and so forth - like you.' She picked up a sheet from the table - a sketch. 'Darling, can you bare it? Just a peak? Really, you must see. He's come all this way; you don't mind, do you Steven?' She held it up to the light. 'I mean. Look at this. See, here? It's a garden - and oh, a divine little wall.' She peered close, in her short-sighted way. 'Breath taking - and the paper - handmade, isn't that right Steven? By you - but what patience.'

'Look, old thing - Steve? Steven, yes? Steven. Look, he's trying to go and frankly, this is hardly - sorry - another time. Breakfast -'

Shirley-Anne picked up another and lifted it above the mantelpiece. 'Oh, Tom - do look. A robin. How sensitive. Won't you spare a glance?'

Tom sunk back into the chair.

'There is little doubt, but that they will sell - surely?' said Shirley-Anne. 'Yours do?'

Tom waved blindly.

'You see, Steven? You've heard it from the expert. When I think of some of those things Harry was showing last night, really you'd make a very good living with these. And this - Red Square at sunset. Oh, Thomas.' Shirley-Anne held it up.

'...pastels and wash...energy...flying ducks...' All the same. Bland. Postcards from nowhere. The maid served coffee from a side table.

'I was telling Steven about your work.' Shirley-Anne spread her hands suddenly, as if admitting a secret. 'I hope I'm not letting the cat out of the bag, telling Steven -' she smiled '- he hates it when people know that he works in advertising -'

'Not now, old thing.' Tom said. 'Nice pictures. Really, I mean it.' He gritted his teeth.

'Oh, Steven understands. He's done posters too, in fact I thought you might show him your studio - a helping hand?'

'A what?'

'Helping hand?' Shirley-Anne, faltered. 'I just thought -?'

A pain - sharp - dry - shot through Tom's skull. 'Yes, why not. Anytime.'

'I did warn you, Steven, he's an absolute devil to pin down.'

'No. No, not at all. Come round. What have I got to hide?' Tom imagined squeezing her neck.

'Oh Tom-Toms.'

For a second and only a second, he felt it - and ah, the silence - 'I had one like that, once -' Tom pointed to Steven's portfolio case - 'torn in the same place.'

'Tom - we can tell Steven can't we -? Terribly hush, hush - do you take milk? There's soya if you'd prefer?' Shirley-Anne rang for the maid. 'Darling. Warm milk, s'il t'plait. Semi-skimmed - you don't mind? Organic?'

'Look old thing, can't you see he doesn't want your coffee. He wants to go.

Let me walk you to the door -'

'Sugar or honey? Tom is going to do some kind of commercial print - oh do tell, Tom. You'll stay for breakfast, Steven? We're really very relaxed, here. After rescuing me like that, you must give me a chance to repay.' Shirley-Anne poured coffee and told Steven's story about how he was just out of prison and trying to find his feet. He was an artist and she thought Tom might lend him a hand. Steven felt his toes curl.

'Oh for heaven's sake!' Tom shook with rage and anguish. Shirley-Anne stopped, dead. Her head bowed.

Steven - his back to them - walked to the French windows overlooking the back garden. 'Another lovely day. People say spring and autumn are the best but I'm a summer person and August is best of all - are those hollyhocks?'

'Look, old thing -'

'No. Thomas, you are right of course. Stupid me. I'm sorry. Stupid. Stupid.' She waved at the maid to take the coffee away. Tom closed his eyes. He had to remember she meant no harm.

'Sorry, sorry -' Tom picked Steven's pictures up and dropped them behind a chair.

'Darling Tom. No, it is we - I - who should be sorry. How unforgiveable, to spring this on you - and with you being so ill. I was excited. I suppose I wanted to help. You'll forgive me, Steven - for being such a bore? Yes, Angel, hollyhocks. Lovely flowers, persistent. Do you see that vase -?' she pointed to a miniature vase on the mantelpiece '- here, take it - no, really - I insist - hand painted hollyhocks. A keepsake.' Who was this man?

'Sometimes I don't stop to think. Mother used to say that. It just seemed like such an opportunity - for you, both. Sorry. Sorry.'

Both men walked to the hall. Shirley-Anne, mistress of the house, stood in the middle of the room, invisible.

****

An hour later, Tom floated on a codeine lift. Steven and Shirley-Anne were at the bottom of the steps in the rose garden. Snatches of conversation came up. 'Glorious - poor Tom - ideal for hollyhocks - suffers so -'

The small outburst earlier was forgotten. Tom would make amends. 'You going to stay out there all day?' he called.

They brought in the warm scent of flowers. 'I was telling Steven about that man, you know, the one you mentioned -'

'Man?' The pain was gone, his sinuses clicked open and he felt great. 'As you can see -' Tom tapped his head '- bit slow today.'

'The posters,' said Shirley-Anne.

'Ah? Yes.' So, it was out - that bit of Tom's not so secret, secret life. 'I'm afraid, it's nothing much. Been doing shots for trade prints. Wind farms, railways, silage plants, that sort of ticket. That's what I do. Old man stuff. Boring.'

'He works so hard - out all hours. You can't imagine. Poor Tom. I worry, so.'

'Wouldn't interest -'

Shirley-Anne cut across 'I just thought - with those long hours, maybe you could take on Steven as an assistant - until he finds his feet. It could help you both. You know how it exhausts you?'

And it was true. There were days when being drunk before ten in the morning was exhausting. Tom stretched, the tips of his feet warmed by the spreading sunlight. 'Well most of the work isn't done here. Unfortunately. No. It's in Holland.' He breathed in deep; this was nice.

'Holland?'

'Amsterdam, actually.' Words came up at random like they had a life of their own. 'Coming to an end - otherwise, of course love to have you along - could have done with a helping hand last winter.' Nice story. Tom almost believed it himself.

'Thomas, I had no idea. You dark horse - but how marvellous. And then you'll be paid?' Shirley-Anne knew more than she said about Tom's work.

'That's the plan.' Tom stretched again, warm and comfortable. 'There it is.' He waved to Steven as he left. 'I meant it though -' he called '- about seeing the studio. Anytime.'

****

Steven went and another batch of scrambled egg arrived. Hot. Tom and Shirley-Anne ate on the terrace. Harold sat on the railing beside them, eying the toast. The front door bell rang.

'Oh, please. Not back?'

'No, Angel, that'll be the driver. Dr Gilmore promised him. He said he'd call round today for the books.' La Petite motioned through the front window, for the caller to go down to the basement door. This was a side to his wife that Tom didn't know and didn't like.

'Darling, tell him they're in those boxes.'

'Oui, Madame.'

'If he's passing a dry cleaner's maybe he could take the dress? It's in a bit of state. No? Ah, well.'

'Getting rid of more clothes?' said Tom, without interest - it was a long time since Shirley-Anne wore anything a man would want. He buttered a piece of toast and looked for the cheese.

'No. We've been going through the library; oh, the rubbish up there, really where does it all come from? At any rate, we're bound to get something for those sets, some first editions. Sort of thing decorators go for - that's what Penelope says and she's usually right about these things. Nice chap. Willing - Victor. He'll take them over to Bonham's tomorrow. It will keep Gordon off my back. When one thinks of those poor men -

years in prison and then out - nowhere to live, nothing. It hardly bares thinking.'

Tom cracked open the newspaper and Harold jumped. 'Oh, for God's sake will someone put that little bleeder in it's cage - shoo - look there's a feather in the butter.'

'Oui, Oui - allez.' Shirley-Anne ushered the maid out leaving the parrot to follow on foot, which it did. 'Bit of a misunderstanding, last night - fuss about nothing.'

'Oh? Fuss?'

'Seems Penelope's dress was torn. She thinks La Petite did it. At any rate, it's in a heap in the pantry, La Petite refuses to touch it. Really, I despair over the pair of them; like children.'

'Tore her dress? Why would anyone tear a dress and anyway, Richmond doesn't wear dresses.'

'I know. I know. I lent her one of mine - well, one of mother's. You remember it? Lemon? Silk. Terribly 60s - but she does have the legs. Perfect fit. She looked lovely. Anyway, apparently there was a bit of a tear in it. I had no idea, of course. Penelope spent the whole time in poor Mr Steiner's kitchen, hiding. Then she got locked out in the rain - oh, really I could lose patience.'

'Get rid of her.'

'Did you want marmalade? It's here somewhere - I'm sure La Petite made some fresh -' Shirley-Anne rang '- hopeless. Deaf as a post.' The maid failed to appear, which was no surprise. She was canny enough to be deaf in any matter relating to Richmond. Tom envied that.

'What did you wear, finally? Last night, I mean?'

'Me? Oh, my grey dress; always a success.'

Shirley-Anne spoke about Steiner wanting to promote her and how things seemed so meant to be. 'Once I get my work out, it'll be better than printing money. Harry said that and he should know. He's keen to get me started; did I say that? Yes. A retrospective. Keen.'

'Oh, yes?'

'Wants to take me over -'

'So you say. Well, good for you. Good for you, both.' Tom reached across and pecked her on the cheek. 'You've always loved painting.' The codeine lift was beginning to wear off and a flat feeling was coming back. He stood. 'Might take a stroll around the garden. Clear my head.'

Shirley-Anne grabbed his hand as he turned. There was something urgent in her voice, which surprised him 'I wish you'd been there Thomas, last night. I wish you'd seen it. Harry says we could be on the brink of something -' her hand pressed hard. 'People say things,' said Tom, afraid of hope. 'Don't worry. He'll have forgotten by now.'

She shook her head. 'We need the money - my poor charity - it's all gone so wrong.' Her voice now, quiet. 'I am afraid.'

Tom sat down again. 'Of what?'

'He wants my pictures - all of them. Not just the ones here, but the others; the ones we left at Sea View. Mother's.'

Tom felt a chill.

'I'll go' Shirley-Anne was speaking quickly now. The last few years had worn away the last of her investments. Her small charity - set up for tax reasons - had taken more than it gave. 'Penelope can come with me. Gordon says if we don't get some money soon, Pilgrim House will close and anyway, Robin says I don't get half enough exercise and we could lose this house, we could lose everything - God, what a mess. Sorry.' She stifled a sob.

'No.' He laid his hand on hers. 'Don't spare me.' Behind the bravado she was a neglected child; neglected by him. 'I'll go down there' he said. 'I'll get your pictures. It's the least I can do.'

****

Back in the pantry, Harold tore a bigger hole in the yellow dress. La Petite kissed the feet of St Expedite. The altar was full but it looked empty and the more she put on it, the emptier it looked. La Petite prayed hard to hold on. It's never too late, said St Expedite. It's never too late, to do something.

1.8

'Looking well -'

'Think so?'

'No.' Tom and Solly were back on the bench in Embankment Gardens. It was early September and the place still had a holiday feel. 'Can't stay. Got those fuckers coming in from XProof at 3.30 - remember them - pest control by numbers? I was never meant for this. What did you get - mmmm - ham and cheese, my favourite.'

'Happy Days.'

'Oh, shove it.'

'You know, I'd forgotten how nice a working life can be.' The river was calm. The smell of hamburgers wafted. Tom tilted his face to the sun. Working for McVie & Co and being here, really were happy days. He'd been a fool to let it go. 'Truth is, I thought I'd hear from you sooner' he said, throwing crusts.

'You always liked them' Solly pointed a toe.

'Pigeons? Yes. I suppose.'

'Didn't do bad out of them. Cleared nearly five million and that's not counting what God stuffed away in the Isle of Man -

not bad, for a beak and a few feathers. Midas, they called you. Remember?'

'Team effort. Team effort.'

'You got the awards. Glory days. Glory days.'

'All gone now,' said Tom. Solly's plastic shoes shone in the sun. 'Still buying from Arabs, I see.'

Solly - 'thank you, yes - go with polyester suit, I feel.'

They laughed. 'And you wonder why they didn't make you Art Director.'

'No. Stopped wondering that a long time ago. Didn't make it in graphics, either - just for the record. You sure this is pork?' Solly told stories, the way he used to - funny and clever and mostly true - about God, the cars, the gambling, who sold who, the magic. Then 'I need more time' he said. 'I'm on to something - but I need time.'

But time was something Tom didn't have. Two weeks without Solly had weakened him. Hope and then silence weakened him. 'God is a reasonable man' he said.

'No. I think you'll find he isn't.'

'He can be impulsive - I'll give you that.'

'Thanks.'

'But then - nothing ventured nothing gained. I don't need you to fight my battles. I always got on well with him.' Tom spread his hands to show his reasonableness. 'I could bring in a few things - mock ups. I've still got contacts - all money in the bank. This is no time to turn business away, you said so yourself.'

'Don't you get it, Tosser? The world has moved on. When did you leave?'

'I didn't leave. I was ejected.'

'Bollocks.'

They argued in a good-natured way. Solly put a positive spin on it. 'Things'll look up; don't know a time when we haven't been on the slide - it's what we do best.' But Tom looked across at the river and felt its pull. 'I'll do anything - I just need to get back with people - real -'

Solly wiped his fingers and leaned back. 'The ham and cheese I don't mind; it's the mayonnaise, I object to. Nice day. Something to be said for this - you know - dining al fresco. Should do it more often - no really.'

The river was calm on top but the undertow could sink a boat. They sat in silence. Then - 'There's more, isn't there?' said Solly, the funniness, gone.

'I'm scared,' said Tom. He couldn't lie to Solly - not if he wanted his help. 'I think I'm losing my mind.' A cyclist cut across the grass.

'That's what's wrong with this fucking country -' said Solly. Tom closed his eyes. His life was a broken thing that just kept going. One day he was fine and the next Severin Brille - a man he hardly knew - killed himself and Butters and a policeman turned up at St James Gardens and a life he thought he'd left behind, was back. 'I've got to go down to that place by the sea - the old girl's place - wants her pictures. I'll go - the police are watching me - they think I don't know, but I do.'

'- fuckers in latex' Solly wiped his glasses. 'Shoot the lot, that's what I say. If you got rid of every fairy in London under 10 stone you'd solve the urban housing crisis overnight. You know yesterday I was going down the escalator at London Bridge. I felt this thing poking in my back I looked round and this - don't cry, Badger - nothing's worth it -'

'It's ok. I'm fine. Really.'

Solly understood. He knew Tom like no one else. 'Worries. Stupid worries -' Tom was a drunk, a liar, a man afraid of himself '- I know this sounds stupid, but sometimes I think I do things without knowing - like a bit of me is out there, doing stuff -'

'You're right,' said Solly. 'Stupid worries. Fucking stupid. Pull yourself together.'

Tom was embarrassed. Saying it out loud did sound stupid - but since Severin died, things just didn't feel right. He told Solly that he imagined things in his study moved on their own - small things, ordinary things like letters, old diaries, just stuff on his desk, on the shelves - just stuff. Things that didn't matter, just wandered. 'How crazy is that?'

Solly sat still and the pigeons pecked. His voice was quiet. 'You say you're imagining this?'

'Yes.'

'What makes you think that? I mean, what makes you think it's not really happening? I mean - and I don't want to state the obvious here, but being drunk will do that. Remember, how Shirley-Anne got me to babysit you - back then - for exactly the same reason?' This was just after Tom and Shirley-Anne married. She asked Solly to 'look after' Tom. It was a hoot.

'No,' said Tom. 'This is different.' What could he say? He was living a happy enough life until a man called DS Rainbow turned up. No warning. No going back.

'What about Shirley-Anne? You've told her?'

'No.'

'Surprised you two are still together - no offence.'

'We rub along. It's called marriage.'

'Wasn't that way with Evelyn. I mean - it's alright to say, I mean - is it -?'

'Yes. Yes. It's all the same mess.' Tom didn't talk about Eve, ever. But Solly was here and the words came. Tom and Eve were part of the old crowd - the same as everyone else except they were happy. In those days, Tom drank little - if at all. He always had an eye for a woman but it was more talk than action. Eve was there and that was that. Then, one day, she wasn't.

'- I mean, Shirley-Anne Brille - dear God, any port in a storm - but - sorry, maybe I shouldn't -?'

'No. You're right. You were there when Eve died. I remember.' Tom wanted to stop, but couldn't. He covered his face.

'It's none of my business, Badger. Consenting adults; happens to us all, if we're lucky.'

'It is your business' Tom said, quiet. 'I forced you into coming here; I'm asking you to help me and that makes it your business. You don't understand why Shirley-Anne and I married?'

'All in the eye of the beholder, but it happened so quick - I'm not saying she wasn't attractive. There are parts of Greenland where big feet are particularly prized.'

Tom said nothing.

'We were all happy for you - don't get me wrong - but, Shirley-Anne Brille? You could have had anyone. What got into you?'

'Eve was gone.' Tom shrugged. 'Shirley-Anne was there.'

'And it worked out? Between you?' Empty question.

'Like, I said' Tom's voice, flat. 'We rub along. She has her life. I have mine.

She's a tolerant soul. Means well.'

'Well then, tell her. Tell her you're ill. Stressed. Imagining things. Tell her you're barking.'

'Yes. Stupid. I know.' Tom eased. Solly could do that. He could take most anything and make it different. Better. They chatted again about the early days when they were a team. Solly and Tom. Tom and Solly. Tom got the women. Solly got the blame. It was a comedy - that's how Tom remembered it. Good times. But there was an underside that Tom didn't see. He didn't see it then and he didn't see it now.

Solly knew Tom a long time before Tom knew him and the pair might never have met were it not for two things that happened in quick succession - the value of the pound dropped against the dollar and Alistair McVie lost his shirt at Monte Carlo. At the time, Tom was working for an American agency just off Berkley Square and doing well. Solly was working in the basement at McVie & Co and dreaming of better things.

When the fallout came, it was quick. McVie & Co halved in size, budgets were cut, clients walked and Solly stopped dreaming. With the agency sinking, he saw opportunity. He would bring in new blood, turn the agency around and be the man of the hour.

Tom Amis was riding high and in the tight world of West End advertising, he was a catch. A risk taker. The big money followed him and so did Solomon Solomon. And that is how Solly knew to turn up at a nursing home in Clapham at the right time and say the right things, to a man who was no longer thinking straight.

Solly was everywhere. He put his arm around Tom Amis' shoulders the day Eve died. He gave him shelter. Tom never forgot.

Years later, when Tom was on the slide, Solly became a friend also to Shirley-Anne. She turned to him to keep Tom out of trouble. Solly told the story now, of how he pretended to faint in the street to distract Shirley-Anne from colliding with Tom coming out of a brothel. It was at the top end of Berwick Market and instead of a graceful slide to the ground, Solly slipped off the curb and fell across the bonnet of a police car. He was arrested for being drunk and disorderly. 'I've never been the same,' said Solly, tears of laughter welling up, 'you know dear Shirley-Anne gave a statement of good character; I got off with a limp and a fine.'

'I owe you,' said Tom, also laughing.

The river rolled on. 'You're right,' said Tom. He should tell Shirley-Anne. She'd help. Of course, she would. 'Still. Hard to understand,' said Solly, drying his eyes. 'Marry in haste, repent at leisure - you sure things are ok? A man can go mad in a bad marriage?'

Tom smiled. It was hard for Solly to understand - hard for anyone. When Eve died, Tom died, too. What remained was a shell. A nobody. Right up to the last, he believed she would live - and every day, he walked to the church on the corner of Clapham Common and sat in the same place and said the same thing. 'Let her live. Take me - not her.'

Eve died, though the signs were good. She'd come through surgery, she was young, strong, the worst was over. Then she was gone. Life mocked him. Tom was ready to follow Eve, but for the hand of a stranger. That stranger was Solly. 'Trust me' he said. And that is how Tom met Solly.

****

Joy rose like a lark. 'A new beginning - a new beginning.' Shirley-Anne shrilled. Harry Steiner was on the phone, giving the good news. There was a bit in one of the weekend supplements. Shirley-Anne Brille - the artist returns. Not much, but enough. Shirley-Anne was out.

The theft of *'Poppies in a Jar'* drove the story. In less than an hour, Steiner was back. He had firm plans. He'd set up an interview with a journalist - Betty Reece Rae - she had space in 2 of the major dailies, on line - he wasn't taking 'no' for an answer. Shirley-Anne whooped. Betty Rae - nice woman. Shirley-Anne skipped around the dining table and Butters - also there by chance - was happy for her. Even Dr Gilmore - so cautious - was coming round. He phoned the day after the View to congratulate her and he was in the best of moods. He wished her every success and said that he looked forward to seeing more of her work, on his return from the Dordoyne. 'I just couldn't be happier' were his parting words.

It meant something; Gilmore's approval. He had kept such a grip on her life over the years - for her own good - it was just miraculous to see it lift now - and to think - the way they'd argued?

All over now.

1.9

It was gone nine o'clock and Shirley-Anne held position listening for the door. Then it came, the click. 'Darling? Is that you? Up here.' Penelope Richmond was away a week and it seemed a lifetime. 'Terrible journey?'

This was the morning yoga and the ambush. 'In here, Angel - just finishing - oh, put your things - yes - there - on the card table.' Richmond came in and sat obediently by a small table in the corner. 'Forgive me, Angel. If I don't do this - can't afford to let my back go, now.' She breathed in deep. 'I'm expecting something from the Guggenheim - apparently, they've got one of mother's early pastels and Harry thought they might lend it. He's stopping by later, dying to meet you again.' Shirley-Anne's nightdress and yesterday's silk knickers were on the floor with a mix of faxes.

'New York?'

'Oh? It's come?'

'I'm not sure - says something about packing and shipping - look, why don't I just take the lot upstairs where there's more room?' Richmond's mind was running in different directions and she needed time to collect herself. She'd arrived late - not a good start - and with so much going on, she had to be careful not to slip. She really needed to think.

Shirley-Anne stood and stretched. 'There -' spreading her arms - 'how do I look?' Her bare thighs dimpled grey.

'Wonderful.'

'Really?'

'Yes.'

'Thank you, Angel. Robin tells me I go from strength to strength, but I sometimes wonder.' Shirley-Anne sat on the chaise long and patted a place beside her. 'Now. Come and tell me what you've been up to. Oh, take off your coat, do. We missed you - a whole week - how did it all go?' Richmond's week away had been spent moving. 'I hope you didn't do any heavy carrying and lifting? Here. Here. That's right. You work so hard, we worry so. Thomas sends his love. I'll ring for tea - still green? You see, I remembered.' They sat, side by side, almost touching. 'Well? Well? Tell all.'

'S-sorry. Head's s-spinning.' Richmond wasn't good when put on the spot.

'Wonderful to be back. W-wonderful.'

'Darling -'

A fax slid under her foot. Big, baby writing with exclamation marks. 'Oh? Give that to me, darling. Hand me my glasses - over there, on the card table. Oh, darling, my clothes - be a dear, pick them up - just hold them, would you?'

'Came in last night - 11.30 pm.'

'Poor Petite, doesn't understand a thing. Where was it - on the floor? She means well - I can hardly scold her.'

'It's from Cordelia Brille.' Richmond scanned the fax. Butters knew Shirley-Anne was being wooed by Harry Steiner. It says '...police are hopeless...take matters into one's own hands...Kitty recommended him...traced Johnnie's violin ...to have come this far...fuck up...' Richmond looked up. 'I think it's about the missing painting - looks like she's found you a detective - Tree? I can't read her writing. Do we know anyone called Adam Tree?'

****

The fax from Butters distracted Shirley-Anne long enough for Richmond to get to the office upstairs, where a surprise was waiting.

When she came down twenty minutes later, Shirley-Anne was still in her leotard. 'Are you alright darling, you seem pre-occupied? Shall I ring for that tea now? La Petite made some of her banana bread, specially. Of course, there are scones, if you'd prefer?'

'Not for me thank you. Had the most enormous breakfast; couldn't touch a thing.'

'So slim; ah, youth. Tell me, still eating the goat yoghurt?'

'Every day.'

'I knew you'd like it. People can be very fussy about unpasteurised milk; sometimes I think we've forgotten what real food is.'

'Oh, I swear by it.'

'Darling, it's just so good to have you back. Are you sure we can't tempt you - a little black bread and dried fruit? It's going to be a long morning? No? Ah, well.'

Richmond's latest house move was still in the air. Shirley-Anne was keen to show sympathy for the trials of shared living and she rejoiced now, knowing that at last Penelope had a room of her own. 'Darling, a new beginning - you must be overjoyed? Do come and tell all, we've missed you so.' Shirley-Anne patted the chaise long again. 'Sit. Sit.'

'Time is flying, I really ought to get started. And what about this Tree person?'

'Nonsense. Sit.'

Richmond sat stiff. 'Well, what can I say? A whirlwind. An absolute whirlwind.' She had a way with words. She could tell a story and Shirley-Anne loved a story. 'So many friends. Pitched up out of nowhere. Surprised more things didn't get broken. Tremendous fun. Good to come back to work for a rest.' And she had a laugh - it tinkled - like she meant it.

'But, what an adventure. I wish I'd been there - and nothing got broken? I would have been hysterical.'

'And when it came to it, we did it all in a day - but never again, trust me.' She told a story about going to the wrong address, getting stuck in traffic and losing a nightdress on Hammersmith Bridge '…at that point, I actually felt sorry for the driver. Poor man. He did his best. I could hardly scold him.' Now in full flow, telling a story half true, half not - Richmond was a very different person to the one who walked in to St James' Gardens four years earlier. She was four stone lighter. She'd lost her voice and found another. She no longer dressed like a girl. Only the stammer and the hatred remained. 'I know, I know. Sometimes it's easier to do things oneself - too many cooks - oh, do leave the fax, there's nothing to be done now. But what an adventure - is that Chanel you're wearing?'

'Yes. But how clever of you.' Richmond tinkled. 'Two Christmases ago, remember? Something for my stocking?' Tinkle. 'How did you know it was my favourite?'

'It wasn't difficult: we are so alike.' Then - 'at any rate - what is the new place like? I want every dreadful morsel; leave nothing out.'

'I hardly know where to begin - head still spinning - wouldn't surprise me to wake up tomorrow on top of a lamp post.'

'But are you happy? You know I cried when you told me about that little walled garden - I knew it would make you happy.'

'Thank you. It's darling. Just darling. A dear little house. Victorian. Architect and his wife. Grow their own herbs - and a beehive and oh, the dreamiest little pond.' Talking together in a sun filled room with gilded furniture and the wide sky outside, it was easy to forget the real reason why Penelope Richmond kept moving. Flatmates found her difficult. During the day, she sailed through Shirley-Anne's moods. She was a hard-working, competent clerk. There was nothing she couldn't do and do well. But at night, she was irritable, demanding and petulant.

Shirley-Anne saw none of this. When she looked at Richmond, she saw an orphan. A neglected girl she could make in her own image; someone who would never leave her. 'I'm glad. At last, a place of your own. You could have stayed here but I know you want your independence; well, who doesn't. Was that you I heard whistling, upstairs?'

'Yes. Me.' Richmond chirped. 'I whistle when I'm happy.'

'But of course you do - a new home, plenty to be happy about. Anyway, welcome back to your other home.'

Richmond smiled and tapped her watch. 'Before I forget, I must collect your dress.' The whistling Shirley-Anne heard upstairs was Vic. He also missed Richmond more than words could say - and he was determined not to let her get away this time. He'd been living off the memory of that shy wave back at Steiner's picture show and now he wanted more. Much more.

'Dress?' asked Shirley-Anne, puzzled.

'Yes. The one you gave me for Mr Steiner's Private View, remember? The cleaners called; they've mended it. You don't mind?' Walking in on Vic today was a shock and in a panic to get rid of him Richmond agreed to meet for coffee up at Nottinghill Gate. And besides, events had moved on and she needed him, again.

'Why, no? No. Thoughtful of you, darling. Of course, I meant it as a present, yellow suits you so. You looked stunning - you were the real belle of the ball. Everyone wanted to meet you. Did you have a good time - it all ended so quickly? I must say, I'd forgotten about the dress. Well, that's age for you.'

'Yes, wasn't it wonderful. You can't imagine what goes on behind the scenes; upstairs it was all so calm but down below in the galley I can assure you it was far from calm. Wouldn't have missed it for the world. I'm sorry though - about the painting.'

'Yes. My poor *"Poppies in a Jar"*. Well, I say mine - did we ever find out who bought it? Gone. Never mind. Did you get home, alright?'

'I was fine. Fine.'

'Good.'

'Anyway, I'll collect it - the dress - thought I'd pop out now? We're low on envelopes and the printer cartridge is wrong. Did you want anything up at Nottinghill Gate?'

'Mmm. No. Nothing comes to mind. Dr Gilmore's driver delivered in this morning; he's been such a dear. Of course, you could ask La Petite just to be sure.

Anyway -' she stretched out both hands towards Richmond '- it's just so wonderful to have you back - where you belong.'

'I'm home.'

'Darling.'

'Well, I'll be off. Won't be long. Any news on that funding application from the Roberts Trust? I sent them photos of the house in Bayswater -'

'It's all in the post upstairs - looks worse than it is. You'll sort it out in no time. Gordon was asking about the bank statements, maybe you'll give him a ring? Why are accountants so dull?'

Richmond ran down the stairs like a cat and the front door sighed behind her. Shirley-Anne felt that. She stood at the upper drawing room window and watched Richmond cross the square. At the corner of Addison Avenue, Richmond turned and waved and Shirley-Anne smiled and waved back. The dress that Richmond was off to collect was hanging in Shirley-Anne's wardrobe. It was delivered to the house last week and as Richmond turned out of sight, something in Shirley-Anne also turned.

1.10

Vic waited on the corner of Camden Hill Road like a well-trained dog. Richmond came into view - a Starbucks in each hand - and without breaking step, she gave him a cup and kissed him on the lips, like it was the most ordinary thing. That was the last thing he remembered until he came back to his senses an hour later in a cheap room just off the Bayswater Road. Richmond was lying beside him, naked and also mildly surprised.

Up until that morning, Vic was nothing - she'd grown bored with him weeks ago and wholly regretted encouraging him, but Betty Rae wanted more from Sea View and for this, Richmond needed Vic. And there was more.

Turning at Addison Avenue and seeing Shirley-Anne at the window with that annoying little wave that said 'you'll never escape' - got her so angry, that by the time she got to Nottinghill Gate, only rough sex would do. And Vic did not disappoint.

All good as far as it went. Except that now, lying in a small room the inevitable come down was hard. Penelope Richmond saw that she was trapped in a life she didn't want and it was going to take more than a big man in a small bed, to get out.

This wasn't her first attempt to escape. Coming to St James' Gardens was an escape from standing in the rain in Portobello Road. Playing the orphan to Shirley-Anne's Lady Bountiful was another. She fought with the maid and played around with Tom Amis - all escapes from a dull life. But nothing worked. She was still trapped. Then came Betty Reece Rae - another escape. Rae said she was researching a book on G.F. Brille and she was interested in Brille's daughter, Shirley-Anne Amis. Richmond was easily persuaded and within a week, agreed to go 'under cover.' The subterfuge at this point was necessary as - according to Harry Steiner - Shirley-Anne kept a tight grip on those around her and a tighter one on her own life. The weak spot, the way in, was her sullen assistant - Penelope Richmond.

Rae wanted information. She wanted things from Shirley-Anne's early life. She wanted to know about Sea View and at first, it was all a bit of a lark. Rae didn't want to come to Shirley-Anne empty-handed, she said. She wanted to show that she had taken the trouble to learn something about her first - a mark of respect. Richmond didn't care. Having a secret from Shirley-Anne was already one foot outside the door.

In the coming months, Richmond went through desks and drawers and copied photographs and personal letters from Tom's study and gave them to Rae. She made secret visits to Sea View with Vic. She found fragments of another life - diaries, keepsakes, address books - but nothing satisfied Rae. Then around August, the time of Steiner's Private View, Rae turned. She lost patience and in Richmond's mind, she turned into another Shirley-Anne - demanding, fickle and petulant. That was the point where Richmond decided to fly solo.

Lying in the Hotel Tunis now, Richmond sighed and Vic blew smoke rings. She was angry with Shirley-Anne but she was angrier with Rae because Rae led her on - made her believe she could be part of something - a book, a film, a life - when all along it was nothing. Beneath it all, she was angry with herself for believing.

She didn't collect the yellow dress that day. She didn't go back to St James' Gardens and she didn't telephone Shirley-Anne. Instead, she left a message on the answering machine saying she had a toothache and that she'd be back, soon.

Ha.

With Dr Gilmore away in France, Vic had the Daimler and insensate with happiness, he drove Richmond to the coast to the place they'd picnicked before. It was a delight. Penelope Richmond, so chatty, told him how clever he was and how much she'd missed him. He ate it up.

He ate it. He ate it. He ate it. The mystery umbrella, the legs he didn't know, Richmond's disappearances - none of that mattered - none of it - she was here now so go and fuck yourself.

At Sea View, Vic scaled the slippery east wall, like before. He picked the lock on the upper walkway and let Richmond in through the front door. If she told him to throw himself down on to the rocks below, he would have. He set out a picnic in the sheltered courtyard, while Richmond went through the house thinking of Rae and looking.

What was it about Rae? What was she looking for? Richmond went from room to room imagining Rae speaking, telling her what to look for - and what came into her head was one word - 'dirt.'

Richmond ran her fingers over window frames and under ledges, between cracks, down corners, behind pictures and - then - her fingernail caught a sharp corner. A triangle of paper, folded tight. A letter. Old, faded but legible. It read like the ravings of a deranged person but there was nothing deranged about the way it was hidden. Careful. Wedged deep behind the frame of a painting.

A letter. In the right hands, it could change a person's life. It could change Richmond's life. This was her ticket out.

On the way back to London, Richmond was quiet. Vic, wrapped in happiness, assumed she was dreaming about the next time they'd be together. Her eyes were closed and there was a smile on her lips and no doubt, like him, she could hardly wait.

Back in St James' Gardens, Shirley-Anne played and replayed the message about the tooth.

****

When Richmond eventually got through to Shirley-Anne, it was soft. An abscess, she said. The tooth was gone but the pain was terrible. They gave her antibiotics and said to watch for infection. She was so sorry. Shirley-Anne listened in silence. Richmond would take the rest of the week off. They would start again, like new, on Monday.

Tom noticed nothing. Breakfast was quiet. 'Thomas? Angel? Poor Penelope. You haven't seen her?' A circuitous conversation followed, in which Shirley-Anne tried to decide whether or not to believe the tooth story and in her mind, Tom was a big part of that. She spoke about how attractive darling Penelope was and how forgiving one might be, if a man should fall. These things happen in the best of families, she said. Sometimes, a small rift can make a marriage stronger, she said. But Tom said nothing. When breakfast was cleared and Shirley-Anne was left alone with her worries, she thought she would burst. Thank Heaven for Robin Gilmore.

Gilmore was back in Wimpole Street, reviewing the day's patients when Shirley-Anne called. After three weeks in pleasant sunshine and mostly in his own company, he was in good mood and happy to talk. He expected to hear from Shirley-Anne, so this was nice. He expected to hear that things had gone downhill since Steiner's Private View and that she was having second thoughts, etc. It was inconceivable that she would still be promoting herself, not after the painting was taken like that. Other people of different temperament might have used the incident to advantage, but not Shirley-Anne - of this, he was certain. She would take it personally. She would have seen it as a warning. She would be lost and fearful and in need of his guiding hand. This is what he expected. It's not what he got.

Shirley-Anne was angry. Opportunities were passing. She was back painting - there was talk of a one-woman show next year. Butters and Harry Steiner were competing for it.

When Gilmore put the phone down, he felt the sting of pride. He'd misjudged Shirley-Anne and that was stupid. His fingertips trailed over a flat package on his desk. *'Poppies in a Jar.'* He lifted it out of the wrapping and held it with care up to the light. Neither its speedy exit from Steiner's show last month, nor the smoke or the rain, left a mark. Even by Vic's standards, this was a job well done. If only it could have ended there.

If only.

Gilmore held it over the shredder and watched it go through. If only it could have ended there.

****

It was Sunday morning and the alley echoed. 'That's Sunday for you - empty like the grave - careful, it's hot.' Steven Witt was in Tom's studio in Bowling Green Lane, drinking coffee and a bit confused. 'Thanks. I really didn't think I'd hear from you.'

Solly had come up trumps. He'd got Tom work. McVie & Co had won a government contract to promote Anglo-French tourism - something to do with Life after Brexit. It was a big thing, for them. Solly sent some shots of men shaking hands to Tom's phone, but otherwise, he was vague on detail. Pictures, he said - 'piccies now'. In reality, it was bread and butter work, but at least it was work. Real work with real people and it went a long way to calming Tom's nerves and so much so, that he contacted Steven. Make it real. Well, why not?

'Sugar? No? Know why you are here? No? Really? No?'

'Drop more milk? Thanks. Yes - Mrs Amis wants me to spy on you. Are those doughnuts raspberry?'

'Oh?'

Steven explained - as if it needed it - that Tom smelling of booze that day, after the Private View - said it all. Tom was stunned. Yes, it was dressed up in a thin film of truth: Steven was just out of gaol and yes, he needed a helping hand and yes, he did ask Shirley-Anne for help. But it came at a price.

Tom started. 'Straight talking - no - I like it.' He told Steven that Shirley-Anne used his old friend Solomon Solomon, also as a minder and how that didn't work out, either. 'Here -' he showed the shots on his phone '- these are the people on this new job and -' he pointed to Solly '- this one is Solly - a good friend - no, great friend. So, you're not the first of her spies and you won't be the last.' Steven put on his glasses and peered close.

'That's Solly? - and you say, he's a friend to Mrs Amis, as well?'

'We go back -' Tom added, although he didn't know why '- I owe him my life.'

Tom laid out some old shots on the bench - things from campaigns, years ago. 'Take a look.' He had no intention of going out taking new shots for Solly's team and besides, in the early stages of a job no one knows what they want. He took down half a dozen back catalogues. There'd be something he could recycle.

Box files, storage boxes, piles of magazines, catalogues and books stood in odd places. There were prints everywhere. 'By the way - how much is she paying you? I mean, to look after me?' Shirley-Anne was a snoop's dream.

Steven told Tom that Shirley-Anne found him somewhere new to live and that was his payment. He'd been living in a doss house up in Islington, but she found him somewhere better - safer - in north London. He was in her debt for that and besides, he really did want to work with Tom.

Poor bastard, thought Tom.

Steven bit into a doughnut, eyes closed. Back at the work bench, Tom put out more prints - black and white, sepia, a few colour (he never rated colour).

'Not on line?'

'No. Low tech. Very low.' They drank in silence. Tom prided himself on how well he hid things. He switched on the light box and put on a few strips. 'Go ahead. Take a look. Like I told you before, old man stuff.' Steven looked up lamely; his fingers covered in sugar. 'Shots I did - oh, a few years ago, now. I'm thinking of resurrecting a few. What do you think?'

'Stills only?'

'Ideas stage. Pitch is Thursday. Here -' he took out some bigger prints from a portfolio '- water, windmills, bicycles under street lamps, bits of mist - what do you think?'

Steven had something to say about everything and the hours passed.

'Tell me, what did you do in advertising. It was advertising, wasn't it?'

'Yes. Trade press, like you - but not the glamorous end. Industrial chemicals; polymers, things that make lino stronger, things that kill - usual stuff.'

'There's a good living to be had in industrial chemicals. We'd go a long way for that kind of work; steady, predictable.' Tom ran his fingers over other files. 'This is one, for example. Insecticide. Here's another; Tex Mex, I think that was. Developed something that melts insects' bodies from the inside - nice work. Anyway, what happened? To you, I mean? Why did you leave it? Or shouldn't I ask?'

The rest of the day went quick. By eight o'clock they were in a small Indian restaurant behind Farringdon Station, still talking. 'Sorry - I don't see where a soft focus adds anything - ' it wasn't hard. This. Being here. Tom wondered why he didn't do it more often but then he was usually alone or with someone paid by the hour. 'Southern Indian. Drinking out of tin beakers takes a bit of getting used to. They don't use glass; unclean, apparently.'

'Funny.'

'Yes. I know, well that's foreigners for you.' They had stuffed pancakes and Tom couldn't remember when they tasted so good and when eight o'clock turned into ten o'clock, Tom called for the menu again. 'Makes you wonder how they make a living - all of those things on the menu - you think it all comes out of the same tin?'

'Don't know. Don't care.' For a skinny man, Steven could eat. He reached across and wiped the lentil dahl with the last of the bread. 'It's got raisins and coconut - and they call it bread?'

Tom ordered more wine although he was the only one drinking. 'How did you meet the old girl? At that bash, I hear?'

'No. She didn't tell you? In prison. I met her in prison.'

'Oh?' The waiter brought chicken vindaloo - another favourite - and milder prawn and lamb tandooris. Steven stayed with the vegetables.

'People say things to me - goes in one ear and out the other. I find it works.'

'I met her in prison.'

'Yes. That bit I get.'

Steven smiled weak. 'I'm sorry - you know - turning up like that. I had no idea she could be so - um - persuasive.' Tom laughed and tapped the menu. 'Kulfi's good. Take a look.'

Steven looked down the price list. 'I'm buying,' said Tom. 'I insist.

Consider it payment for today. Maybe even for tomorrow?' It was a good feeling.

A strange feeling: despite himself, he was happy.

Steven pushed the plate away and wiped his mouth. He closed the menu and shook his head at the waiter. 'We met in Belmarsh. VP wing. Heard of it? No? Want me to go on?'

'No. Really - I was just being polite.'

'You asked. I'll tell if you want?'

'Oh, well - please yourself.' Tom pictured men in a sunlit room weaving baskets. He imagined Shirley-Anne and her friends making it all so nice with flowers and tea and homemade cake.

'I don't remember exactly - you lose track of time - I was in isolation - yes, that bit I remember.'

'What's VP?'

'Vulnerable Prisoners.' Steven coughed. 'Sick.'

Silence.

'How long? That is, I mean, how long?'

'Eight years.'

'Oh?' said Tom. 'So - not a parking offence?'

'No. Not a parking offence, although -' Steven laughed '- it did involve a car.' The kulfi came. Steven waived his away and Tom took both. 'Tastes like rice pudding. Not bad - make it from condensed milk. And Shirley-Anne -?'

'You're not going to ask what I did? That's what usually comes next.' It bothered Steven, it had always bothered him that what little respect he got from the street was because he'd done time for murder. The first month or two inside were easy, because of it; but death is a thing you give off - and it didn't take long to get around that he was no kind of a killer. Then the beatings started.

Tom closed his eyes and leaned back. 'Honestly, I'm not that interested - I meant it, when I said I was just being polite.'

'Yes, sorry. Where are my manners?'

'Curious, that's all - about the old girl; what she gets up to when she's out.

Curious about what she wants, from you?' Tom was saying it straight, for once.

'Told you. Information - that's what she wants.'

'No,' said Tom 'there's more.' At different times in their marriage, Shirley-Anne surprised him, and not in a good way. He strayed, because he was bad. She sulked, because she was good and so he strayed more. No one got hurt; at least, that's how Tom saw it. But with her minders, Shirley-Anne got fed bits of information about him and always the wrong bits. It made her worry in a way that was stupid. At a drinks party one Christmas Eve, she threw a martini in the face of a woman talking to Tom. He hardly knew the woman but Shirley-Anne called her a whore and made a lunge for her face, much to everyone's amusement (they were plastered at the time and it seemed like a bit of a joke - except to Tom). And there were other things. Shirley-Anne went through a phase of having a driver pick him up and stay with him when he was out on a shoot - in those days, he did actually work. Weeks later, she would question him on the most innocuous detail - about a model or a female worker and when he couldn't remember, she'd fly into a rage. And then there was Solly. Solly a few years ago - when Tom was sliding and sliding fast - she paid him to befriend Tom. Stay with him. Keep him out of trouble and the not very subtle subtext to that was that Solly was to tell her about Tom's women. All of them.

Tom knew Shirley-Anne did this because she loved him and because there was a side to her that wasn't right. He put it down to a sensitive nature and tried not to look further.

'No. You're right. Sorry.' Steven shook his head. 'Being banged up changes you. Hard to see straight. I stumble, sometimes - sorry.'

Tom looked at his watch and called for the bill. 'Time.' He put his card down and calculated how far it would stretch. The machine printed out a receipt, and he breathed again. 'I know that most of her boys as she calls them, do time. She likes to help -'

Steven shook his head. 'It isn't going to work, is it? This?'

'You're just not what I was expecting,' said Tom. 'You're different, that's all - not like her usual victims, sorry, that came out wrong - '

Steven had an urge to say more. He wanted to say that prison was bad but getting out was worse. He wanted to say that he'd been picked in prison to befriend Shirley-Anne and Severin Brille. He wanted to say that Vic and the silent ones in Danbury Street were going to get Severin's fortune and that Steven was helping them because he was afraid.

'We are all victims' he said.

It was late when they left the restaurant and Farringdon Station was closed. Highbury was a good four hour walk, so Tom hailed a taxi and paid the driver to take Steven back. Something in him needed to do that.

1.11

The yellow dress was a problem, but it was the tooth that did it. Shirley-Anne knew about Tom and Richmond and the scuffling in the library and she lived with it - after all, Tom was weak and poor Penelope was needy. But since the tooth, Richmond had an air about her, like she was hiding something. Part of Shirley-Anne feared it was Tom, but another part of her knew it couldn't be. It just couldn't.

When Richmond returned to work after the tooth, Shirley-Anne recommended herbal remedies. She praised Richmond's work. She praised her looks, her diligence, her dedication. Richmond tinkled her tinkle like everything was fine - and as far as Richmond was concerned, it was.

****

'Great -' it was five in the morning and Richmond stretched one leg then the other. This was the daily run - a new thing. Since moving to Shepherd's Bush, there were other new things: Richmond ate less, she went to the gym more and in between, she ran. She ran to work and she ran home and sometimes to stop herself thinking, she ran at night.

Meanwhile, back in St James Gardens, Shirley-Anne persuaded herself that Richmond's distance was due to an embarrassing personal problem. She'd made a mistake moving to that slum in Shepherd's Bush. No doubt she wished she'd moved into St James' Gardens, instead. Shirley-Anne wasn't good at telling the difference between what went on in her own head and what went on in another person's and while it led to misunderstandings, it also made for short worries. It wasn't that Shirley-Anne was cut off. No. She was well aware of the currents around her, it was just that the currents inside her were stronger.

Richmond was preoccupied. Shirley-Anne got that. Richmond had a false gaiety, a sharpness that was suspicious. Shirley-Anne got that, too. But when she put these things together, her conclusion was wrong. She believed it all pointed to the fact that Richmond missed her, but was too embarrassed to say. Blinded and comforted in equal measure, Shirley-Anne set about drawing Penelope back and part of that was being sure - no, really sure - that Tom was not part of the problem. Meanwhile, Richmond went on fading.

Richmond's mind was on two things. First, the letter - she could sell it and buy a new life. But now things were not so straightforward and this was the second thing on her mind. Love. She was in love.

There was a man in her life. A real man. His shy smiles and bashful ways were signalling to her. He was saying - in so many words - that he was hers but she needed to ditch the letter. She could have a life with him or she could have a life with that letter but she couldn't have both. That's what occupied her now.

It wasn't an easy choice. This man was real but still a stranger. She felt sure there was a relationship there, waiting - but it hadn't exactly happened. Not easy. Money or love? So, she ran, hoping it would sort itself out. 'Great - to be alive.' It was now ten past five and a new day and a new run and this time it would be ok.

Without knowing it, Richmond's runs made her easy to spot, easy to follow and easy to predict. She stopped as usual at the corner of Shepherd's Bush Green at twenty-three minutes past five, readying for a diagonal sprint. The path was slippery in places and with the first lunge, she slid backwards and hard. She would have cracked her head were it not for the sudden arm of a stranger. Three minutes later, Richmond and John Smith were sitting in the Buttered Bun, drinking skinny lattes like the best of friends. How lucky that he was passing. How lucky that she was so light. How lucky. It started to rain, more coffee came and one thing led to another.

It might have been the fright, but when Richmond started talking she couldn't stop. Waves of gratitude swept over her. She liked this man. He was clever and funny and he saved her life. Breakfast came. Cheese omelettes, toast, more coffee and talk. Richmond ate and talked without thinking and it was a relief. She had a problem, she said, and she ran because it helped.

Smith was a good listener. 'People don't spend enough time talking - would that be one sugar or two? Oh, thank The Lord, it's white - Italians - don't know what they see in the brown stuff, well that's foreigners for you - so, a problem, you say? Would that perchance, be a man? Don't tell me - older? Man of the world? Married?'

Richmond was amazed. He could see right into her.

'You know,' said Smith 'if you took all the unavailable men in London and put them somewhere else, you'd solve the urban housing problem overnight.' He made her laugh. Yes, she said. It was a man and yes, unavailable but no, not married. Definitely, not married. 'Oh -' said Smith '- gay as moonbeams? Well, good luck with that.' He went on to tell a funny story about something or other and Richmond floated.

When the rain stopped, she left renewed, and the man who saved her from falling paid the bill, satisfied. Richmond waved at the corner and disappeared. Smith waved back. He knew where she lived, where she worked, how much she disliked her employer, her landlords, ex-flatmates, ex-friends, ex-partners. He knew where she hid her sweaty trainers, how she liked to put things in straight lines and that her favourite colour was green. He also knew that there was someone in her life and it wasn't her employer's husband.

A week later, Richmond met John Smith again. Same time, same route, same breakfast in the Buttered Bun. He liked the routine and she liked him. He was not what she'd call good looking - not someone you'd fall for but he was easy to talk to and he wanted nothing from her. They met several times after that - in cafes - he gave her his phone number and told her to call, which she did.

John Smith never did get to the mystery man in Penelope Richmond's life. What he did know and what really mattered was that it wasn't Tom Amis. What he didn't know was that these contacts with Richmond were beginning to matter - to him.

****

The internal phone buzzed; Shirley-Anne with another herbal remedy for complaints of the tooth and jaw. Tea, this time. Nettles. Yesterday, it was Royal Jelly and Mint. The day before, smelling salts from Prague.

Down in the garden, Harry Steiner stood in the studio, his back to the window. He was a frequent visitor these days. He brought flowers and gossip and as far as Richmond could tell, plans for Shirley-Anne's exhibition were well under way. Richmond calculated now that Steiner would be down in the studio with Shirley-Anne for most of the morning - and this gave her time. She took off her shoes and walked on the edge of the stairs down to the library.

Tom Amis was there, waiting.

****

The maid's lot was not a happy one. There was fumbling in the library and sulking in the pantry and she knew it was only a matter of time before Vic did something. He was not a stupid man and La Petite could see torment in his face. It was two weeks, since the Hotel Tunis. Two weeks since Richmond resurrected him from the dead but now she was gone again. He accepted that women - real women - were hard to read and that maybe this blowing hot and cold was normal. But still - something wasn't right.

Vic was pretending to peel apples at the table. Harold sat on his shoulder, also morose. La Petite sighed. This couldn't go on. She liked Vic but there was a side to him that scared her - the way he tested a blade with his finger, the way he looked through half closed lids when he was thinking - it wasn't normal.

Vic sighed. The parrot sighed. Then the world exploded.

Glass shards spat through the air for a million years.

In the unreal quiet that followed, La Petite's sparrow like body stopped shaking. She looked down on the Sevres plate smashed on the floor and she knew - that plate was Richmond. She had to go.

****

Two hours later, Tom was back in the studio in Bowling Green and Steven was with him. He was telling more about Solly's job and hoping Steven would stay. 'This is what I had in mind - see? Landscapes - not what you'd call cutting edge. What do you think?' They were viewing contacts on the light box when Steven swayed. His face glistened grey like putty. 'Steady. You alright? What is it? Not coming down with something - not ill?' Tom opened the studio door for air. 'Been at the sauce? Stopped that sort of thing myself, years ago. Can't tell you how much better I feel. No - really, are you alright?'

'It's OK, OK.' Steven steadied himself with the flats of his hands. 'My legs go, sometimes. Low blood pressure. I'm fine, really.' Tom hadn't seen this kind of sudden wilting since his drinking days.

Steven puzzled him. He was a young man and not a drunk yet he was worn out.

'You look like a ghost.' Tom wanted to believe that Steven deserved what he got. 'Burning the candle at both ends. Catches up with you. Mark my words.' He didn't want this - a man who just stood there and took it. 'Look - remember those pancakes -?' he phoned the local Indian and ordered. Billy the cat was off his food; Tom imagined Steven lying on the record player. 'And nan with currents - yes, fucking sultanas, whatever.'

The food came and the afternoon was pleasant. They ate and talked about everything and nothing and it wasn't bad at all. 'What's wrong with you?'

'Nothing - sometimes I forget to eat.'

'Liar.'

Steven was getting skinnier and he smelled of fish. If Shirley-Anne was paying so much - and, she did pay - why was he like this? 'I get giddy myself, sometimes,' said Tom. Then he did what he didn't expect he would ever do. 'Well, like I said. Boring old man stuff, but if you wanted to help with the layout - when it comes to the design bit - that is, if you're still up for it? I don't want to take up your time, if you've got other things?'

'I'd like to,' said Steven. 'Glad of anything. Do you mean it? Really?'

'I can't pay much - bus fares - that sort of thing. Just wanted you to know that.'

'Yes. I don't mind - I can't thank you - really, to work with a professional -'

****

Tom opened his wallet and gave Steven forty quid - all he had. Thank God the rain stopped because the walk from Clerkenwell to Holland Park was hideous. It cost Tom three hours of his life and a lot of thinking. He knew no good could come of this - with Steven. Shirley-Anne would tire of him and Tom had no work, no real work to give him. But he liked him. He just liked him.

By the time Tom got to Holland Park Avenue, his feet ached and the traffic rattled in his head. He stopped at the station and found enough change in his pocket for a bunch of yellow roses for Richmond. He was sorry. She was young and alone and he blamed himself. He'd give her the flowers and they would call it quits and this time he really meant it.

When he got home, the sweet smell of apples met him at the door. The maid was baking - always a good sign.

1.12

Shirley-Anne smiled in the mirror and blew a kiss when Richmond walked in. Harry Steiner was coming to lunch and Shirley-Anne had made an effort, she said. She was wearing an ankle length Chinese green silk dress, she hoped Penelope approved? Richmond barely noticed. She was shivering, her bones and her head ached.

At eleven o'clock, she walked down to the garden studio, braced. There were new service contracts and funding applications for the Bayswater charity and seven emails from Gordon Watts, the Treasurer. It was late November and never a good time for Gordon. He'd been going through the books and as usual they didn't balance. Each year, he said he wanted a thorough review of spending and each year he didn't get one. It was a bit of a dance. He'd tell Shirley-Anne that the charity bank account was not her personal property. She'd agree. He'd give her a simple ledger. She'd take it. He'd wait. Several months later, cash withdrawals would turn up for increasingly implausible reasons. Over the past year, nearly £70,000 was unaccounted for - that was the content of these emails from Gordon today.

As Richmond knocked on the studio door, something cold ran down her spine. 'Darling. Sorry, did I make you jump?' Shirley-Anne squeezed by and unlocked the door. Richmond dropped her folder, shaky.

'Come in, darling. Just put those anywhere - there's nothing that can't wait. Look at these - what do you think?' Shirley-Anne spent most of each day down here, sorting through old works and making sketches for new ones and it was only these short morning meetings, when the two women met and when they did meet, they talked art. Richmond liked it. It made her feel trusted.

Richmond wisely, now hid nothing about her visits to Sea View. She spoke quite openly about the doctor's driver and all the help he had given her in making an inventory of the works still stored there. She made a point of listing her meetings with Betty Rae, although in an edited way. Richmond was on Shirley-Anne's side and she had nothing to hide. She wanted her to know that.

'You spend so much time down here in the studio; I hardly see you -'

'Darling, you've missed me? And your tooth - how is that, now?'

'Fine. Thank you. Yes. I just wish I could do more, to lighten the burden. You've got a lot on your plate, what with this and keeping the Charity afloat - can't be easy - if there was anything I could do, you know, here -'

Richmond swept her arm over the studio '- I don't know much, but I could learn.

I've always loved art.'

'Angel.'

'Don't get me wrong. I'm very happy working for the Charity, I'm not complaining -'

'Sweet.'

For Richmond, getting Shirley-Anne's approval was like catching a wave.

If she got it right, it would carry her. 'What are you thinking, Angel?'

'You carry so much, alone. That's what I was thinking -' and before Richmond could say more, Shirley-Anne fell upon her shoulders and cried. That was a shock.

Shirley-Anne was alone. She was in such trouble. Such trouble. She had so longed to confide in Penelope but - oh - oh - oh. Richmond wondered if this was about money - the usual worry. Or, was it Steiner and his constant demands for new pictures, bigger pictures, better pictures or was it Butters still trying to undercut Steiner and leaving Shirley-Anne caught in the middle? Whatever it was, it couldn't have come at a better time.

Shirley-Anne sobbed like a child - real and shameless. Richmond couldn't have been happier. She put her arm around Shirley-Anne and said soft words about no matter what was wrong, she - Richmond - would be by her side. 'You're more than I deserve, Darling. More than I deserve -' and in that moment Shirley-Anne would have given the world, to have meant it.

The doorbell and the smell of soup came together. Steiner was punctual, as usual. He brought a large bouquet prompted he said, by the vase of fresh flowers he'd seen in Shirley-Anne's bedroom below the portrait of mother and also there was something to celebrate. He'd got something in the press about Shirley-Anne's stolen painting. His contact - Betty Rae - was going to do a feature for one of the Sundays. She really was very clever, he said; the way she turned disaster into gold. Lunch was protracted and difficult. Richmond was definitely coming down with something. It was made worse by the evident trouble the maid had gone to, to please. Each course - five in all - was vegetarian, in Richmond's honour: warm choux pastries filled with Gruyere cheese, clear ginger soup with mango dumplings, followed by artichokes a l'anglaise, then mint and pea mousse shaped as a castle with carrot and celery swirls and finally an apple merengue of such lightness that La Petite herself, insisted on serving it.

Shirley-Anne cooed, Steiner beamed, Richmond shivered. By the time the mousse was brought in, Richmond was seeing double. She wanted to make her excuses and leave, but now was not the time. She had to stay. She had to prove that she was steadfast - trustworthy - she needed to be part of what was going on. So she stayed and she ate. Everything.

Everyone was pleased; even the maid. Especially, the maid.

****

As lunch was served upstairs Alan Tree tripped the latch and came in the basement. This was against his better judgment but Butters insisted. Butters knew about Steiner's visits to St James' Gardens and that he'd hang Shirley-Anne out to dry if Butters didn't get there first. Tree was to find *'Poppies in a Jar.'* Butters would make it her coup and Shirley-Anne would follow. Butters fully intended to beat Steiner at his own game.

But Tree saw it differently. Back at Steiner's Private View, when the fire engine was edging out and guests were still singing, Alan Tree got into the CCTV room in the basement of Chelm House. He was security, he said. He re-ran the evening's recordings and saw Vic - Dr Gilmore's driver - ignite a small fire at the end of the courtyard and as smoke and confusion spread through the house, CCTV also picked up Vic, letting in a stranger through the back gate. The stranger was Steven Witt. Witt went direct to Shirley-Anne and stayed with her for the rest of the evening. Meanwhile, Vic walked to the upper storey, lifted *'Poppies in a Jar'* off the wall, cut it out of its frame, rolled it under his jacket and left.

None of this was remarkable to Tree. But what did surprise him, was Harry Steiner. The following day, Steiner feigned shock. He said the CCTV discs had been accidentally wiped. He didn't want to take the matter further. Too embarrassing. He never spoke to Tree again.

The missing painting certainly gave Steiner the publicity he needed to re-launch Shirley-Anne. But did he need it? If he intended to promote an artist, he could. He didn't need to stage a theft. So, what was he doing?

Tree had no idea. But what he did see and didn't like, was that as a result of Steiner's Private View, a criminal walked into Shirley-Anne's life and no one noticed. This was the same man who walked into Severin Brille's life just before he died. It irked Tree that he watched Severin spiral in the last months of his life and did nothing. He felt he owed Severin something and that's why he was back now, in the pantry in the basement of St James' Gardens. Witt was targeting Shirley-Anne and Tree would stop it.

First, he needed to know more about Shirley-Anne and no one knows more about the Mistress of the house than the maid. True enough. La Petite could tell him that the Mistress was a changed person since that tea at the Ritz. She knew the Mistress met Severin Brille secretly and that she gave him money. She also knew that the Mistress was out the night Severin died.

Upstairs, a roar of laughter - time was short. Shirley-Anne was in danger. Tree felt his way in the half dark to the pantry where something on a shelf was growling. This was Harold, knocking small ornaments on to the floor. The cooing and shrilling upstairs increased as Shirley-Anne insisted on a second serving of the apple merengue. Steiner's flowers were on the centre of the table and taking up so much space that La Petite served dessert from the sideboard. 'Oh, Angel - and on our best Sevres plates. You spoil us, so.'

Tree listened and waited. Did Shirley-Anne know what was closing in?

Harold bobbed and knocked St Expedite onto the floor and into a hole in the skirting board. Then came the crash.

Silence.

Then the scream. 'Penelope. Penelope.'

****

Footsteps ran overhead and Tree left quick and silent. He closed the basement door but in his speed, he didn't engage the lock and five minutes later as he hailed a taxi in Holland Park Avenue, Harold hopped off the shelf and wandered into the street with no intention of going back. Meanwhile, everything upstairs stopped.

Up to the scream, it was all so light. Then Penelope began to sway. She thought the room was underwater. She saw things lifting and floating away. She tried to swim to the ceiling but fell to the floor. That's when Shirley-Anne screamed and Harold walked.

When Richmond opened her eyes she was lying somewhere soft and quiet and someone was there. 'No. Stay.' A hand touched her shoulder. 'Don't move. I'm Robin Gilmore -' he leaned over and drew back the winter curtains '- shade your eyes, now.'

'Where am I?' A soft light came in. 'What happened?'

'You fainted. They brought you up here. You're in Mrs Amis' bedroom.' Richmond tried to sit up, but couldn't. 'God. Sorry.' Her tongue felt swollen.

Was she dribbling?

'No, it's nothing. They were just worried. I was passing.'

'Sorry.'

'You've had a bit of tooth trouble?'

Richmond nodded. Did she?

'There's a nasty 'flu virus doing the rounds -' a fragrance - beautiful and from another world, filled the air '- the maid's just getting over it. How do you feel, now?' He held her wrist. His hands were silk - smooth and cool - 'bit of a temperature.'

'I don't know what came over me. I'm sorry. Oh, I keep saying that - not sleeping well.'

'Oh?' He touched her forehead. Could this go on, forever? 'Headache?'

He replaced her arm.

'I'm trying to find somewhere better, but it takes time.' What was she saying?

'Digs?'

An old-fashioned word. She nodded. 'I'm not really like this.' Words flew out before she could stop them. Sad things. Bad things - ever so slightly mad things. 'Things that bring other people down, don't touch me. I'm strong. I can be strong, that is, I think. I don't want the money -' what was she saying?

He was here and so was she and it seemed like a dream and she could say anything because in a dream, you can. None of it was easy, she said. There were times when she felt so alone, when it seemed it would never end - times when she thought she would never get out. She did want to tell him - so many times - but it was hard - 'I can save you' she said. She gripped his arm. She had the letter - hidden. She knew. She knew it all and it wasn't too late. She could make it work. He needn't fear because she loved him and she knew he loved her. They could be together forever - she was his - she had always been his. 'Trust me' she said.

Dr Gilmore heard none of this. What he did hear was that Penelope Richmond didn't like where she was living and that she was going to move again, soon - and yes, her tooth was fine. I meant no harm, she said. You must believe me. I had no idea - we all make mistakes - I've made mistakes myself, God knows - and in her mind she told him about standing in the rain in Portobello market and how a warm house is hard to turn down. She was telling him about black worms that dripped in the rain and fell on paper but it was alright because only she could read them.

Gilmore heard a few ramblings about rain and buttered buns, but that was it. Richmond was burning up. 'Lie back now. Rest. You're dehydrated.'

He knew from Shirley-Anne that this girl had recently moved and that it had all gone wrong. He was sympathetic. 'Living with other people can be hard. I remember when I first qualified - dreadful - nothing worse - other people's laundry -'

Richmond tried again. He needed to know that she was valuable to him - that only she could protect him - there was still time.

'Things will settle, you'll see. Sore throat?'

'A bit. Comes and goes, but fine. I'm sorry, I know I'm gibbering.' Why didn't he hear? What would it take, to make him stay?

'Taking anything?'

'No.'

He hesitated. 'Nothing? A lot of people do - I mean, that is to say - there's a lot of stuff around and -'

Richmond's face twisted. Is that how he saw her? A victim? Just another one of bloody Shirley-Anne's bloody victims?

'Well, you'll be as right as rain here.' He opened his bag and wrote something. 'Mrs Amis tells me you're all fired up for the exhibition. That true?'

What should she say? She nodded and sniffed. He handed her his handkerchief. Linen. Folded. Sharp corners. Beautiful. 'Take a few days off. Doctor's orders.' He chuckled but she grabbed his arm - 'it's not the way it looks.' What was she doing? Her grip was fierce and Gilmore froze. 'I found the letter' she said. 'I know what happened. I can save you -' she wanted to say more, but fell back exhausted.

The worms drifted by. 'Sleep,' said Gilmore. 'You're over-tired.' He clicked a syringe and a small arc of silver bounced. 'This will help.' And it did.

'Don't worry - I'm rambling -' then it all dissolved.

The door closed quietly. A hundred years later, in another life a woman screamed. 'Filthy Bitch.'

****

'Oh?' Richmond felt something cold at her fingertips.

'Here.' Dr Gilmore was back. He put a glass into her hand. 'Drink this.'

'How long?'

'Since the day before yesterday. We thought it best to let you sleep. Flu -' he read a thermometer '-temperature's down. I'll get my driver to take you home. There's no letter that can't wait until tomorrow.' He was smiling, now.

'Letter?'

Gilmore sat by the bed, patient and kind. It felt like he had all the time in the world. 'Is there anything Mrs Amis or I can do? To help, I mean - with, anything?' Richmond began to cry again and more words came out before she could stop them. She was sorry. Sorry for what she'd done, sorry for what she knew. Just plain sorry.

Gilmore smiled. Every crime has its price.

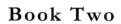

Book Two

2.1

It was January. The sun was low and the snow was fresh. Nir Grobstein stamped his feet and blew into his hands as he watched two women walk towards him arm in arm. They were late. 'Mr Grobstein?'

'Yes,' he hoped this wouldn't take long.

'Darling, this is the man; this is he. What an Angel you are, to wait so. The traffic in Mayfair was dreadful. Simply, dreadful. Have you been up there, recently? They sell such rubbish.' Grobstein held out his hand. 'Pleased to meet you, Mrs Amis. I'm a great fan. Harry's told me about the exhibition; glad to help.'

The woman tinkled. 'No -' she bowed to her companion '- this is Mrs Amis. I'm Penelope Anne Richmond.' She walked past him and into the gallery. Shirley-Anne took off her sunglasses and smiled awkwardly. 'So this is it? This is where they're interred?'

Nir Grobstein was well regarded and the art world is tight. A few years ago, Harry Steiner saved him when his stock got damaged in a flood and later - when those pictures came up for sale - Steiner, correctly, kept their water damage to himself. It was how they did things. So, Grobstein owed him and the favour Steiner was asking wasn't big. Take in a few canvases. Eight. They'd been in store in a place by the sea and all things considered, they were in not bad condition. No one knew of their existence and Steiner wanted to keep it that way. These were the few remaining works of G.F. Brille, thought to be lost - but, thanks to Shirley-Anne's absent mindedness, they'd been locked up and forgotten. Forgotten, until Penelope Richmond.

A lot happened after La Petite's apple surprise. Penelope Richmond got promoted and went to live in Pilgrim House in Bayswater. Now, she virtually ran Shirley-Anne's charity. She was also involved in setting up Shirley-Anne's exhibition - now a certainty, with Harry Steiner. It also looked like it was her idea to include some of G.F. Brille's work in this exhibition. She was everywhere.

Shirley-Anne and Dr Gilmore were changed, too. There was a kind of peace between them - an understanding - and Shirley-Anne was beginning to get some backbone. 'Yes' she said to Harry Steiner. 'Why not.' The idea of exhibiting some of mother's pictures was no threat. No. Let the world see that Shirley-Anne was an artist in her own right. A person. Not a tag along. Let them see the rubbish that G.F. Brille really produced. So, bringing up G.F. Brille's pictures to London was a good idea. What Shirley-Anne didn't expect and what surprised her now, was that Steiner had not included any of her own works in this shipment. All of Shirley-Anne's works were still at Sea View.

The exhibition date was not set and Grobstein would store the eight G.F. Brilles until then. 'We've started to unpack them -' he went down the spiral staircase '- down here - we've put them in the long term stock room. Mind the step. We've had new lighting put in; just there.' He pointed to a small control panel at the bottom of the staircase. 'There are arc lights, over there - black lamps, there. When did you say the conservator was coming?'

'Presently. Presently. You know how hard it is to pin these people down,' said Richmond, still tinkling. Shirley-Anne stopped. 'What's that, please?'

'New,' said Grobstein. 'Air conditioning.'

'It cleans the air twice before it comes in,' said Richmond. 'That's what made dear Mr Grobstein so valuable to us.' She pointed to the grey box on the wall. 'Climate controlled?'

'Yes.'

'And you've adjusted it - you know - what with the dampness in some of our pictures? Variable dampness. Did you see the bloom on - oh, let me see if I can find it - '

'The humidity is stable, Miss, er -'

'Richmond. Penelope Anne.'

Grobstein went gently. Steiner warned him that these women were difficult; the younger one, pushy, the older one, slow. 'Yes. Well, you're both very welcome to stop by again, once we've put them in racking. You'll have to excuse me -' The gallery assistant called down. 'Ring the bell if you need anything.'

They travelled back to St James' Gardens in silence, Shirley-Anne, lost in the passing traffic. She told herself she was doing the right thing. So much had changed since Harold went missing.

****

It was all about Richmond, now. Back in November, she was a worry - pale and nervous, living on borrowed time. It was no surprise when she keeled over. Dr Gilmore sat by her bedside, day and night. When the fever passed, Richmond gazed up at a new world with absolutely no recollection of what had happened. 'It's going to be different, now,' said Shirley-Anne, when Richmond came back to her senses.

By the end of the week, Penelope Richmond was promoted, given a pay rise and moved into a flat of her own at the top of Pilgrim House - the shelter in Bayswater, run as Shirley-Anne's charity for ex-offenders. It was a whirlwind and there was something in it for everyone. Gordon was pleased because, in a way that defied logic, Richmond's new appointment enabled him to write off cash losses that otherwise looked like fraud. Shirley-Anne was pleased because she needed more space to paint, Tom was pleased because Shirley-Anne was pleased and Dr Gilmore was pleased, because he just was.

The story was that Penelope Richmond was exhausted. She'd worked hard and living in a damp room in Shepherd's Bush had damaged her health - which was frail, anyway. All of it true, almost. The story was that Shirley-Anne had worried for the longest time. Poor Penelope was troubled - and so alone. She lived only to please and at an Extraordinary Meeting of the Board of Trustees of Pilgrim House - aka Dr Gilmore, Gordon the Accountant and Shirley-Anne Amis - they all agreed to give something back. As Penelope Richmond lay delirious in Shirley-Anne's bed, she was duly promoted to Site Manager of Pilgrim House, in Bayswater. With this, came a flat rent-free and a small increase in salary.

It made sense.

The other bit of the story - which no one knew - was that Penelope Richmond was also poisoned and it was this, not exhaustion, which finally did for her. This bit of the story started the day the Sevres plate got smashed in the pantry and Tom came home to the smell of apples cooking. Before she'd swept up the fragments, the maid made up her mind that Richmond would leave St James' Gardens and never come back. From there, it was but a short step to the apple delight.

The way La Petite saw it, Richmond was trouble and she needed to go and a special lunch for Harry Steiner was the time to make it happen. She knew how many of the Mistress' pills would rob Richmond of her senses and that is how and why Penelope Richmond fell to the floor after two mouthfuls of the maid's apple delight. She had ingested a large amount of powdered Diazepam - and that was why she gazed up at Robin Gilmore from Shirley-Anne's bed and told him things she shouldn't.

It was a simple plan and God knows, the maid meant no harm but no sooner had Richmond hit the floor, than a cold wind blew up from the basement.

For someone of belief - regardless what kind of belief - the ability to read meaning into meaningless things is swift and cruel. When La Petite came down to the pantry and saw that door open and Harold and St Expedite gone, her victory was dashed. Something wasn't right. So, when Richmond skipped off to a new life in Pilgrim House, La Petite took to her bed plagued by doubt.

Richmond was out of St James Gardens but she wasn't gone. She was hovering - out of reach but still there - and the maid had no idea what to do next.

Then there was Vic. No one was more hurt by La Petite's apple surprise, than Vic.

As Richmond lay drifting and murmuring, Vic went to Shepherd's Bush to pack up her belongings. This was no simple task. In their short and unpredictable relationship, Vic had never been to the place Richmond called home. He knew so little about her and he saw so little of her that a large part of what he thought was Penelope Richmond, lived only in his mind.

In his mind, he talked and she listened. They made plans for the future. She told him she needed him, she couldn't live without him and soon they would never be parted. He promised to go straight - maybe be a bus driver or a taxi driver; she'd work in Tesco's by the frozen peas. They'd be happy forever and even though none of these ideas reached the daylight world, they were real to him.

Vic executed his mission with reverence. He folded Richmond's clothes without looking - although he wanted to. He smoothed down the cover on her bed and that was hard. One by one, he wrapped her small possessions, packed them in boxes and taped each box tight. He wanted to show to the world and to himself that he could be trusted and that he deserved her. It all went well until the last box and a dip in the pavement and that's when he tripped and a book fell out. A diary.

It lay there - open - like a wanton thing.

He didn't want to look but he did. He read a few lines and they drew him in and at first, it was good. He saw his name and the days they met and where they went, routes, weather, length of journey, etc. The divine Penelope was one for detail. Interesting. But then other names, other dates and other places and who was John Smith? "Breakfast with JS. Cheese omelette. Toast. Rained."

That was November.

By mid-February, snow mixed with sleet and Vic sat for hours in parked cars outside Pilgrim House - tormented. "John Smith?" Each day a different car and a different place, but all within sight of Richmond's window. He watched. He knew when she put the light on, when she went to bed. He knew who called at the house, but what he didn't know, was why?

Why did she lead him on? Why did she work so hard to get him? The clothes that got ripped were his. The body that got thrown on that bed at the Hotel Tunis was his. If she didn't want him - then, why?

Vic found solace in the criminal within. He learned the routines of Pilgrim House. He knew when the bins were collected, when the post was delivered, when the caretaker swept the front steps and cleared the drains. He knew the residents; their habits, their arguments, the places they went and when they came back. He also knew the callers - the kind that came calling at Danbury Street and for the same reasons. And there were others - one, a woman - came by most days. Skinny. He noticed her legs, he didn't know why. She rang the bell and shouted through the letterbox. There was also a man. Always at night. Hat and long coat and quick. But the door didn't open for him, either.

Vic learned the habits of that house so well, he could have been part of it.

****

La Petite - a frail old lady with the wit of a sparrow - spent a week in bed then rose renewed. All was not lost. She could still get to Richmond.

2.2

Solly and Tom had an arrangement now. They met once a week at the el Saoud café off the Bayswater Road. Tom gave Solly working ideas i.e. simple line drawings and black and white shots from other campaigns. Solly gave Tom money, not a lot but enough. Cash. Solly liked the place and Tom liked the routine. They sat facing the window, watching the people outside.

It wasn't easy to lie to Solly about re-cycling this stuff and Tom fiddled with his phone, which was something he did when he was nervous '- obviously, those shots - I took them before the weather turned - anyway, going over to Greenwich tomorrow - still have a cavalry there, did you know that? Big black fuckers - horses, I mean.'

'Oh? Right. Pass the sugar. Thanks.' Solly took the folder without looking. He handed over the money without looking. His mind was somewhere else.

'I could put them on a stick, if that's easier - it's just that I thought, well, you know - what's the matter? Not ill?'

'Me? No - nothing. So, what's new at home, then? - and for fuck's sake, put that bloody thing down.' Solly took Tom's phone and put it on the next table. 'Did she ever find out?'

'What? Me being out of work - or me, being broke?'

'No - you being mad?' Solly asked a lot of questions; personal questions and coming from another person, really quite offensive questions, but this was Solly and he had to know everything. That was the deal.

'No.'

'You didn't tell her? You think she won't find out?'

Tom gave the weekly report. He told Solly he was drinking, but not much. He was seeing the occasional prostitute, but it meant nothing. He was selling off bits of Shirley-Anne's jewellery to pay for it all - but that meant nothing either. He told Solly about Steven Witt - 'brains of a herring. He's supposed to be spying on me -' Tom laughed '- like you.' Tom said about Richmond and the fumbling in the library and how that had all finished too. All true.

Solly revived at the mention of Richmond. 'Nip?' He poured from a hip flask. 'So, this Penelope creature? What happened? Why the sudden exile - the frozen wastes of Bayswater, you say?' It was Solly who caught Richmond the day she slipped. It was Solly who bought her breakfast and made her laugh and it was Solly who got her talking. Of all the small jobs he'd done for Shirley-Anne, this was by far the most amusing. And Shirley-Anne paid well and that amused him too. It was nice for once to be the barer of good news and telling Shirley-Anne that Richmond had no interest in Tom Amis, was good news indeed. It got him a five thousand quid bonus. But Richmond's sudden disappearance came as a shock and the hole she left behind came as a bigger one. He'd grown fond of their meetings. It was like a bit of him was gone.

Tom tried to keep it light, so he gave the official version. Shirley-Anne's shelter for ex-offenders had taken on the tail end of a lease - a run-down house somewhere - and they needed someone on site to run it. Apparently, putting Richmond there solved a lot of problems and everyone was happy. What Tom didn't say was that the happiness didn't last. After Richmond left, La Petite took to her bed and Shirley-Anne stopped eating. Tom believed he was the cause of it all - Shirley-Anne must have found out about him and Richmond and it shouldn't have mattered, except that it did. 'Thing is, the old girl's got enough on her mind. No point in making things worse and besides, I'm better now. Not mad. Not broke. All gone. Better.'

'She's always got something on her mind.'

'No. This time it's real. Spends all day in that damned studio. Gets upset at the smallest thing. Brought down a brandy and soda - wouldn't touch it. Just went on splashing paint.'

'Why? What's happened? Thought you two were swimming along?'

Tom looked into his cup. 'What is it? This exhibition thing? Bitten off more than she can chew? Well, that's ambition for you.' Solly got back to Richmond. What did Tom really know about her? What was her background, what did she like, who was in her life? Did she have a boyfriend? Did she ever speak about anyone - any acquaintance?

Tom sighed. 'Anyway. The maid and the old girl are fed up. They miss Penelope. Thought I'd try and get her back - she can't be liking living in a place like that. Have you seen it?' 'No' said Solly '- what do you mean, back? She's coming back?'

Tom visited Pilgrim House just before Christmas, left a few small presents and a card at the door. He stopped by again at New Year's with a bunch of flowers. He wanted a truce. He wanted Richmond to know that she could visit St James' Gardens, that there were no ill feelings - at least, not from him. In fact, he'd visited Pilgrim House again today, just before meeting Solly. Richmond wasn't there, so he left a note - another note - he said that it wouldn't kill her to pick up the phone. He made up some kind of lame reason for her to visit St James' Gardens; he hoped she'd bite.

'Why don't you just call her?'

'Yes. Maybe.'

Solly called for more coffee. It seemed odd, he said, putting a young, attractive woman in a house full of criminals. He held a spoon mid-air, like an unfinished thought. Tom drank and said nothing. The two men parted at the corner of Bayswater Road. Solly took the train. Tom waited and then walked back to Pilgrim House. He'd forgotten his phone. It was snowing again.

****

Richmond rounded the corner as the snow started to settle. She'd been running in Kensington Gardens. Tom saw her in the distance and he stumbled. He was not the only one caught in that moment. Vic was there, too.

Tom didn't wait. Now standing alone, Vic called over to Richmond. He smiled and held out a wicker basket Mrs Amis sent him, he said. More snow on the way. Mrs Amis worried that Richmond would be stuck. He made it easy. Richmond took the basket, relieved. He wasn't going to make a scene, he knew his place - and for less than a second, Richmond liked him again. There were pastries and cakes; sweet and savoury, still warm in greaseproof paper. Like a shark nudges its prey, Vic touched her arm as he gave it to her. He wanted that. He wanted her to know that he could get to her. Anytime. He said he hoped she was settling in and she said, yes. She thanked him for packing up her things in Shepherd's Bush and no, nothing was missing or damaged - not as far as she knew. Richmond waved from the front door of Pilgrim House until Vic was out of sight, like everything was fine. So much had gone right in her life that losing her diary in the move didn't register. She'd left St James' Gardens and Vic far behind. Yes, they'd had a few dates but things move on - letting go, that was the key. It made sense. Well, of course it did. Richmond could see that. So could Vic.

She closed the front door with her foot and as she did, a faint smell hit. It seemed to come and go. Going up the stairs, it got stronger. Drains. Cold weather, a cracked pipe, she made a mental note to call a plumber.

Pilgrim House was one of those mid-19th century terraced houses, built in west London when times were still good. It was designed as a grand residence but never made it. It started life as a multi-occupancy tenement and stayed that way. The stairs creaked, the light was poor, it was drafty and noisy and it was starting to get on her nerves. Above, in her flat, Richmond locked the door and put the basket on the kitchen counter. She made a list. The phone rang and went straight to voicemail. Rae, again. She was coming round and this time Richmond had better answer the door. Richmond unwrapped one of the warm pastries, as she listened. Little did she know - or care - what effort went into the cheese choux melting in her mouth. La Petite had been up all night baking and thinking and the contents of this basket were without mercy. Richmond licked her fingers and took another.

Rae meanwhile was hard to fathom. Why wouldn't she let go? She was waiting today at the round pond, to catch Richmond on her daily run. Yesterday, she rang the bell and shouted through the letterbox. Richmond stole her story. The message droned on. 'We all know - we all know -,' said Rae '- you stole things from Mrs Amis. How long do you think you will last - a thief - when she finds out?' Rae was willing to trade. Richmond licked the icing off a poppy seed bun and slowly, the idea of meeting Rae again didn't seem so bad.

An hour later, the Landline rang.

'Pilgrim House -' but the voice wasn't Rae's. It was Alan Tree.

Remember? Harry Steiner's Private View last August - the painting that got stolen? He was speaking to people about that evening - could they meet? Richmond hesitated. Her mind and her speech weren't quite in sync - she felt a bit tipsy. On the other end of the line, Tree listened and picked up fear.

2.3

Steven Witt had two masters. He loved one and hated the other and most of the time it worked. When he was with Vic, he loved him and that made him a criminal. When he was with Tom, he loved him and that made him a fool. It was all based on fear and Steven Witt knew a lot about that. He was feeling it now, curled on the floor.

'Once - once - just once in five months, you've been inside that place.' Vic stood over him apoplectic. This was about Shirley-Anne's fortune. 'She saw you coming -'

Steven clamped his head.

Shirley-Anne, like her brother Severin, had a thing for the gutter, so why was Steven Witt failing? 'She trusts you -' screamed Vic '- she visited you in Belmarsh - how fucking hard can this be?'

Steven stayed in a tight ball. Lucky for him, Vic was torn between killing him slowly, and just walking away, because - what was the point? Put another way, the criminal within wanted Steven Witt punished for failing to deliver, but the other part of him was too empty to care.

That was the part with Penelope Richmond - blowing kisses, waving - making love and making everything else pointless. Was it real - what they had? If it was, where was she now? If it wasn't - then, what kind of a world was he living in?

Vic was not a reasoning man, but he knew Penelope Richmond had weakened him. He wanted to blow her brains out and he wanted to be with her sitting on the cliff and laughing in the wind and no matter what he did, he couldn't let that go. She killed him and made him live at the same time. He was basically fucked.

Steven sneezed. 'Sorry. Dust. Can I get my inhaler?'

Vic jolted back. He picked Steven up by his collar and pinned him to the wall. He explained in simple words that the time for waiting was over. He told Steven to get Shirley-Anne's fortune or he would personally and very slowly, take him apart. Then he dropped him. Steven stayed where he was for a long time after that.

Vic drove back to Danbury Street tied up. Women used to be like things in the funfair - you shot at them and forgot them. It used to be so easy.

Certainty and blame were the cornerstones of Vic's world and he clung to them now. 'You must have known what you were doing. Don't sit there and tell me you didn't - you did - how could you not know?' This was Vic talking to Severin Brille, which he did a lot these days. 'What possessed you? Why? Really, I mean, why? You tell a bunch of scum you've got money to throw away - did you think we would just sit there?' In Vic's mind, if Severin hadn't wandered into the Soup Kitchen, if he hadn't tempted broken souls, none of this would have happened.

He swerved, narrowly missing a cyclist. He could hear Severin on the car seat beside him. 'You thought you knew me - but you didn't. You thought you could go on like that - and never get caught -?'

'You, with your stories of money - money to throw away - what the fuck did you expect? Of course we came after you - it's what you wanted - admit it - what kind of sick fuck spends

116

his time with the likes of us?' Vic worked hard to make it Severin's fault - everything. Severin dying was Severin's fault.

Penelope Richmond was Severin's fault. Steven Witt being a useless piece of shit was Severin's fault. All of it, Severin's fault - because if it wasn't, then it meant there was something out there, cleverer than Vic - and if that was the case, it was still out there.

****

Next day, Steven was back in St James' Gardens with a cracked rib and under the eye of a woman betrayed. 'Your tea Mr Witt, is getting cold -'

He tried to smile.

'- and I don't have all day.'

He wanted to help Shirley-Anne. He was so grateful for all she had done and for all she continued to do for him, that - with Miss Richmond being so busy and all - was there something he could do - for Mrs Amis - so to speak? Anything?

Shirley-Anne sighed and looked at her watch. When she first met Steven Witt, he was an orphan in prison. When he got out, she forgot him. When he turned up in the smoke and the mess of Steiner's Private View, she opened her heart to him. That's how and why Steven Witt turned up just after seven on the morning after the Private View. Tom was still drunk and before he'd opened his eyes, Shirley-Anne had let this stranger into her house and into their lives. That's how she saw it.

She wanted Steven to keep an eye on Tom - not to spy, because that would be wrong - but just, keep an eye. Tom could be wayward, she said - and after all, a man just out of prison like Steven Witt, would have some sympathy for that? And she was good to her word. She persuaded Tom to take Steven under his wing, she also found him a better place to live - away from the riff raff of Islington. She gave so much and asked so little. That's how she saw it.

'Well?'

117

Steven squirmed. He had no idea what Tom Amis got up to. He didn't know if he was seeing other women. He could try lying but what was the point? And he was right - on that at least. There was something determined in Shirley-Anne, something non-negotiable. A knot in her stomach said Penelope Richmond was betraying her and - despite regular messages from Solomon Solomon to the contrary - she still feared it was with Tom and the more she wanted Tom and Penelope to be blameless, the more that knot tightened.

'Mr Amis works hard -'

'Oh, please.'

Shirley-Anne was ready to forgive all, if only Steven Witt would say the words that mattered - 'you are wrong. Tom has nothing to do with Penelope Richmond - how could you think such a thing? Penelope really did have a bad tooth and the thing with the dress was a misunderstanding -' but that's not what he said.

'I could do filing.'

'What?'

Steven floundered. Shirley-Anne wanted to sink her teeth into his face.

Back at the studio in Clerkenwell, Steven put a good spin on it. 'She thinks you're having an affair. That's why I'm here.' Tom tried to sound surprised but Steven's dog-like trust disarmed him. 'I know. You told me that before' he said. 'A lost cause.' In his own way, Tom was faithful. Prostitutes didn't count and stealing Shirley-Anne's jewellery to pay for them, didn't count either, so it annoyed him that she had such little faith in him. But then - like most things - he forgot about it. He didn't care what Steven told her. She wouldn't believe him. She didn't believe anyone.

'Problem is, she's given me the sack.'

'Oh?'

Tom put down the eye glass. There was something in Steven's voice - an edge. Tom mistook it for shame - which is something Tom knew a lot about. 'She'll come round. Don't worry. Happens to us all.'

Steven trembled. He could see it now. Vic was good with an iron bar and this time, with nothing to trade, he'd finish him. He'd seen it in Belmarsh. So quick, so easy, so dead. He looked up at Tom, desolate.

Tom didn't understand and thought, incorrectly, that Steven was wounded by Shirley-Anne's rejection. That his wife should mean anything to anyone, was always a surprise to Tom - and he hated himself for it. But that she should mean so much to Steven, moved him. With no awareness of what he was doing, Tom told Steven to contact Penelope Richmond at Pilgrim House. He was sure, he said, that she'd find plenty for him to do and that in no time - no time, at all - he'd be back in favour. It just came to him. He honestly had no intention of using Steven as a bridge between Shirley-Anne and Richmond - but once the words were spoken - it was there. The answer.

Steven would bring them together and everyone would be happy.

****

Richmond was learning that the one thing worse than not getting what you want, is getting it.

When she first moved in, Bayswater was a dream. Really. Up there in the clouds. Early morning walks in Kensington Gardens, coffee in that Moroccan café on the corner, the picture market on Sundays. The world was hers. So it was inevitable that the love affair would begin here.

He stood on the doorstep. He'd admired her from afar and for the longest time, he said. But it was only now - now that things had changed - that he could tell her. He was in a delicate position.

Yes, she said. The need for discretion - obvious.

'Chateauneuf du Pape. House warming.' He gave her a present, so it had to mean something. He came by the next day and the next and every day and always with something - flowers, chocolates, small cakes from the Moroccan café. It was so easy - like he'd known her all her life - and they talked for hours even about small things like her favourite colour - his favourite was green. They walked in Kensington Gardens, went to the local cinema, she cooked dinner, they talked and talked and talked and then, it stopped. Just like that. Gone.

Looking back, it was hard to pinpoint. Maybe, sometime around Christmas he started to come late, leave early, not come at all. At first, there was always a reason. He was busy, she understood. Then the glow faded. Days drifted. Unpaid bills and lists of jobs to do lay around like dead things. Where did it go?

The hampers at least were reliable. Every Wednesday and Friday from St James' Gardens. Vic left them by the door without knocking. So polite.

On New Year's Day, the boiler broke. Then came the ice in January and the cracked pipes and the smell again. The house that was a delight back in November, was turning against her and slowly with nowhere else to go, she turned against herself. It came to her that this place smelled bad because of her. She was not taking care of things. She was the reason he didn't come back.

Well, a problem seen is a problem half solved. She paced, moved furniture, emptied cupboards; she took down the curtains, washed them, ironed them, hung them up and took them down, again. She took up the stair carpet and rubbed linseed oil into the exposed floorboards, she polished and re-polished the brass fixings. She whitewashed the steps outside.

At the end of January, he came back - like nothing happened. December - always a busy time, what with the cold and all. She understood, she said - but she didn't. She'd been busy herself. He spoke some more and she spoke back and agreed with what he said and it all seemed OK and then he went and she waved from the front door like it didn't matter. But it did. He went round the corner and a piece of her went with him.

Then she went back to waiting. She sat by the front window and waited and the longer she waited, the more the smell bothered her. That was it - that was what was keeping him away. She told herself that if she saw him coming next time, she would open the windows and spray air freshener and it would be alright. So she went on sitting and watching. This was a stupid idea and a dangerous one because, sitting for hours can make a person see things and it wasn't long before Richmond saw that she was being watched from the street below. It started with a car, parked on the corner, side lights on. Next day, there was a different car in a different place. Then a sharp knock on the door and a man calling 'Miss Richmond - open the door. This is Alan Tree. I need to speak with you. I want to help -'

She didn't answer.

Tom Amis also stopped by. He got as far as the flat door and rustled about and left something or other. He came back the next day on his way to meet Solly at the el Saoud café, but still she didn't answer.

Known and unknown callers came to Pilgrim House and all were ignored. Then another man came by. A man in a long coat and he had a key. He knocked on the flat door and with no answer, he left a note and a small bunch of roses. The note read 'ring me -' and it was signed 'John S.'

Richmond never got the note but Vic did - on one of his night visits to Pilgrim House.

****

A wind of a strange kind blew through Pilgrim House after that. It came up the stairs and rattled the doors and at night it spoke.

'You are dead,' it said.

2.4

As Richmond watched from her window, Shirley-Anne watched from hers. She stared across the square, willing Richmond to appear. She would yield if poor Penelope ran back and threw her arms around her and begged for forgiveness. It would be hers. No matter what - it would be hers. But no one came. No one that is, except Solomon Solomon and he wasn't about forgiving.

Back in Bayswater, Richmond was now 5 nights without sleep, sustained only by the hamper in the kitchen and her own thoughts and when both ran out, fear ran in. She sat in darkness - the better to see outside - and what she couldn't see, she imagined. She had done wrong and retribution was out there, waiting. Where did it all go so wrong? Shirley-Anne Amis rescued her, gave her a life and a good life - warm and dry and smelling nice.

She didn't see it for what it was and now she was going to be punished. Every nerve in her body rang.

Who would they send? How would they do it? Down in the street, a car pulled up. The driver turned off the main beam and sat there. She'd seen this car before. She recognised the broken side light. Was this it? A couple with a dog came out of the house opposite - was this it? Another man crossed at the corner. He walked quick, his head down. He came straight to the house. He was carrying something - it glinted as he passed under the street light. A knife.

The door downstairs opened and closed and there was a step on the stairs. This was it. Hacked to death. The steady tread got nearer. Everything spun. She was helpless. The door opened, slow - and death spoke. 'I've come about the plumbing.'

It was Steven Witt and he was carrying a spanner.

****

Tom gave Steven the spare key and a good story. Old houses have problems and women have no idea. Say you're a plumber. It'll be easy, he said.

Trust me - women always need a plumber - and Tom was right, Penelope Richmond certainly did need a plumber. She slid from the chair like jelly.

'God. Sorry -' Steven fanned her with an envelope. '- oh fuck oh fuck fuck fuck.' She convulsed. She was trying to talk - trying to say - thank you. It looked like she'd swallowed her tongue. 'Lie on your side - try breathing -' First Aid from Belmarsh was the best he could do and whether or not it was right or that Richmond sensed safety in this stranger - she did eventually calm down.

Steven's interest in the perils of sudden frost were still beyond her, but what she did grasp and grasp well - was that he was here to help.

When he left Pilgrim House three hours later, Steven was holding £120.00, a shopping list and Richmond's mad gratitude. He'd got himself a job.

Handyman. He would come back the following day, do as he was told, prove to Shirley-Anne Amis that he was twice the man she took him for and they'd be firm friends and she'd tell him where she hid her money and Vic wouldn't crush his skull with an iron bar.

But as Steven's footsteps receded, so did Richmond's faculties. Sleepless nights, La Petite's baking and a miraculous saving did for her. Then came Betty Rae. Rae walked in as Steven walked out. He held the door for her. But unlike Steven, Rae didn't stay long and she didn't leave happy. She'd come with an ultimatum.

She'd got interest - real, paying interest - in Shirley-Anne, the artist recluse. But it wouldn't last. Rae needed something from the underbelly to make it run. She came straight to it. A place like Sea View doesn't close down for no reason. And a person like Shirley-Anne Amis - on the brink of celebrity - doesn't disappear overnight for no reason. Richmond had been snooping into her employer's life and now Rae wanted what she got. Hand it over, she said - or your employer will know that you have been stealing from her and selling things and really very private things, to me - and I am the scum of the earth. She didn't belabour the point.

Richmond listened in silence. She agreed. Yes, she'd found a letter - although it was not what she was expecting. Yes, it was worth a lot to those who wanted it out and more to those who didn't. Yes, she was tempted to sell it. And yes, maybe - probably - she would have sold it anytime up to now but - now things had changed. In her blunted reasoning, Richmond was as grateful to Rae now as she had been to Steven. They were both messengers from Heaven. Steven would take away the smell and Rae would take away the letter.

Yes, said Richmond. Rae could have the letter. No, it wasn't here. Yes, it was hidden and hidden at Sea View and no, no point in looking - you'll never find it. Richmond would get it but she needed a few days. Her calm was chilling.

****

'Would that be emulsion or gloss?' It was eight in the morning, next day - Saturday.

Steven was back and Richmond was full of it. The furniture was under a dustsheet, bin liners slid on the landing. She'd been up all night. Her man - yes, hers - would see her without blemish. He'd come back and she would be there - transformed - in white. They would be happy together, forever - just a lick of paint would do it.

'Mr Witt?'

'Yes, miss?'

'Thing is, Mr Witt, I need it done today. Not much - just one room. This one. What do you think?' She wanted the walls painted. He wasn't keen. 'I mean, just the walls, not the ceiling. Emulsion. White. See?'

Steven did as he was told and it wasn't easy getting white paint at that hour.

'Kitchen's in there - well, you know that - anyhow, place is all yours; plenty of hot water. There's a hamper; help yourself. What do you think? Done by this afternoon? No rush.' It was February. The windows were open and it was colder inside than out. The hamper was empty because the food from St James' Gardens was hard to resist and Richmond ate more than she knew and the more she ate, the more she got unhinged.

Steven blew into his hands, he was losing sensation in his feet. Tom told him not to argue. Whatever it takes, he said - just do it. Do it and tell her to ring Shirley-Anne. 'Depends' said Steven, considering his options. Richmond was scanning the street. Someone was waving up. 'Depends? Depends on what?' A car pulled up. That same couple with a dog came out of the house opposite - was that the same dog as yesterday? Were they all in it together? 'Well?'

'How quick it dries.'

'What?'

'Depends on how quick it dries. Won't be able to sleep in here. Not tonight.'

'What?'

'Tonight. I'm just saying. If you do this you'll have to move out. Is there somewhere you could go? Friends? Just for the night? You sure you don't have a drain or something that wants mending?'

She walked between the door and the window. Steady, even steps. One word, one step. How fucking hard could this be? 'Just the walls. What if I helped? I mean, it's barely eight o'clock. We could start in half an hour. Everything is here. Two people? Done in an hour, two - tops?' She put ten folded £20 notes into his hand. 'We'll need bigger rollers - and an electric fan. Don't argue. Get them or don't come back.'

With Steven gone, Richmond calculated how long it would take if she helped. No bad thing - two pairs of hands. There was no time to waste because "He" - her man - would be back tonight. He'd walk in but this time, she'd be ready - in the middle of a bright white room. No smell. No regrets. She'd tell him about the letter and how sorry she was and that she'd never do anything like that again. In ways that made no sense she thought this would be an OK thing to do - under the circumstances.

He'd lift a lock of hair out of her eyes and see that he couldn't live without her.

She kicked the last bin liner down the stairs. It landed, spilling out the clothes she'd outgrown. She spread newspaper across the floor and prised open a 5 litre drum of paint. She could see him now in the doorway. 'Decorating' she'd say, in her special voice 'ghastly smell - the chaps downstairs tried to help and they've made such a mess - I can hardly scold them.' He'd laugh. She'd tinkle. All white. All bright. All right.

The phone rang under the dustsheet. It was Shirley-Anne. 'Darling - at last -' her voice soft and sharp '- where have you been? I've been trying for days - you didn't get any of Gordon's e-mails?'

'Sorry. Problem with pipes, you know plumbers never come when they say. I was about to call you.'

'We sent round that nice driver - Victor - he couldn't find you. He tried to deliver a hamper - poor Petite, she worries so. They said you were out?'

'I know. I know. The thaw - leaks everywhere - and we're in for another freeze tonight. Madness. Anyhow, nice to hear your voice, at last. No leaks at your end, I hope?'

'I miss you, Angel. You never visit...we worry so...' Shirley-Anne's voice went on and Richmond wandered about, kicking bits of paper and then something pulled -

'...if it's not too much to ask -?'

Did she hear right?

'- Penelope? Penelope?'

'Yes? Sorry - not good reception here - missed that - what did you say?'

Shirley-Anne hesitated. Apologetic. 'Only, if you have the time? And of course we'd pay your train fare, in fact, Victor - you know him? Yes, of course you do - he's offered to take you himself - he knows the way - you're busy of course you are, but you're the only one I trust.'

'Wait. Wait. Say that again.'

'Oh, Angel do wake up. It's my jewellery. I could have sworn I put it in store but apparently not.' Unknown to Tom, the storage facility at Whitley Industrial Estate where the small valuables from Sea View were stored, sent Shirley-Anne an annual inventory along with their annual invoice. She was looking at the one that arrived yesterday and for once, paid attention. There was no jewellery listed. A call to the warehouse manager confirmed this.

It must be wrapped and safe somewhere in Sea View. She wanted it back - that is what she told Richmond.

'At the house? Sea View?'

'Darling. I'm in your hands.'

Richmond hadn't seen any jewellery - then it got worse.

'...such a nice chap...'

The doctor's nice driver had offered to take Richmond down to Sea View, to look - in fact, it was his idea.

'Angel? Are you well?'

'No. Yes. Yes. Yes, why wouldn't I be?'

'Are you sure? You sound distracted. Is it the tooth? Do you want to come back - there'd be no shame? Poor Petite, she misses you so - she doesn't say it, but she does.'

'God no.' Richmond laughed. 'My duty is here, I mean.'

'Well, there it is. The Charity's gain is our loss. At any rate, the jewellery? You'll look?'

'Yes. I'll do it. If it's there, I'll find it. You know I've been down there quite a bit, recently?'

'Yes, Angel. So diligent and here I am, burdening you again.'

'No trouble. You know me: thorough. And besides, now that it's opened up, it does need watching.'

'Watching?'

'Yes. You know - when you lift the lid -' Richmond laughed her laugh '- well, you know - anyone could walk in; just thinking of you.'

'Yes, of course. Well, whatever you think best.'

'I'm a bit tied up at the moment. When did you have in mind?'

Shirley-Anne explained that - as far as she could remember - she kept most of her small personal effects locked in a cupboard in the main bedroom, upstairs. 'I'll give Victor the key; I have it here, somewhere. You could make a day of it. Take a picnic. At any rate, he'll give you a call. I just knew you wouldn't let us down.' She rang off.

Richmond stood still but her thoughts raced. She remembered the way Vic touched her arm - a nudge - like a threat. He planned this. Was he the executioner? Dark spots appeared on the wall in front of her, damp to the touch and spreading.

'Damn.'

Another burst pipe. God alone knows what was leaking out.

'Plumber. Make a note. Put the bin liners out. Make a note.' She felt under the dust-sheet for the plumber's card. She went to the kitchen, then to the bathroom looking for a pen. She marked the bathroom mirror with soap. The plumber's number.

****

At noon, Richmond was still waiting for Steven to come back and she couldn't stand still any longer. It was turning into one of those hazy bright days that can happen in the middle of a freeze and a good time to go for a run. As she crossed the road to Kensington Gardens, a man in a long coat walked slowly towards Pilgrim House. He was carrying a bag. Richmond came back thirty minutes later, warmed and in good spirits. She was thinking about what to wear tonight and got as far as the first landing before she slipped. Water was dripping through the ceiling light. The occupant of 1-C ran past, barefoot and splashing. A black film was creeping down the stairs. 'Steven' she screamed. Other residents came out of their rooms and ran into the street. 'Stev - switch off the power - Steven.' She stumbled up the stairs. 'Fire. Fire. Fire.'

On the top landing, the bathroom door was open. The bath was overflowing and the tap heads were gone.

'Oh for fuck's sake. Who did this?' She went down the corridor; the doors were open and all the rooms empty. The lights fizzed and went out and the sound of running water got louder.

Plumber. Emergency number.

She had it, she knew she put it somewhere. She ran to the bathroom. She'd written the plumber's number on the bathroom mirror. And there it was, written in soap - in large letters.

'Get out,' it said.

****

'No heat? What do you mean, no heat?'

It was early evening and dark. The caretaker from next door cleaned his hands and shrugged. No water, no heat. It meant nothing to him. Steven was missing and the place was a sink hole. 'But they did say tonight? Right?' It was quarter to seven. Tonight of all nights.

'Fucking beyond belief.' There was nothing to be done but face it. She felt her way into the kitchenette and found a box of candles and matches. In the dim light, she reached - as if by instinct - for something from the hamper, but there was nothing. Her mobile rang. It was Shirley-Anne again. 'Darling? What a catastrophe - are you alright? What happened?'

Richmond fought to remain calm. 'I don't know. Someone left a bath running - the taps came off apparently and the electricity's gone - bloody nightmare.'

'Angel. Come back this instant - at least for the night. I'll get La Petite to make up the Pink Room. I insist. Darling, you need to be pampered.' A log fire. Linen sheets.

'Drop everything. Just leave it,' said Shirley-Anne. 'What can happen now that hasn't already happened? Get in a taxi. Leave it. Come back.' Hot water. Rose soap. Weak and cold - who would blame her? Pilgrim House was desolate like Portobello Market and Shirley-Anne beckoned to a better place. On the ground floor, a man's voice echoed up - Steven - at last. Shirley-Anne cooed on the other end of the phone as Steven's even steps came up. Slow. Measured. Shirley-Anne was talking about cup cakes - Penelope's favourite - the maid had just made a batch. Dainty things with flowers - all colours. Richmond could smell that sweet smell - that fragrance - rose. Steven's step reached the landing and he knocked although the door was open.

Without looking she beckoned him in as Shirley-Anne cooed and soothed - '…we'll have the place to ourselves…early night…darling…together…'

'Yes. Yes. You're right.'

Was St James' Gardens so bad, after all? What silliness made her leave it?

'…just you and me…'

Give in, said the Tempter. Is it so bad? Shelter? Give in. Be what she wants you to be - what have you got to lose that you haven't lost already? I can hardly scold you. Be me.

Richmond nodded and silently gave up. She turned to tell Steven to go home - there was no point - she was going back - then - she gasped.

The phone dropped.

'...darling?...are you still there?...Penelope? Penelope?'

Emptiness yawned over the Universe.

Shirley-Anne heard a man's voice on the other end of the phone. What she didn't hear was what Richmond said next.

'Robin.'

2.5

Shirley-Anne hung on a thread '- darling - Penelope - what's happened - what's happened -?' then it broke.

She knew.

She'd always known, but now she really knew. Tom. He was there now, at this very moment, with Penelope. They were there together in Pilgrim House, laughing.

That fuck of a girl.

Shirley-Anne went numb. She must have screamed and screamed loud because the next thing she knew was the steady hand of Victor. 'Oh?'

Victor was in the pantry when he heard. Was anything wrong? She was on the floor - did she have an accident? Could he help? Yes, he had time. No, not too much trouble. No trouble at all. 'Dearest Victor - my rock.'

Tea and toast had never been so good. Vic - now a frequent although unpredictable helper around the house - had a way with Shirley-Anne. He did what he was told. He knew his place. There was no problem, he said, that tea and toast couldn't solve and on this point, he was talking from experience. For a man who couldn't read women, Vic read

Shirley-Anne well. He didn't need to know that Penelope Richmond was the cause of Mrs Amis' anguish. He knew it already. He didn't need to know that Mrs Amis wanted her gone and gone for good. He knew that too - and all communicated over the Darjeeling and sliced white, without a word.

As Vic poured a second cup in St James Gardens, Tom ordered another cognac in the el Soude. He was alone and watching the snow and thinking of nothing. He'd been there all day, lost.

****

Richmond was not in good shape. The on / off relationship with Robin Gilmore took its toll and she could think of nothing anymore, but him. "Love" she thought - but she was wrong. "Forever" she thought - wrong, again.

But the highs and lows that carried Richmond were only in part to do with Robin Gilmore. The greater part was to do with what got delivered each week in greaseproof paper. Richmond was an addict. She lived for sweet relief and when it came, nothing else mattered. Diazepam will do that. And when the inevitable down started, she could hold out because she knew, relief would come again. In fact at this stage, the pain of longing was part of the pleasure. Diazepam will do that too. So here she was in the velvet embrace of Robin Gilmore, accepting everything, good and bad. He was passing, he said. She was ok with that. He'd seen a lot of commotion in the street earlier and wondered what happened. He was sorry to see her all alone and he blamed himself.

Gilmore could see Richmond was nervy - unpredictable. He said he had something to calm her and she believed that too.

Gilmore and Richmond spent that night together in the Piccadilly Suite at the Ritz in Piccadilly. He gave her an injection - vitamin D - and she floated. When she woke next day - Sunday - breakfast was served, the bill was paid and Gilmore was gone. He did however leave a message. He would contact her later and Richmond was just fine with that. She returned to Pilgrim House later that morning to find the front door open, the lock broken and a card from Thames Water on the mat. The house was hollow but the lights worked and the heating hummed.

It was snowing.

Back in St James Gardens, Vic was long gone but Shirley-Anne remained on the chair, where he left her. She'd been there all night. Thinking.

Upstairs in her flat, Richmond checked the answering machine. There was a message from the evening before. Tom Amis. He was coming round, he said. Mrs Amis wanted the building secured and he was to bring Penelope back to St James' Gardens - she absolutely insisted. What Tom didn't say, but what was clear from his voice, was that he'd been drinking and that it was extremely unlikely that he'd had a rational conversation with anyone in hours. He rang from a public phone in the el Saoud. After he hung up, he swayed out into the snow. He was going to wait outside Richmond's door and say he was sorry - for everything - it seemed like a good idea, at the time. 'Oh, fuck off.' Richmond deleted the message and paced. She needed to stay focused. Vic and Tom were trailing her but if she could stay away from them until tonight when Robin would come back, then it would all end. A new life was waiting. She hung on to the magic of last night - what Robin said - what he did. How they laughed. How she told him about the letter and how good it felt to be unburdened - and Robin was a good listener.

Tonight "The Marriage of Figaro". Tomorrow, breakfast at Claridges. Iced vodka, smoked salmon and then - 'Who knows? Who cares?' He had plans for her, he said. They would get the letter. Together they would destroy it. It was the last thing standing between them and happiness.

The day passed quietly; the heating hummed, air in the pipes gurgled. Towards evening, she looked into the street. It was darkening and the snow was coming down hard. There was a car under a street light and someone sitting inside. Was it the same car as before? Did it have a broken sidelight? She couldn't see. There were people pushing against the wind - who were they? Why were they out there - in this weather? Someone was standing in the pubic phone box - that phone didn't work - why was that person there?

Her mobile rang and she jumped - 'Robin - at last -'. It was the plumber. He'd done the emergency work and needed paying. He'd be back next week to finish the lagging. The place needed to dry out, first. 'I see.' She made an effort to sound upbeat but it was getting hard. 'Well, if you are sure. Yes, yes e-mail it now and I'll get it settled. No, no trouble.'

The snow was whipping up. The heating made the floorboards creak but the smell was gone. She switched on the computer and waited for the plumber's bill on email. The screen blipped -

'Darling. What's happened? Where are you? We need to talk. Your best love, SA.' It was sent last night at ten past ten. What it didn't show was that Shirley-Anne waited through the night, for a reply and by the following morning when the screen was still blank, she'd made a decision. Richmond deleted the message and went to run a bath.

This time tomorrow - where would she be? Where would *they* be? That was all that mattered now. 'Oh?' She stepped on a loose nail. She pulled at it and absent-mindedly wrote "sticking plasters" on her list of things to do. Everything on the list was ticked off; the plumbing was done, repairs done, paint bought, carpet lifted, old clothes binned, all jobs done - all, except one.

'Get out,' it said.

The phone rang.

'Pilgrim House.' The call was short. Richmond listened in silence. Following the directions given to her, she left the house two minutes later, carrying a white overnight bag. She walked to Paddington station, bought a ticket to Holland Park and made her way to the Circle Line platform. She jumped to her death in front of the next incoming train.

The bath was still running.

Book Three

3.1

Richmond was gone. The police were back. The oven was cold and there was something in the dustbin like a dead cat.

Upstairs, La Petite tapped on the office door and waited. She carried the morning post to the card table in the summer drawing room, she collected faxes off the floor, she deleted phone messages without listening. Back in the pantry she threw bits for the birds. The birds came and pecked and they didn't die.

DS Rainbow was in the drawing room looking out onto the square; white with settled snow. A young woman in uniform was talking on her phone.

'…nothing…CCTV   down…no   nothing…weather…I know…yes, well ice will do that …' It was the third visit since Richmond died. They were nice and polite and they believed what they were told, but they kept coming back.

La Petite closed the pantry window. She could hear muffled voices upstairs and guessed what was being said after all, it wasn't the first time this happened. A young woman? Everything to live for? Where was Shirley-Anne at the time? La Petite was back to Sea View twenty years ago and the young woman then was Veronica Lakey. DS Rainbow was gentle. Mrs Amis lost her brother just last year. 'None of this is easy,' he said. Snatches of conversation came and went. 'Are you sure? Anything? Was she depressed? Worried? Did she leave a note - did something unusual happen - did she have enemies? Was she ill? When did you last have contact with her?'

'No, Constable. Really, I keep telling you - darling, don't touch that - it's Meissen.'

Last night, La Petite dreamed of Harold. He was running along the edge of a cliff. In the dream she was trying to call. She was saying you can't just walk into other people's lives - but he didn't hear. She saw it all, but it made no difference, Harold still fell. He had wings, the sky was up there and he could have flown but he ran to the edge and bumped all the way down to the sea where a train was waiting.

The voices from the drawing room were calm but firm. Rainbow spoke, again. 'You don't mind us looking? Routine - under the circumstances - upstairs?'

'But you've been up there. She moved out months ago. There's nothing. I assure you. She was really a very private person. We hardly knew her.' Shirley-Anne was growing plaintive, the way she did when things didn't go right.

'And you say she was messy? What do you mean, messy?'

'She - poor Penelope - I can hardly believe we're talking about her like this - well, she had her ways, not always easy. It was a trial for the maid, not for us - we adored her.'

'What do you mean?'

Shirley-Anne looked down into her hands, blameless.

'And your charity - Pilgrim House?' said the policewoman. 'She ran it? Lived there? In Bayswater?'

'Yes?'

Rainbow looked back to the square, like he was trying to remember something. 'Lodging house?'

Shirley-Anne sighed. 'Yes. If you say, so. Yes. Yes.'

Then he said again, about Richmond's flat - the way they found it.

Shirley-Anne squirmed. 'She was working class - really, does any of this matter? There's been an accident. A terrible accident. I don't know why you're here.' He went through the story, again. Richmond dropped her house key on the station platform before she jumped. 'Which is strange' he said. 'Jumpers don't usually take keys - it's not like they're going back'. He described again the broken furniture, the slashed curtains, wallpaper torn from the walls - like something wild was trapped. This was Richmond's flat an hour after she died. 'Bit more than messy, wouldn't you say?'

Shirley-Anne sobbed. 'A burglary. Robbery. The house got flooded - someone passing saw it open - how can people be so wicked?'

'Did she have enemies?'

'No. No - of course not. She was a simple girl. A nobody. We looked after her. She had no one.'

'Did anyone else have a key?'

'No. I don't know. How should I know? There's a key here, somewhere -

I don't know.'

'To her flat?'

'No. No, I don't think so. I don't know. The house was empty - there'd been a burst pipe or something - well, you know that.'

'You have a key Mrs Amis - I mean, do you?' Another pointless question.

She'd just told him - why didn't they listen? - Pilgrim House was run by servants - why, even her doctor's driver knew more about the place than she did.

'Penelope worked so hard. She was so dear. An orphan - did I say that?'

'Mrs Amis this wasn't a robbery. The computer, the phones - even cash on the floor - nothing was taken.' Shirley-Anne looked blank. Then the policewoman spoke. 'I know how you feel.'

'You do?'

'Terrible shock - thing like this, out of the blue.' She hesitated. 'And your brother? And that painting - stolen?' Pause. 'And Mr Amis? You knew he was - what I mean is - Penelope Richmond?'

The scream and the servant's bell slapped La Petite out of her reverie. 'Cherie. Cherie, darling. Angel.' The police were standing now; they made a nice couple. A tall man in grey, a short woman in blue. Shirley-Anne remained in her seat, straight backed and staring. 'Would you like to speak to someone?' said the policewoman. 'We can give you a number? Confidential. It might help?'

'You're very kind - Cherie - be so kind, the police officers are just leaving. So kind.'

'We can see ourselves out, thank you. You'll - er - call us, if - anything?'

'Yes. Yes, of course. We are indebted. Truly - hearts full of gratitude.'

La Petite led the way down the hall. At the front door, Rainbow stopped and called back. 'We need to see him - Mr Amis - routine.'

'But what are you saying?'

'Penelope Richmond didn't jump - that's what we are saying - she was pushed and pushed by someone she knew.'

'But - but -'

'- and whoever pushed her, wanted something from that flat. Tell Mr Amis to call us.'

Shirley-Anne gripped the sides of the chair, knuckles white. She saw Richmond in pieces, alive, twitching. 'This is outrageous. How dare you make accusations against an innocent man -' Rainbow leaned against the doorframe. 'Strangest thing though, now that I recall - with all those people living there -?'

'Yes? Yes? What of it? What of it?'

'No fingerprints. None. Not even hers -'

Shirley-Anne slumped back in the chair, uncomprehending.

'- wiped clean.'

'It wasn't an accident -,' said the policewoman softly, as if speaking to a child '- and we will find him.' The police left and the maid closed the front door quietly behind them. Back in the basement, she poured the last of the Master's gin over a dark furry mess in the dustbin. It was a tight bundle - woollen clothes. She dropped in a lighted match and it burned quite well.

****

Steven and Solly gave Tom strength. They believed in him and that is why he could give up Richmond. They believed he was not such a bad person and that is why he really did want to heal the rift between Penelope Richmond and Shirley-Anne. He wasn't a strong man and yes, he relied a bit too much on Dutch courage but aren't there some clever words somewhere about more rejoicing in Heaven over one repentant sinner than over a whole load of good people - so, how come none of that rejoicing helped him when he needed it? He was with Solly now in the el Saoud.

'Thaw on the way -' Solly raised his chin to the window '- Spring - just round the corner.' Richmond was dead a week.

'You've been saying that since Christmas.'

'You know me. See the good in everything. Pass the sugar. Met the account handler, yesterday - did I say?'

'And - ?' It wasn't easy. The freelance work that Tom was doing for McVie & Co was proving erratic '- the job, Solly. The fucking job?'

'I know.' Solly chewed on a piece of Baclava. 'I'm trying. I am, really - you know what it's like doing work for the government - first they want it this way, then they want it that way and now they've changed the account handler - still, if you've lost interest -?'

Tom looked into his coffee.

'Come on Badger, it'll come right, you'll see. You've always had the Midas touch.'

'That was then. Things have changed. They're following me - the police -'

'Oh?' Solly looked over his cup.

Tom had been up at Ladbroke Grove nick and it didn't go well. A man in a suit, a woman in uniform, cup rings on the table. Routine, they said, but he knew they were lying. When he left, he was followed. He wasn't stupid.

'You sure? I mean - had an old aunt once, swore she was followed by a greyhound.'

Tom's eyes closed. The thing with Richmond was nothing. They'd done nothing wrong and anyway, it was ended - a tussle in the library, nothing, just nothing - but the police twist things. 'Look -' Solly was sympathetic '- we've been over this -'

But no. They had not been over this. Solly had no idea how frightened Tom was - how could he? How do you tell someone that you've spent half your life running and you wake up one day and realise it was all for nothing? Twenty years ago he was lying in a hospital bed thinking he'd escaped the police. Oh, what a joke. They were there all along, waiting. 'They think I pushed Penelope Richmond, that's what they're saying. What do you know - you must remember something?'

'No,' said Solly, firm '- and I don't know why you don't let it drop.'

'I won't let it drop because the police won't fucking let it drop how many times do I have to tell you -? Sorry.'

The night Richmond went under a train, Tom was there. He didn't know how but he was on the platform, behind her. That's what they told him but all he could remember was the snow. He needed Solly to help him remember or he would go mad. 'So, what did they say - I mean, what did they really say?'

The police told Tom he was on the platform when they arrived. Standing still with black stuff down the front of his coat. They took his coat. They showed him photographs of his coat today. What did he remember? Nothing. Tom's only recollection of that night was coming into the el Saoud café. He was wet and cold. Solly was there. It was a dream full of holes. 'You must know something? What did you see?' He needed to remember because he would rather be a murderer and know it, than be anything and not know it. 'Tell me, Solly - for fuck's sake - what happened?'

Solly stirred his coffee and sighed. 'OK. Fine. Here we go again - yes, I was here and yes, you came in. I was here because the snow stopped traffic and fucked if I'm going to break my neck walking through a storm like that - it's the black ice, people don't realise, under the snow it's the black ice, that gets you - anyway - you were a mess - we ordered a few cognacs, got plastered and after that your memory is as good as mine - probably better.'

That jogged something. More bits flew up. 'Yes - it was cold -'

'- and your mac? Where was it? You never go anywhere without that thing?'

'They took it. The police. I was wet. You were dry. I'm sorry, I know you're tired of this -'

Solly shrugged. Yes, he was tired of it but he was Tom's friend and he wanted to help and if Tom couldn't remember, Solly was happy - more than happy - to remember for him. 'Badger, it's a bad business. You were fond of her. She was a tramp, but - you'd had a few, thought you'd fuck her one last time - after all, when it's on offer - anyway - you followed her to the station then lost your nerve. It happens. You don't remember because you were plastered - well, nothing new there.'

'The police - they said I called Richmond just before she left the house. My mobile.

They said I arranged to meet her at the station. I pushed her.' Most of that, true. Penelope Richmond did get a call and it was from Tom's phone and she did leave Pilgrim House a few minutes later.

That was the general gist of the interview up at the nick this morning. But what they didn't say - and what Tom couldn't remember - was that he was nowhere near Richmond when the train came through. He was on the platform, yes. His coat was splattered with her brains, yes. But someone else was there - and that is what interested them, now.

'They think it was me. They couldn't get me for Veronica but they knew I'd do it again - they've been waiting for this -'

'Did they arrest you?'

'No.'

'Oh? They tend to arrest murderers - I think you'll find. Cognac?'

'Shut up.'

'Look, Badger -' Solly reached over and touched Tom's arm '- you've had a bit of a shock. No. Be fair. It's been rough - easy to, well -'

'Yes? Easy? What, easy?' Easy to see what he'd become? He used to be a man - now, look at him. An ape led by a monkey. 'Pass the sugar.'

'Look -' Solly coughed. 'We can talk. I don't mind -' and in a way that only he could do, Solly brought Tom back. He asked questions, he helped Tom remember Richmond in a way that didn't hurt - what did he like about her? What annoyed him about her? What was she hiding - and everyone hides something? 'Remember that tart in Praed Street? Turned out to be a man?' Solly had a gift. He could lift Tom out of the mess - any mess. Another bottle of cognac came and the job that wasn't happening, the girl that was dead, the money that wasn't there and the police that were - didn't matter. Solly was talking and Tom was listening.

They left the café, a little unsteady. When they parted outside Queensway tube, Tom assured Solly he'd got a portfolio of prints and Solly assured Tom he was near to nailing the budget. They went their separate ways, happy.

****

Next day was grey. Tom stood outside his wife's room, hovering.

It was midday and he was back from the nick again. Same questions. Still routine. Just a bit of info on Shirley-Anne but

146

didn't want to upset her - they thought he might help? He didn't believe that, either. The door opened and the scent of sweet decay hit him. 'Gilmore? How's - what I mean is, how's -?'

'Come in Mr Amis.' Dr Gilmore was carrying his bag. He never said much. He never stayed long. 'I'll see myself out. No, it's best you stay. Thank you. Good day.' Tom knew Gilmore suspected him. Inside, Shirley-Anne was dressed and sitting by the window. A familiar plastic bag was knotted behind a Chinese umbrella vase in the corner. The maid would take it away, later. 'What-ho old thing. Roses back in your cheeks.'

'Ah. Thomas.' She was pale. Drawn. She pointed at the roof of the house opposite. 'I was looking at the crows.' Her voice, light. 'Up there, on top of that chimney. See them? I couldn't understand at first. One isn't moving. The other is pecking at it, but it just doesn't move. Why is that? I can't understand, why.'

Tom looked for somewhere to sit. Sickness made him uneasy. There was only one chair. It was not a room for visitors. He rang for the maid. 'Frenchie - fetch in a chair -'

'No. Leave her. She has enough to do. The police made such a mess.' La Petite bent into the corner and picked up the bag. Despite himself, Tom followed it with his eyes.

'Feeling better? I mean, what with everything.' He was out of place in this room. He was the visitor.

'Robin wants me to have surgery - a procedure, I believe they call it these days.' She gave a short laugh, a snort. 'Apparently, it's all the rage.' She looked back to the window. 'It's gone on too long, just nothing seems to make a difference, and -' her voice broke '- the shame.'

'Now, now, old thing. Chin up.'

'I can't bear it. It came on bad, last night. I had to call him.' It wasn't like her to show emotion. She was the strong one. He pretended, but her strength was real.

'Now, now.'

'He's right. I need to do something. I can't go on -' her tears were open and shameless. 'I see people looking at me. I think all the time they are looking at it - the dirt.'

147

'Don't.'

'They mean well, but I see it in their eyes. The pity. The revulsion.'

'No. It's not true.' What could he say? He stroked the back of her hair; it was lank. 'Perhaps, it's for the best' he said. 'You know, no more of - this.' He coughed and sat on the edge of the bed, afraid the blood would touch him.

'You worry so, for me. I know you do. It's been hard for you, too. But the pain -' her eyes closed '- you know, sometimes I think I will lose my mind. There's no rhyme or reason; it comes on out of the blue. It's like I become a different person. No one understands; how could they?'

'I know' he said, but he didn't. 'I know you want me to - that is - you want your privacy, but -'

'Darling, Tom -' her hand on his. 'Endometriosis gives no one any privacy.' He shot a glance at the window, looking for a way out.

'I'm afraid to leave the house. I stay here for weeks, hidden away and then - then, I just can't stand it anymore and I run out like a mad thing.

Yesterday, I was up at Clarendon Cross before I realised I was wearing sandals.

Sandals in the snow.' She sobbed. 'You know, I even thought of going to Lourdes. Can you imagine? Yes, I thought you'd find that funny.' She sobbed and laughed and sobbed, again.

'No. Not funny. We all believe in something.' He gave her his handkerchief. She cried quietly now; more like herself. Modest. It was hard to believe that this was the body that once set him on fire.

'Darling, what are you thinking?'

'Oh, nothing - this and that. Clapham Common. Funny.'

She looked up, surprised. It wasn't like Tom to reminisce.

'That day. Remember? The heat wave. Remember?'

'Yes, I remember.'

'I turned round and there you were: out of nowhere.' It was a day in August. Dry and tired. He was running from sickness then, too. Running from love. Just running.

'Thomas. Always the romantic.'

'Do you remember - the fair?' Shirley-Anne Brille, spinster. A friend of a friend - one of the crowd. A nobody.

'Yes. I remember. The steam. The noise.'

But Tom wasn't thinking of the Fair now. He was thinking of nights sitting by a bed, holding a hand and promising the earth. He was thinking about his first wife, Eve. The nights of watching, the days of walking, time standing still. He remembered the rain and taking cover. He remembered sitting in a corner, listening to the bell for eight o'clock mass. A church - shelter from the rain, that's all. He had no idea how he got there. He was an empty man. When Eve slept - and that was most of the time (a good sign, they said) - he sat in a corner and bargained. 'Let her live' he said. 'Name Your price' and he meant it.

Then came Shirley-Anne. In the middle of the steam, in the middle of the Fair, in the middle of the mess - Shirley-Anne. Bright. Smiling. Her arms outstretched. Somewhere to run.

He stroked her hair again, now. 'Is there anything I can do?' he said. Wiping her eyes, she looked up at the crows. 'People say they look like policemen. I suppose they do, in a way; but I think they look more like an old married couple. A couple who've run out of secrets.' The maid came in with a tray.

'Ginger tea, old thing. Your favourite,' he said.

'Et pour monsieur?' asked the maid.

'Du café.'

Why did the maid always ask -? The coffee was already on the tray. Why did she ask? They drank in silence. Then 'they called me in again,' he said.

'Darling. I'm sorry.'

'Routine, they said.'

'But Angel, they're speaking to everyone, even the maid - yes, I know - got in an interpreter specially. Was it awful?'

His back was beginning to stiffen. 'Look, let me get a chair from the drawing room. I could read to you. You've always liked Keats -'. How could he tell her? The sniping, peevish remarks they made. He knew what they were doing - they attacked Shirley-Anne to make him angry, to make him say things '- what's it like -' they said '- married to a saint?' and they laughed. He wanted to hit them but he was scared. 'You're not under arrest - you can go anytime - it's not you we want.' They were playing games - but why? 'Tell me, Mr Amis - or, is it Tom? Tell me, Tom - your first wife? Died? Can't have been easy - watching her go like that? We've got the post-mortem notes - oh, sorry? Didn't we say? Want to see? No? The word "irregularity" comes up nine times. What do you make of that?' and they laughed, again.

DS Rainbow didn't laugh. Watching Tom through the one-way glass, he drew circles on paper - each a death, each a woman close to Tom Amis: Evelyn Amis, Veronica Lakey, Penelope Richmond. Each standing between him and Shirley-Anne. Then, he drew another circle for Severin Brille. Why did Severin Brille die?

Shirley-Anne rang the bell for the maid. 'On second thoughts, maybe a few crackers. Keats, you say? Yes, of course dearest. I can hardly lift a finger. I'm not myself. These damned pills, I have no idea what he is giving me - could be anything.'

'At five hundred quid an hour, I hope it's not just anything?'

She smiled. 'Actually, it's rather more.' That smile. It brought him back from the grave, once. 'Darling, you should see him. You know, he's very good.'

'A man with expensive tastes.'

'Doesn't stop him being a good doctor.'

Tom never liked Gilmore. He wanted to say, if the good doctor was so good then why was she still so ill - but he didn't say it. He stopped saying that a long time ago. 'Don't need doctors. In my prime.'

'You've stopped drinking? Alcohol? Of course you have, forgive me, Thomas. I worry so, what with your health and the way you work.'

'It isn't my health, though - is it? We have to talk. You know that.'

She put the cup down and sighed. 'Yes. Penelope. I know.' This was part of the unspoken story that kept them together and apart, at the same time.

'They think I killed her,' said Tom and then he went quiet. This was all about Tom and the slide. It was a story of different bits, all successfully avoided by Shirley-Anne and Tom, most of the time.

For Shirley-Anne, it was easy. She had goodness on her side. But not so for Tom. He attracted trouble. He was a philanderer, a coward who used women and killed them. But she loved him, still - because that's what she did. She assumed - rightly - Tom believed that too. That's how they stayed happy. Tom had an affair with Richmond - well, why wouldn't he? - just as he did with Veronica Lakey, all those years ago. It meant nothing then and it meant nothing now.

'You're smiling, Thomas. Why are you smiling?'

'Good times' he said. He was thinking of Veronica. Back then it was all about fun - except, like Richmond, when it came to it - it wasn't. He never really understood what happened to Veronica. It was the end of another summer and the best party, ever. Golden times - or at least, that's how this bit of the story went. Tom and Veronica got very drunk. They argued, he hit her, she fell and he would have fallen too, had he not passed out. They found him unconscious and slumped on the edge of the walkway. When he came to his senses two days later in a hospital bed, Shirley-Anne was by his side. She nursed him back to health. She comforted him. He would not be arrested. The secret was safe with her. She forgave him.

How far this story departed from fact, didn't matter. What mattered - at least to Shirley-Anne - was that it allowed them to be happy once again with each other and with themselves. It allowed Shirley-Anne to be good and Tom to be grateful.

'They're off,' said Tom, looking up at the crows. He wanted to be with them. She nodded. 'Darling - no, don't put me off Thomas - I have to tell you; tell someone.' She looked up, helpless. 'You know, sometimes I go into a room and forget. Why? Am I mad? I pick up a brush, a piece of paper - then, I forget. I just stop, in the middle of things - I think I hear her calling or running down the stairs. I turn - I think she's there. Hours go by, I do nothing. I look out of the drawing room window across the square, expecting to see her. You miss poor Penelope - but Angel, we all miss her. We berate ourselves. We think we could we have done more. It's the price of love.'

Tom's coffee was cold and so was he.

'It's been hard on us all' she said.

The police showed him Richmond's phone record, the calls from him highlighted in yellow - and one from his mobile, twelve minutes before she died. They showed him a torn note - 'kill you' - his writing. What could he say?

'Filthy bitch,' Shirley-Anne whispered.

'You don't mean that,' he said. He patted her shoulder. He knew no one missed Richmond more than his wife. She was the one who sat by the phone, waiting. She was the one who loved - he only pretended.

****

Two hours passed and the heavy beat of the hall clock called them back.

'I've become a vampire,' said Shirley-Anne, her voice hoarse.

'Quiet now. You were sleeping.'

'You must have a million things to do, don't stay.' She tried to sit up. 'You know, with this stuff I hardly know I'm alive until the afternoon and then - through the night I'm awake. Sometimes, I wonder, what's the point - taking medicine, or trying to change things - after all, the sun rises and sets, for a reason. It must be for a reason.'

'What do you mean?'

'The natural way of things, it's there to help, surely? If you fall out of it - fall out with what nature intended -?' She looked up at the portrait of her mother and her head fell back heavy. Tom hated that picture. 'You are mine -' he said '- that's all that matters.' He leaned over and touched her cheek. 'I am nothing without you.' He wanted his words to mean something but that slight flinch, said different. It said what the portrait had been saying for years. He was speaking a language his wife didn't understand.

'I'll go back. Yes. Sea View. It's been years. I'll go back and take that chap - what's his name - Steve? - Steven? - we'll finish off what Penelope started. We'll sort it out. You'll have your show. Why not? Just think of it: "Artist Returns!" It will be great.'

'Oh?'

Tom brightened. 'We owe it to Penelope - it's what she wanted.'

Shirley-Anne smiled but her eyes were full of tears and when she spoke, it was soft. 'Darling, Thomas. You don't know? Poor Steven - darling, he's dead. I'm sorry. So sorry. Forgive me Angel - I wanted to spare you -'

3.2

Shirley-Anne took Dr Gilmore's advice. She had surgery and spent four comfortable days in a private clinic off Wimpole Street, wondering what all the fuss was about. At the same time, Tom stayed in his room looking at the wall and La Petite sat in the pantry scratching her face until it bled.

Sitting up in bed now with a dry sherry and the Luncheon menu, Shirley-Anne thought kindly of the maid. She was old, she'd given good service and a time comes when the sun sets for us all. There were brochures for Care Homes on the South Downs. Shirley-Anne was still in pain but her spirits were high. 'My poor darling maid. We were both so terribly fond of her, but, well, what must be must be.' She was addressing a visitor, sitting crossed legged and smiling. Solomon Solomon. He lifted his glass and they toasted each other and life and the way people come and go. In his pocket an envelope. Cash.

In his mind, words. Written in soap.

Back in the pantry, La Petite's gaze stayed with the sky but she only saw what was in her head. The day after Penelope died, La Petite was filling the kettle for the Mistress' morning tea, when her foot touched something under the sink. The

Mistress' coat. An old thing, heavy and rolled up and wet. Then the police came. The mistress shrieked and after that, La Petite set fire to the dustbin. Flutter. Flutter. Flutter.

That's when the baking stopped, the house ground to a halt and Shirley-Anne concluded that the maid was losing her mind. By a stroke of good fortune, the doctor's nice driver had time on his hands and at Dr Gilmore's suggestion, he offered to help out - just until the maid got better. Gilmore tried to persuade La Petite to take a short course of iron tablets but she resisted, doubting the intentions of anyone dispensing tablets. She would have continued to resist but for an injection of vitamins, which the doctor told her would do her no harm and she believed him. It swept through like a soft wind and after that she was grateful for anything.

She never recovered and Vic stayed.

'One for the road?' Back in the Chancel Clinic, Solomon Solomon poured another. 'Cheers' she said. 'Here's to not getting left out in the cold.' Shirley-Anne raised her glass and smiled. Well, they both did.

****

Alan Tree watched and waited and when the maid was alone, he paid a visit. It didn't go well.

His mother being from the same part of Haiti, he assumed a warm welcome. He didn't get one. His Creole was good and hers was not bad but she was slippery and feigned ignorance which annoyed him. Tree explained that he wanted to help. He was trying to recover Mrs Amis' painting and although the painting no longer belonged to her, she - or the maid - might know something about it, to help him? He asked about Vic. He seemed to be a regular visitor now and why was that? He also asked about Vic's friend, Steven Witt - what did the maid know about him?

The maid shrugged. She stayed looking out of the window and said nothing intelligible. It made for a short visit.

Tree was a precise man but he'd let two lives slip through and it irked him. The drive back to Pilgrim House helped to clear his mind. The place looked different now, smaller. He parked on the corner and tried again to piece together that last weekend of Penelope Richmond's life. What did he miss?

He remembered sitting in his car - just here. He tried to reach Richmond - he called through the door - but she wouldn't answer. It was late Friday afternoon and already dark. Then Witt arrived. He was hiding something under his coat - a weapon. He got straight into Pilgrim House, so he had a key. Tree recognised him from the CCTV at Steiner's Private View back in August - Vic let him in the back gate then and he went straight for Shirley-Anne. The following day, he was in St James' Gardens and within a week he was working for Tom. Now he was here, with Richmond. The pattern was simple: the target is identified. The criminals move in. They become friends, servants, lovers, even doctors. They make themselves indispensable. They watch and wait. It happened to Severin Brille and now it was happening to Shirley-Anne - the inheritor.

Witt came back to Pilgrim House early next day carrying heavy bags. Tree watched Richmond up at the window, waving her arms like they were arguing. Witt left soon after. Tree followed but Witt was too quick. He dipped into a small hardware shop on the Bayswater Road and then doubled back into the tube and Tree lost him. When Tree got back to Pilgrim House, the street was cordoned off. Someone said a gas leak; someone else said a bomb. He couldn't get near.

Within the hour, a bathroom flood was located and Tree went back to sitting in his car at the end of the street, waiting for Richmond to show. What did Steven Witt say? What was in those bags? A trap - was that it? Was he forcing her to trap Shirley-Anne? Tree remembered listening to the car radio and drifting off. He woke when something bumped against the car. It was night. The wing mirror was pushed back. A man skidded across the road and went into the basement of Pilgrim House. This was Saturday night.

Inside, a light flashed up. It went from room to room. It stopped just below Richmond's flat and went out.

This was Steven Witt. Back and waiting.

What Tree didn't know then but realised next day, Sunday, was that Richmond was no longer in the building. She'd left at about seven the previous evening with Dr Robin Gilmore, when Tree was dozing.

When she re-appeared at the end of the street on Sunday morning, she was smiling - her face tilted to the sky. It was starting to snow again. Tree stayed in his car. He knew he could get Richmond now - save her. But Witt was watching - yes, Richmond would agree - but then what? Witt would disappear for a while. He'd wait. But he would be back. They always come back.

Tree weighed his options and watched her go by. He needed hard evidence. He had to wait.

An hour went by and nothing happened. Richmond sat by the window, looking out. Tree sat in his car, looking up. By mid-afternoon a light came on in the room below and a man's face showed at the window. Witt. He was going to make a move. Tree was about to signal to Richmond but then two things happened in quick succession. Shirley-Anne appeared from the phone box on the corner and walked towards Pilgrim House and Tree wet himself.

When he looked up, Shirley-Anne was gone and Penelope Richmond was in the street - heading for the tube. No doubt, Witt had used her as bait to get Shirley-Anne here. No doubt, she saw a chance to escape and took it. No doubt.

Tree called and ran and slipped. The snow was driving hard and by the time he got to the corner Richmond was out of sight. Cars were stalled in a white fog. He followed her footprints and behind them another pair. Large. Tree called again but nothing came back. When he got to the station, Richmond was gone and the alarm was up and Steven Witt was running out of the station.

Sirens screamed. Tree retraced his steps but slow. By the time he got back to Richmond's flat it was wrecked. Wallpaper was stripped. Holes gaped. Wires hung. The mattress was cut down the middle like rape. Witt did this. He did it when he came to Penelope Richmond the day before. No doubt, showing her what would happen if she didn't comply. No wonder she sat like stone. No wonder.

Tree heard commotion in the street. He left by the basement as the police arrived.

He went to the el Saoud café and sat. He didn't know what to do. An old man problem caught him out. It was like a part of him was saying 'give it up - you're too old for this - you and your weak bladder - who do you think you are?' A stab. Unusually for him, Tree stayed at the café and started drinking. He didn't notice Tom Amis walk in. It wasn't until he heard his voice - high pitched, shakey - that he looked up and saw him, drenched.

A man already at one of the tables called over 'Badger -' he slapped Tom on the back and ordered 2 cognacs and then a bottle. They sat talking quietly in the corner for over an hour and Tree lost interest. He didn't see Tom's phone on the table when he came in, neither did Tom. He didn't see Tom put it in his pocket without thinking.

The snow had stopped when Tree left and the night was still. Everything was buried including his car, so he decided to walk. He passed various small hillocks of snow on his way to the station. One whimpered.

That was Steven Witt.

****

After Steven's death, Tom was like a wind-up toy, run down. 'Mr Amis?

Are you in there? Are you alright, sir - it's Victor - Dr Gilmore's driver. I've got a newspaper and those blue cigarettes you like.' Vic took the tray untouched from yesterday and tapped lightly. He wanted to speak. Steven was missing - did Mr Amis know?

'A bloke called - said something about stuff in store? Invoice? I said you were out. I'm lending a hand - until the maid gets back on her feet, sir.'

The door unlocked. 'What?'

Something got through and by a series of lightening connections Tom realised - this was the Whitely Industrial Estate and he'd forgotten to pay the quarterly bill, again. Within the hour he was back there hearing more bad news.

Over the years, Tom pilfered more than two hundred thousand pounds worth of things stored at Sea View. This alarming news came to him today, when a girl in sharp glasses called him in to the manager's office. 'Pride ourselves on our records,' said the manager, Fred Pond. 'Thought you'd like to know - had a word with your wife -'

Yes. Surprise. What started out as a harmless bit of borrowing to tide him over, slid into something hard to deny; so, he didn't. It was a tight spot but lies still came easy. Tom said he'd taken these things for repair and restoration and once done, they were put in the bank. 'God. Sorry - thought I'd said?' The matter came to a head because Shirley-Anne now wanted these missing things located. 'Fuss about nothing.'

'Back to the station, sir?' In the taxi going back, Tom's mind was elsewhere. 'I'm aiming for the eleven-forty.'

'You'll be alright - rush hour's over; see? Up ahead - cleared already.'

A lifetime later, he pushed open the door at Bowling Green Lane; mouth dry heart pounding - it was back - that mad thing that pushed and pulled and followed - 'thought I'd make myself at home. Mind?' Denise. Tom's peccadillo. There. Tipsy and naked and part of the mess.

'So? Denise - nice weather' he undid his belt and after that he felt nothing - nothing but the savage loneliness that Steven Witt left behind.

****

Two hours later, Tom paid Denise and she left Bowling Green Lane, sore and slightly confused. Tom stayed. It was hard to breathe, his jaw ached, Richmond was everywhere, the police were everywhere and Steven was dead - how did that happen? How? The man was such a coward? Tom sat back and tried to breathe slow. The police worried him - the way they laughed. They showed him pictures of his coat, covered in brains. Why?

If he killed Richmond, why didn't they arrest him? Why did they keep calling him back? 'Bit of a drinker - Mr Amis?' they laughed because they had a lot to laugh about. Tom Amis was on the platform when the train that sliced Richmond went through. He was standing near her and his coat did get sprayed with her brains. But, the trail of the spray and the undisturbed snow showed that Tom was more than four feet from the platform edge when Richmond was hit. He didn't touch her and that is why they kept calling him back - he saw who did.

****

Without knowing or caring, Tom took a taxi to Highbury. Maybe he just wanted to know what happened to Steven or maybe, a mad part of him hoped that it was all a mistake. He found the house. A typical, large north London, run down place like Bayswater. Purgatory. The street door banged. 'Sorry? Can we help?' A small man, skinny, easy to hate, looked up from the desk.

'I rang. I'm looking for -'

'Tom -' something shrieked behind the filing cabinet '- Tom Amis - I can't believe it.' A fat hand shot out. 'Topper. Remember? Yes, of course you do - well who'd have thought? How is darling Shirley-Anne? Yes we're expecting you - this way.' She waddled down the hallway. 'Won't find him in - transients - can't keep the room empty indefinitely - refugees - where do they all come from - ha ha.'

Tom wondered how much horsepower it would take to slice that up? She led him to the basement stairs at the back where the air thickened.

'Tom?' Another voice called, weak, thready. 'Mr Amis? Tom - is that you?'

Tom stopped. Then screamed. 'Fuck - you're dead. Oh, fuck.' Stars burst and the world went golden again. Yes. It was true. It had all been a joke. Yes. Yes. Yes. Yes.

Over. Over. 'Fuck. Fuck. Fuck. No really - fuck - oh my God oh my God oh my God. No - really - fuck - you're alive.'

'Ah,' said the fat woman, also surprised 'Mr Witt - thought we'd lost you. You know we can't keep these rooms empty forever -'

Steven moved slow, dragging a dead leg. 'Watch your step' he led Tom down the basement stairs. 'Just a minute - I tripped a few weeks ago and -' a fluorescent tube flickered overhead. In the dim light Tom saw a bare hallway and waves of steam. Naked men in towels passed between them. Steven was on crutches. He unlocked a door at the foot of the stairs next to the lavatory. 'Come in. Just a minute, I'll put on the lamp.' He shuffled and Tom imagined a room full of nice things, like in St James' Gardens - soft, clean, soft, soft, soft and safe.

It wasn't.

A small orange light clicked in the far corner. The room was high ceilinged with a large window at one end facing a brick wall. 'There -' said Steven.

He pointed to a bare socket overhead '- went a few days ago, needs a new fixing. But this is fine - I like a softer light.'

It was a pit.

'What the fuck happened? Where have you been? They told us you were dead.' Tom hardly recognised him. 'You're a mess. A complete fucking mess - and believe me, you were no cupcake to begin with - what happened?'

In fact, Steven was a good shape. Considering. After three weeks in hospital and a free taxi back, he'd been lying in this room since yesterday, drifting. Today was his first day up. He'd lost weight. His face was still livid with bruising.

'What happened?'

'Fell.'

'Liar.' Tom feared suffering and he didn't really want to know. What he did want was a good story - he wanted Steven to say he'd been out drinking - having a time of it with wild women. What he didn't want was this - a man in rags.

There was a narrow bed against the wall and not much else. They sat side by side on the bed and Tom tried not to hear as Steven told him what really happened. It didn't take long. 'You were right,' said Steven 'Miss Richmond did need a hand and she was grateful -' ok, good so far '- in fact, she was quite pressing.' Yes. 'She wanted me to paint her flat - no, it didn't need it - but, she'd got it fixed in her mind that the thing had to be done and done in a day. Stupid.

Paint takes time to dry.' Steven explained in unnecessary detail how he brought four tins of white emulsion and one tin of gloss up to Pilgrim House on Saturday morning. Richmond was determined to get the job done and in the face of all reason, she sent him out again for bigger rollers and an electric fan. Rollers he could find. But an electric fan - in February? In the snow?

Tom yawned. 'A fan?' He was starting to think it was going to be OK - boring, but OK.

'I had to get it right. I needed to get what Miss Richmond wanted - an electric fan - the way to her heart - the way back to Mrs Amis. Remember?' Steven said he went to a small hardware shop on the Bayswater Road. They had electric fan heaters but quick drying with these would make the paint peel so they sent him to another shop down on the Goldhawk Road. After Goldhawk Road he went to Hammersmith. In the end, he got six hair dryers and a multi-socket connection and anyway - '

'- this is going somewhere?'

'God was I tired - the thing about hair dryers is that they do actually blow cold air -' all true. No sooner did Steven find a seat on the train back, than he fell asleep. He woke with a start at four in the morning - Sunday - still on the train, in a siding -

stiff and cold. He went back to his room in Highbury. Another man would have given up but Steven had fear that knew no end.

That evening - Sunday - he came back to Bayswater with two bags, three hair dryers in each. He forgot the rollers.

'Unbelievable -' said Tom, anticipating a happy ending and soon.

'I saw,' said Steven '- what happened - and yes, she was.'

'What?'

'Pushed.'

In one of those strokes of bad luck that seemed to dog his life, Steven got off the train just as Penelope Richmond arrived on the opposite platform. He saw her wave to someone already there, waiting under the shelter. She was holding a small white bag. The snow was falling heavy.

Tom went cold. 'Yes' he said. 'It was me. I killed Penelope.' In the silence that followed, both men sank. Tom lived again the brightness that was Richmond and how he tried to keep away and then on that last weekend when he couldn't keep away any more. He'd been sitting alone in the el Saoud, since Saturday midday, drinking steadily. He saw her leave Pilgrim House in her running kit. He thought he'd wait, speak to her, tell her she deserved a better life and then he'd walk away. That's what he wanted but it didn't happen. Instead, stayed in the café and drank steadily through the afternoon, waiting and hoping.

By evening, he was still there and drunk. He paid the bill and called Richmond from the pay phone in the corner - said something about taking her back to St James' Gardens. Next thing he knew he was outside. The street was quiet. He bumped into things. He crossed the road and was going to speak to Richmond face to face - have it out - whatever, 'it' was. He slipped in the snow and fell down the basement steps. The door was open. He groped his way upstairs by torchlight, after that, he passed out.

He didn't hear Richmond come back next day - Sunday. In the quiet of the hours spent looking out of the window, she heard him snoring downstairs and assumed it was air in the pipes. Towards evening, he woke with a start. He remembered putting on the light and for a moment, not knowing where he was, he went to the window and looked out. The street lights were on. Now mad with thirst, he groped his way to a bathroom down the hall. Then the front door banged. He saw Penelope Richmond go down the front steps and without thinking, he ran too. He had to catch her. He had to say - say - sorry. Sorry for meeting her, sorry for being happy with her, sorry for ruining her life. The snow was blinding, his chest pained like someone was squeezing it but he would catch her. When he got to the station platform, she was there - she turned and waved and it was going to be OK then it all went blank.

'The police -' said Tom now '- they found me. I don't remember. They didn't arrest me. Shock, they said. They took my coat and told me to go home. I don't know why. I still don't.'

'It wasn't you,' said Steven.

Steven was shaking now, his head in his hands. He was seeing again that moment - when he called across and Richmond turned. She heard him. She looked at him. It happened so quick - the turn, the shadow behind, the train, the screech - but now in his mind, it was slow and he saw every detail. Her face. She knew. Just before she went under, she knew - her eyes, screamed - 'Save me.' Then gone. Another face flashed up - in less than a second it was gone, but not before Steven saw it - and it saw Steven.

Steven knew that face.

****

Fright plays havoc. Tom and Steven both saw Richmond killed - and both saw it differently. Now, in Steven's room and calmed by the faint smell of mint from the steam seeping in, Tom began to take heart. 'You know what this means?'

'Yes,' said Steven.

When Richmond went under the train Steven panicked and ran. He didn't see the gates closing or the car that followed. Slow. Lights off. Somewhere near Pilgrim House, he stumbled and hit the ground hard. He remembered the smell of fumes and red brake lights. Just before he passed out, he thought he was rolling down a hill but he wasn't. Heavy hands dragged him into a corner. He looked dead. He regained consciousness early the following day when the bin men arrived and mistook him for a carpet.

'The cold saved you -,' said the doctor in A&E. Text book. Concussion and bruising '- got off lightly - few bits broken - seen worse on the rugger pitch. That's what comes of drinking.' Yes. Steven did get off lightly - until now. The person who pushed Richmond followed him and ran him over and left him for dead. Dead and safe. But now, Tom was here and Steven wasn't safe anymore. 'Cheer up,' said Tom, warming to it all. 'Young man like you. Few bruises, nothing a few gins wouldn't put right. We can tell the police.' For Tom it just got better. 'Tell them what you saw - we'll both be off the hook.'

'You reckon?'

3.3

Tom was happy. Gilmore was happier and Shirley-Anne was happiest of all. 'Oh, Thomas' she was back from the clinic '- you tease - don't pretend so. You did miss me, admit it.'

Tom was glad for them. He knew they felt the loss of Penelope and he admired them, for not letting it show. 'Smile and the world smiles with you,' said Shirley-Anne. She was still in pain but life was good. Harry Steiner was full of ideas - even Butters wanted to make peace. They were all in a good place.

'I'm a dead man,' said Steven. 'I swear, if you tell anyone - anyone at all - I'm dead - no really, not even your wife.' In ways he couldn't explain, Steven was now on the run from not one, not two but three people. And of the three, Vic with his lead pipe was the least of it. That was why Steven was now in Tom's studio in Clerkenwell with six doughnuts, a bottle of gin and The Racing Post. 'I'll get you out of this,' said Tom. 'I'll get us both out.'

****

Not everyone bore the loss of Penelope Richmond well. Vic for one. It was just too big - she was gone and that was bad, but there were dark moments when he wondered if she'd ever been there at all? He was torn between suspicion and longing and were it not for the criminal within, he would have gone mad. But that part of Vic that preyed on the weak and foolish came to him now. He was sitting behind the wheel outside Gilmore's consulting rooms in Wimpole Street quite calm, watching his consolation prize approach. Mrs Shirley-Anne Amis.

When Gilmore opened the door, Shirley-Anne threw up her hands in delight. 'Surprise. Surprise. Now tell me, what was all that fuss about?' Gilmore bowed like a butler '- and what a pleasant surprise.' This visit was expected.

'I hate it when things go wrong between us - it's so unlike us.' She walked in giving him her gloves. 'Nice place. Hasn't changed.'

'How are you feeling? Well. Obviously.'

The way Shirley-Anne saw it, Robin Gilmore was up and down and hard to read. Back in August, just after the Private View, he was so encouraging. Fully behind her, he said. Then, he came back from his little place in France and went moody again. Admittedly, the searing pain of endometriosis and the mess of it all, can't have helped but now - here she was - ready for a new life. Going up in the lift Gilmore took her wrist.

'Well?'

'Pulse normal.'

'Not that. This. Me. Here. By myself. What does that tell you Robin?'

'Victor brought you? I see the car -?'

She laughed. 'Oh, you hate it so, when you're wrong. As a matter of fact, I walked through the park. Do you know the bluebells are out? Isn't it marvellous to be alive?'

'Walked?'

'Yes - part of the way, at least.'

'Not too soon?'

She shrugged. 'Tom says it's about time I stood on my own two feet and you know - I think he's right.'

'You're looking well - remarkably so - but it really doesn't change anything, Mrs Amis. You know my views. What you propose is -'

'- yes?'

'Ridiculous.'

She needed above all, to stay calm. Being well and being here was not enough. She needed to prove that he couldn't keep her in a box any longer. 'You know, you never visited me - at the clinic?'

'Did Tom?'

'Ah, that's unfair - you know how he hates hospitals. Anyway, the last thing one wants is a man mooning about. Poor Butters was on the phone everyday - desperate for mother's picture. She wants to lend me her boat - yacht thing. Says Tom and I could do with getting away.'

'Tom? How is he? Baring up?'

'What do you think? Butters says she'll give me a good price - even sell Mother on commission?'

Gilmore wasn't listening. 'And, Tom? The murderer?'

'Apparently -' said Shirley-Anne now warming to the real reason for being here '- we're quite a marketable family. Remember my poor picture? The one that got stolen - well, Harry Steiner says it's pushed me back into the public eye. He'd buy it himself, if it ever turned up.'

Gilmore tensed. He would have tensed more if he knew the theft had been watched on CCTV by Alan Tree and that at this very moment, Alan Tree was thinking - 'why would Gilmore's driver, do that?'

The lift bounced to a stop. Gilmore slid the gate and Shirley-Anne stepped back in time. The wood panelled hall looked smaller. Meaner. 'You know it must be years - when was it, we moved you in here? Oh - that little chandelier, still here?' A grandfather clock struck the hour. 'From Clapham Common to Wimpole Street, in one step - and what a step. Do you ever think about it - when we first met? You were such a young thing - so tall and thin. Young men can be elegant in a way a woman never can. We are just lumpy creatures at heart - beasts of burden.'

'Just as you say, Mrs Amis. A long time ago.'

'Remember your socks? Darned?'

Gilmore said nothing.

'Lovely view.'

His suite was on the middle floor where the rooms were best proportioned and quietest. At the back, a picture window faced south - an enclosed world of terraces and courtyards. 'I realise I'm taking a chance - when is your next patient?'

'We have time, please -' he held open the door to the inner consulting room. It was a simple room, almost bare.

'Is that a Warhol?'

He nodded.

'Not afraid of burglars?'

They sat opposite each other. His hands joined as if in meditation.

'Robin, I really can't see what's so wrong in any of this. Me getting back into the swing of things, I mean -' the first ripple came up hot '- a small exhibition - really, even the doctors at the clinic say I should be up and about - Robin, I'm too young to disappear -' then the real thing broke through '- surely, you can see, that?' - the fear.

Gilmore sighed. His voice now soft, measured, as if speaking to a child. 'It means a lot to you, I know.'

'It does. It does. Oh, darling I knew you'd understand.'

He nodded and sighed. 'I would be the last to stand in your way, I think you know that, but sometimes -' here it came '- there are things - that is to say - once you start, there is no going back. Have you thought about that? No, Mrs Amis, don't interrupt - I mean, have you really thought about that?'

'Will you stop treating me like a mental defective.' It was hard - fear slips so easy to hatred. 'Look, Robin, I took your advice. I ignored Penelope Richmond, but she went ahead anyway and now people really do want to see my work. It's art. It matters. I matter. Harry says -'

Gilmore stood - sharp. 'Oh, Harry says - Harry says - have you no sense? He wants what he can get from you. Have you any idea how these people will use you? How much you have to lose? Sorry - I didn't mean to shout.'

'I can't be ill forever. No one can.'

'You're twisting my words.'

In the silence that followed, Shirley-Anne fought with herself. 'Darling, I know you want what's best, but really - look at me. I'm here. I'm fine. My health is good. There is nothing I can't handle. Surely, you can see that?' Those words were part of the story that was Shirley-Anne and Robin Gilmore. In it, Gilmore was young, newly qualified, with an eye for the main chance - a man who still believed in himself.

'Do you remember, Mrs Amis, there was a time when you couldn't leave the house and do you remember why?'

'Dearest,' said Shirley-Anne, 'I owe you so much - you think I don't know that?'

'Have you any idea what publicity will do? To you? To your husband?'

'But Harry says it will be private. Another little show. Friends. Only friends. Just like the thing at his home last summer. So dear.'

'And no one watching? No one asking questions? Who was Penelope Richmond talking to - a journalist? Friend of Steiner's - did you know that? He needs publicity. He will expose you - your life - everything. These people are predators. They don't care - '

'Well - there will be a little publicity, of course there will - but, discrete.

Harry promises -'

'And the police? And Penelope Richmond dying like that - and that fucking letter - need I go on?'

'Poor Penelope, a tragic accident but there it is. These things happen in the best of families. No one cares about a stupid letter - written years ago - if it still exists and I doubt it - people have short memories.'

'And, Tom? Are you blind? He murdered Veronica Lakey - you covered it up - and now the police are interviewing him about Penelope Richmond. And this fool - Witt - where is he - dead? You think? Have you any idea, any idea at all, what you are dragging us all in to?'

'Oh, really, Harry says - '

'- Fuck Harry -' Gilmore screamed and time shattered and they were both back 20 years, to another part of the story.

Shirley-Anne lived again what it was to be a good person - to be someone. When she was someone, she had pity. She gave her help to a man in grief. She meant only well. What she didn't see then, but she did see later - was the monster stirring.

Robin Gilmore lived again what it was to have hope - to be more than he was. In this place, a rich woman showed him a way out. What he didn't see then, but did see later was the monster. Stirring.

Back now to the quiet room in Wimpole Street. They looked at each other like strangers. Shirley-Anne was the first to speak. 'I lie awake at night, afraid and I don't know why. The house is so dark, so small. Being out there, in the galleries - I'd forgotten what life is like. I've missed it. The people. The lights. Life. I'm a creature of the here and now - well, most of us are, aren't we?'

Gilmore said nothing.

'You do see, Robin? Tell me, you see.' She clasped her hands. 'I can't explain. I can't stop this, even if I wanted to - I just can't.' When Gilmore spoke, it was soft, as if to himself. 'He needs help. Covering this thing up -'

'...what? Covering what up? That bitch? Tom didn't kill her.'

Silence.

'It's an illness.' This was the honeyed voice - the voice of reason - the voice that said it's someone else - it's always someone else.

'It's not an illness' she said. 'It's me. My fault. He needs more than I can give.'

Gilmore looked out of the window. Pensive. Shirley-Anne continued '...if I hadn't hid in marriage. If I left him alone ... if -' she raised her hands in despair.

It seemed like only a moment ago, when she was sitting up in bed in the Chancel Clinic, hearing nothing but good news. Every obstacle gone. Now this. How can life be so cruel?

'What's done is done.' Gilmore was mentally re-arranging the day's appointments.

'I failed him. He wanders - well, who wouldn't. Penelope, too. Headstrong. Heaven knows, he never liked her, nor she him - sex seems to get in the way of everything. You never married, Robin?'

He shook his head. 'I think you know the answer, to that?' Yes. They both knew the answer to that. 'You've had a terrible loss. You've had surgery. This is grief. Delayed grief. You're tired. Overwrought.'

'Yes. I miss her, I won't deny it. But it's almost four months - you'd think it would ease - but it doesn't. I lie awake - I think of all the people I've wronged - '

'Not sleeping?'

'When do I ever sleep - at least, like a normal person? Normal -' she laughed '- I've been trying these.' She took a bottle out of her bag. 'Made from nettles.'

'I could give you something?'

'I've relied on your ministrations too long. I've got lost.'

Gilmore smiled. 'Tell me about this yacht. You've been cooped up too long. Fresh air is what you need. Fresh air. A holiday away from it all.'

'Tom was a noble spirit, when we first met. Remember? Everyone admired him; he was so successful. An inspired man, not a "good" man - but inspired.'

'Envied?'

'Yes. I think other men believed he was more attractive to women than he was. I remember, Veronica - you remember Veronica? Yes, of course you do. I did so love Veronica. She used to say his hands were everywhere. And there were others - but then, that is what I did to him - and now look -'

'Go away. Take a holiday. Summer is coming, take a month or two. It'll all come right, you'll see.'

'Yes,' said Shirley-Anne, her eyes closed. 'You said that once before.'

When Shirley-Anne left Wimpole Street, both she and Gilmore were at peace - another truce reached. She agreed not to commit to an exhibition with Harry Steiner until "that letter" was found. She believed it would take no time.

He believed it would. That was the truce.

****

La Petite turned, restless. During the day, she dozed in the chair but at night her sins ran under her skin like fleas and only the cool in the night air would do. It was eleven o'clock and raining and dark and she was on the other side of the square when she saw Shirley-Anne leave the house. Shirley-Anne stopped under a street light and waited. A man approached. La Petite recognised him from her night time walks before. The Mistress gave him something. He left - but not before they both saw the maid and the maid saw them. It didn't take long.

****

Next day, Tom and Solly were back at the el Saoud café and Solly was bright. 'You're looking well.'

'I could sit here with a paper bag over my head, you wouldn't notice.'

'Yes. I think I would. Oh, will you look -?' Solly called over to the waitress '- real sugar, please. White. Yes. Here. Thank you. Bloody Italians.' Turning back, he caught his foot on a bag under the table. 'What's this - not another tart?'

'They're not Italian and no, as a matter of fact -' Tom looked at his watch '- going down to the old girl's house. Aiming for the three-thirty.' The bag wasn't a bag and Tom wasn't aiming for the three-thirty. It was an old portfolio for Steven, still holed up in the studio in Clerkenwell. Tom found the scraps of drawings Steven left behind when he came to St James' Gardens and he was in such bad shape now, that Tom reasoned, doodling might help. 'Yes. Take advantage of the weather - bit of coast line work - everyone likes the seaside.'

The team - Solly's team - were taking Tom's pictures, now. He said they liked them and that they wanted more with boats. He gave Tom an envelope with two thousand quid, in fifties. This was a steady payment until the budget was agreed.

'Odd though?' said Tom. 'Cash, I mean?'

Solly sniffed at his coffee. 'This smell off to you? No? Odd? What's odd about money - and regular money, I don't mind adding?' The team were so pleased with Tom's work, they'd agreed the two thousand a month as a non-refundable expense. 'Problem?'

'No.' He put the envelope in his coat.

'I know Badger - I hate this cloak and dagger stuff as much as you - and let's not forget, I'm the one with something to lose. Anyway, they like what you're giving them. Trust me - as soon as your work is written into the contract, you can have it by wire transfer or cheque or stamped on the back of your hand. In fact, drawing a regular salary, there'd be no reason not to bring you into the agency; short term contracts to begin with, of course.'

'Oh?' Tom looked up. Did he hear it right? 'No? You think? I wouldn't mess up this time, I swear.' He'd give anything - to be back. 'What about God?'

'On the way out - and this is just between ourselves - a certain person not a million miles from this table is tipped to take the mantle.'

'What?' Solly? The plodder? 'You?' Tom was incredulous. He realised too late, what he'd said. Solly stirred his coffee, slowly. 'Rain again,' said Tom.

'Yes, rain again,' said Solly. 'Brown sugar. Fucking French. What a life. Still -' he closed his eyes and smiled '- God's about to fall and not get up - so, not all bad.' For a second, the mask slipped and a side of Solly that everyone knew except Tom, showed. The side that liked it, when big people fell. In the old days, Solly was known for the webs you didn't see until it was too late. No account handler lasted long at McVie & Co, but Solly did. Funny what you miss.

'Remember the Max Max campaign?'

'The what?'

'You know - Max Max - happy days? Oh, come on. Good times,' said Tom. The Max Max campaign. The one time when the hatred showed. 'Yes. You're right. Stupid. Bloody rain.' Too late. Solly's eyes narrowed. 'No. No, you're right. Max Max - I remember - and Eve? That bit I forget - tell me, how was she at that point - just before you joined us?'

'Eve?'

'Yes. She was dying and you were fucking - I think that's how it went. Ah, sugar, thank you dearie. Bleached white; nothing like it. I had an aunt once who swore white sugar was poison.'

Tom looked into his coffee and said nothing. They sat in silence until the waitress went. 'Anything else?' Solly dropped in a spoonful slowly. Tom fixed his gaze forward; forward passed the bedside he wanted to forget, past a hand that waited.

Solly tapped his spoon on the cup.

'Oh? Sorry. Miles away.' Eve was dying. Tom was drunk. Shirley-Anne was everywhere. 'Happy days.'

'Happy days.' Solly wiped his mouth and stood. 'Well, back to the coal face. Same time next week, assuming you don't get a better offer?' He turned to go but his foot got caught again. 'What the hell have you got under there?' Tom reached down and the broken clasp of the portfolio opened. Three of Steven's sketches slid out.

'My God -'

'What?'

'- you're not? You are - you bloody are -' Solly picked up the sketches.

'You're in bed with someone else.'

'No. You don't understand. This isn't for you.'

'Not for me? What do you mean, not for me? Oh, don't tell me - not those fucking Pakis? Oh, you haven't? Bloody nothing fucking changes, you two-timing old tart -'

'- no, really; you don't understand.' Tom panicked. He didn't want Solly to think he was being two-timed; he didn't want him to walk away. 'Put them back. They're doodles. Nothing - rubbish - a hobby.'

Solly held him at arm's length and put the sketches on the table - genuinely surprised. 'Oh? No. I like it - light touch. Arty. Well. Well. And the paper - rough - different - a bit like bread.'

'Handmade.'

'Nice. No. Really. I like them. River scenes. Is that the canal round Islington?'

'Yes. I doodle - eases my mind - passes the time. Not for you.'

'I can see that. So -' he turned them over slowly '- pitching to the highest bidder? Bloody ad men; nothing changes.' He tapped their edges together and bowed. 'I thought I was slime, but you sir, are in a league of your own.'

Tom shrugged. What could he say?

'Tell me. How long?'

Why resist?

'Long enough. There it is. You have me.' Tom raised his palms and smiled. 'Found out. Oh, whoops.'

Solly cocked his head to one side. 'Here. Let me see that one again. That one. Are those turtles?'

Tom gave it to him.

'Well? Worth a try, I suppose. Never know with the French -' he put the sketches in his briefcase.

'No, you can't take them.'

'If you're doing photography and drawings, no reason not to get paid twice. Any objections?'

'Yes. Maybe - no. No.' Double two thousand a month. Cash. No questions. With that kind of money, he could maybe take out a short let flat somewhere. Just enough to get Steven back in shape - maybe set him up abroad - Greece or somewhere.

'Ah. Yes. Not bad. No. I like it. Different. Free spirit. Why not? Why not?' Solly took them - six in all. As he closed his briefcase, he smiled. 'Still the sly dog, eh?'

'Yes -,' said Tom '- still the sly dog.'

Solly called for cognac and late morning melted into a pleasant afternoon and a walk by the round pond. They were both drunk but upright. Tom led the way - there was a bench on the west side that caught the afternoon sun. Solly, less of a drinker, was beginning to slur. He admired Tom, he said. He'd always looked up to him but what he couldn't understand - and he really wished he did - was what women saw in him.

'That girl' for example 'Penelope Richmond - you were having it off with her - go on, admit it.'

Tom closed his eyes and pretended to doze and Solly rambled the way drunks do. What did she - Richmond - see in him? What did they talk about - and, why did Shirley-Anne really put her in that place in Bayswater? Solly asked questions about Richmond, questions about small things - what did she like? Who did she talk about? What did she say - about anything?

Did she ever mention John Smith? It was the cognac talking.

3.4

'Bingo.'

In the mess of it all, Tom forgot about Denise. She had a habit of turning up unannounced and it was a stroke of luck that he cut her off just yards from the studio last week. What resulted, was a pleasant lunch for Denise at Rules and a nice surprise for Steven.

'You are joking?'

Tom and Steven stood at the bottom of the steps looking up at Sea View.

'Only thinking of you,' said Tom. 'No one will get to you up there. Trust me.'

'I'll be a fucking sitting duck.'

'No. No. Trust me. No one will know.' Sea View was a nice place, in its way. After a month or two, with his health returned and no doubt grateful, Steven would see things differently. He'd tell the police what he saw the night Penelope died and it would all work out fine. By that time, Tom would have saved enough to send him on his way - win - win.

Shirley-Anne was pleased too. So, the story was that Tom was here at Sea View, by himself, ready to open the house up and sort out Shirley-Anne's pictures, ready for the shippers to bring them up to London.

'What about my leg - if I put any weight on - the doctors said -'

Tom pointed up. 'See those clouds -' he gripped the rock and started climbing the steps, steady, methodical - quick for an unfit man. Steven followed slowly, leaning on his stick. Wind pushed in from the sea. On the first landing about 30 feet up, it started to rain. 'Only another three flights - you OK with that?'

'What? More? Up there? No.' Steven lost balance and Tom grabbed him. 'Here -' he wedged his shoulder against Steven and pushed them both into the rock face. Then - 'Go on. I'm right behind you. Go - you can't fall; I'm right behind you.' The drop was steep. It was meant to be.

'What about the tools?'

'Just move - I've got a bag here -' Tom pushed Steven again '- bloody mac's ruined - when I think of what these things cost.' Sea View couldn't be seen from the road or the sea. It was visible from the cliffs behind, but only in places and even then its stone roof looked like the surrounding rock. It wasn't on the Land Registry or local maps. It was a house of sorts, cut into the cliff face. A folly built from slaving and extended over the years as the Brille fortunes grew. A shrine to pleasure. Steven reached the top and vomited.

'Made it,' said Tom. The terrace at the front was overgrown. Tom pulled at some of the lower branches. 'You know people come walking along those cliffs and no one has broken in. At least, not as far as I know.'

'You said you haven't been here in years?'

'There, look -' Tom pointed to a small tunnel in the undergrowth.

'I'm sorry. You go - I can't.' Steven sank to the ground. 'I can't do this. Really, I'm not kidding.' He took out an inhaler and puffed.

'You're in worse shape than I am.'

'I'm in worse shape than anyone.'

Tom bent into the tunnel and called. 'You'll have to come - it won't give.'

Steven, still light headed, followed slowly. 'Really, I'm not up to - where? - Hallo -?'

Tom lifted the torch. 'Here. Come on. Over here - wait.' He moved the torch closer. 'It's the door - key's jammed.' He pushed against it. 'We'll have to do it together - ready?'

'No.'

'For God's sake.'

'I can assure you -' Steven screeched and jumped '- are there bats in here?' Tom wasn't listening; he moved his fingertips along the vertical edges of the door frame looking for a place to force. 'Ready? On the count of three, ready?'

'No. This is pointless. There's a fast train at eleven thirty-two. God, my leg - my rib - you know it takes months for a cracked rib to -'

Tom reached down for a crow bar. He levered it against a crack between wood and wood. 'Hold the torch. Come on. Here - shine it along the edge - there, there - see if there's enough space to get purchase. Here, run your fingers along -'

Steven screamed and fell back into the clearing. 'I can't do this. I can't.

Something just ran down my back.'

'God Almighty - you bloody girl.' Tom took the torch and tried again.

Sand trickled down and it was hard to see. 'Problem with wood - it expands. There's just nothing, no space - no - just a minute -' he shone the torch closer. A fresh splinter went under his nail, new and strong. He pushed in the crow bar and called back to Steven. 'I've found somewhere. I think we can do it -'

Steven lay, belly down and still. After a minute, Tom came out.

'Kill me now.'

'Oh, pull yourself together.' Tom gave him the crowbar. 'Here, take this. As soon as we're in, you can go up to the top terrace, watch the rain come over the Channel -' he pointed to an indefinable place higher up ' - see for miles - you'll be glad, really. This place is Heaven, if you give it a chance.'

'I feel strange.'

'Asthma?'

'No - I just don't have any strength - I think I'm diabetic -' Steven got to his feet and followed '- we shouldn't force it.'

'No choice.'

'Don't. If you break the lock - just a minute -' he pulled a can from his inside pocket '- where is it? Here? This? Right - move your hand -' he squirted it into the lock '- now try. You sure there're no bats? What about lizards? Spiders? - please God, not spiders - spiders can live in your ear -'

Tom rattled the key. 'It's moving. Give it another -' Steven shook the can and squirted again. The key slipped. 'It's gone. I felt it.' Tom turned the lock. He pushed the door and the house breathed.

****

Twenty minutes later Tom was on the fast train back to London. 'Sorry Old Thing, there it is - no - line breaking up - break -' he clipped the phone shut. He tried to make it like it was the most normal thing in the world to travel for three hours and then turn round and come back. He left Steven at Sea View. The parting was terse.

'Electricity?' said Steven. 'It didn't occur to you to check?'

'No. The Richmond creature had been round so many times - assumed she'd have sorted that out.'

'You brought two bottles of gin, six cans of tonic and two lemons -'

'- limes -'

'- two fucking limes and no fucking electricity? And I climbed those steps - look at me, I'm still shaking.' Steven was right; in his girlee way, he was right. It was stupid. Getting Steven to Sea View was not enough. 'You say Miss Richmond was here - in the dark? You sure? Alone?'

Tom shrugged.

181

'Impossible.'

'Oh stop complaining.' Tom promised to return next day. He had a business meeting in London, he said - a meeting he couldn't put off. The train was cruising now, through soft curtains of rain. It was warm and Tom drifted. He felt Richmond beside him, happy. He remembered her leaving St James' Gardens. Standing in the doorway. Waiting for the taxi like a sick cat. He still didn't know why they moved her to Bayswater. Why did they do that? It made no sense - even to Solly. And why did the police laugh? What did they mean when they said it was Shirley-Anne? It? What was this 'It' - this thing that everyone seemed to know except him?

The train rocked gently. Sleep and worries merged. Tom dreamt he was back at Ladbroke Grove police station in a small room with two men. He was covered in bandages and couldn't speak. 'Black out, sir? Recognise this do you Mr Amis - got your writing on -' They showed him the letter he wrote to Richmond. All the words were erased except two: 'kill you'. Then he heard Solly's voice - letter? What letter? He woke with a start.

The train was in. He needed to speak to Solly.

****

Tom took the Northern Line down to Clapham Common. He had two things on his mind - somewhere to hide and the money to pay for it. 'Solly? Solly? Yes, it's me - I know -' the line went dead. There was a moodiness to Solly which was new. Of course, he was carrying a burden - keeping up a front - feeding work to Tom as two people can't be easy. But still. Since Penelope Richmond died, something about Solly was different.

Tom left Clapham Common tube by the south side and walked down the hill to King's Avenue. He phoned Solly again '- well, later? Yes, yes I know, but I still - when? Right, yes. OK. Yes.' Tom needed to talk money.

He turned off King's Avenue and into the Crescent and although it had been years since he was last here, nothing changed. A young man leaning against a car with his arms folded, called over - 'Mr Amis?' He'd been watching Tom from across the road. 'Ah -' Tom extended his hand. 'Phipps, is it? Sorry - meeting up in Canary Wharf - flew the team in from Chicago, especially - I know - I know - delegate.'

'Don't worry,' said Phipps. 'Just arrived myself. Well, here we are -' he swept his hand towards the house the way estate agents, do. 'Shall we?'

This was the bit about hiding. Tom needed a flat where he could hide from the police and from himself and this was it. A love nest. A place where no one knew him and where the police couldn't get to him. A place to run to.

Phipps led the way. Tom knew this house. Inside, it was as he remembered. Big hallway. Velvet quiet. Clean. Empty. There was a large stained-glass window on the first floor landing. Was that new?

'Say you know the area?'

'Stayed near here. Long time ago.'

'Yes. A lot of our clients come back, we find. Good schools.'

'Do they? And this place - know who owns it?'

'Broken up into flats - such a shame. He's an inventor -'

'Who?'

'The owner. Number 2. I've got the keys - ah, yes.' Phipps turned keys in three locks and pushed at the small door. Tom smiled. 'Going to South Africa for a few months; short lets - gold dust.' Tom closed his eyes and the room embraced. The quiet. The same no questions asked. This was the flat he used with Shirley-Anne when Eve was dying. This was where nothing mattered. Eve didn't matter. Being alive didn't matter. Now he was back.

'This way -' Phipps opened the curtains '- South facing. Nice view.'

The bay window looked out onto a semi-circular front drive. Beyond, a laurel hedge. High. Dense. 'Yes, South Africa.

Six months, maybe longer - just came on the market - here, let me -' Phipps moved an empty packing case and pointed towards the grate. 'It's real. Wood that is - not coal.'

'Who else lives here? Do you know?'

'No. This is the only one we have in this property - but we've got others nearby if you're interested. Just for yourself?'

'Yes. I won't be living here. More a base for working.'

'Absolutely. So many people doing that, these days. What is it - er -?'

'Writer. I'm a writer. Stories. I make things up.'

'Very nice. Well, I don't think you can do better than this.' Phipps left Tom to wander round. The room was small, it didn't take long.

'Nice view - front garden.'

'Yes. Quiet.'

'Private.'

'Oh, very. Absolutely. No one can see over that hedge. Quiet road. Residential.' The curtains were brown crepe, the furniture was odd in size and shape. Nothing fitted. 'Real fire,' said Phipps, again.

'Yes,' said Tom. He could see Denise here - curtains drawn. 'Broadband?'

'Yes, well I think so. Take your time. Like I said, new on the market.

We've got another viewing this evening.'

'Here?'

'Yes. Like I said - get snapped up. You're lucky. First come, first served.' Phipps patted his pockets. 'You've got my number? Here.' He gave Tom two name cards.

'Gerald Phipps?'

'Assistant Manager, yes.' Phipps pointed to an alcove the size of a large wardrobe. The kitchenette. When Tom was last here, it was a shelf with an electric ring and a kettle. 'Functional. Water heater - immersion, I think - runs on some kind of energy saving thing; I can get the details. Cupboards on top and below. Just about all you'd need.'

'Fridge?'

'Yes. Small fridge, larder. Well, enough for a pint of milk. Very clean.

Shops about ten minutes away - did you come from the station?'

Tom could see himself here, again. Safe. It worked before, didn't it?

'There's a doctor's surgery, across the road - well, you probably won't be needing that.'

He liked the bareness - like no one lived here, no one made any mistakes here. 'Is that a window seat?'

'Yes. Nice feature. You could sit there and read. Not overlooked - oh, I've said that.'

Tom turned back to the room. 'You can love two people at the same time.

They say it's impossible, but it isn't.'

'Pardon? Sorry, missed that - head in the fridge -'

'Nothing. Talking to myself. I do that.'

'Ah? Right.' Phipps' phone rang. Tom wandered around. He would always love Eve, but he also loved Shirley-Anne, in his way. He pitied her - and that is a kind of love, isn't it? He looked into the fake gilt mirror over the fireplace. He could see Denise in it, naked. Soft. Easy to pick up, easy to put down.

'I like it.'

Phipps clipped his phone. 'Sorry. Running late.'

'Yes, I kept you. Sorry.'

'No. Don't worry. We open at nine, if you're interested. You know where we are - the High Street, by the station? Anyway, you've got my mobile?'

Tom nodded. Standing outside on the gravel driveway, he asked 'Is it safe?'

'I know what you are thinking,' said Phipps.

'I doubt it.'

'No. No. You're right. You won't be here all the time - security is everything. Here, let me show you -' Phipps unlocked the front door again and then the door to the flat. Just inside, he flipped open a small cupboard. 'Digital. Straight to the alarm company. They'd be here in minutes and besides -'

'Yes?'

'- police are just round the corner.'

****

So, that was the flat. Now for the money.

'This had better be good.'

He was back in the el Saoud with Solly. 'I thought we agreed Mondays and correct me if I'm wrong, this is not Monday?' Solly cocked his head to one side, the way Harold used to do. 'Want to hear something good?' He slid a brown envelope across the table. 'Count it.' Tom was on the agency books as two people - Tom the photographer and Tom the illustrator. This was the second two thousand quid this month. Yes.

Tom would keep Denise in the flat in Clapham, Steven at Sea View and in no time Steven would give his evidence, the police would be history and he'd get his life back. Yes.

'Well, you look happy. We'll need more pictures and soon - how about next week?' Solly passed Tom the menu. 'This is real work, Badger. I hope you know that? No more playing around.'

'Those days are gone,' said Tom, envisaging his first day back at the agency. 'I swear - sober as a judge. Never did really know, why God gave me the boot - you didn't have a hand in it, did you?'

'You got fired because you were shagging God's wife.'

'Oh?'

'You got fired because you were paralytic most days before ten in the morning. You got fired because you made a lot of money and other people didn't and they hated you for it. Dover sole looks good.'

'It was never like that.'

'I think you'll find it was.'

'Things were different then - more relaxed.'

'No, it wasn't. The only one who was relaxed was you and that was because you were plastered - or, cod in batter? What a choice.'

'You know, you can be very judgmental.'

'You want to know why you were sacked - really sacked? You were a fucking embarrassment. That's why you got sacked. Happy?' Solly called the waitress. 'That'll be two Dover sole, dearie. No chips and another bottle.'

'I remember things were happening that I couldn't explain.'

'Yes. It's called being drunk.'

Solly crossed his legs, impatient. He fiddled with his knife and fork. He looked at his watch and sighed. 'Rain again. What about that Richmond girl - heard anything more from the police? What was that you said last time, about a letter?' Solly was back on Penelope Richmond. 'Just curious' he said. 'And you say you don't remember anything about - when she went - under - sorry - you know, just curious. Talking helps, you said so yourself.'

Solly could be spiteful and malicious and often very clever but he could also be stupid and this was him being stupid. Tom knew he meant well. He was trying to help. He knew Penelope meant something to Tom. 'Yes. Right. Good to talk.'

The fish came. Tom looked at it lying there, helpless. He pushed the plate away and poured another cognac. 'It's a blur. One moment she was there, the next - nothing.'

'Sure?'

Tom shook his head. 'Like I said - I was a mess - well, you know that.'

Solly ate in silence. Then - 'let's suppose, for argument's sake, that someone did push her - any idea why? You knew her - did she ever say anything? Was there anyone like - annoying her - she must have said something?' Solly took away Tom's glass and called for two coffees. 'Look. You left the agency because you were burned out. Happens to everyone - we run, but life runs faster. So tell me - are you going to go off the rails again? Was Penelope Richmond in trouble and will it come back and bite you - or, more to the point, me?'

'You think I pushed her - don't you?' Solly waved to the waitress. 'Hey, dearie - bottle of Pelegrino. Pull yourself together, Badger. You're a prick, not a murderer. I think you'll find there's a difference.' The cognac bottle was empty, the waitress cleared the plates and asked Tom if he got his phone back. He nodded without thinking.

When Solly called for the bill, he turned and put his hand on Tom's arm. 'You didn't push Richmond. Now, leave it. Move on. You've got the rest of your life to ruin.' It was reassuring. Mad as it was, Solly was right. Tom had to let this go. 'Sorry. You're right. Penelope. Shirley-Anne was so fond of her - I wanted to bring her back - to Shirley-Anne.' It did not escape him that if he'd still been banging Richmond she might still be alive. That's how he saw it.

3.5

Tom was back at Sea View with the tail end of a storm. The porch light was out, the wind was up and Steven shook with the cold. 'I must have been mental.'

Tom groped in the dark for the lever and it clanged on. The kitchen at the end of the hall flickered up. The old fridge buzzed back. 'Well, thank God for that - nothing worse than warm gin.' They had supplies. Picnic things from Marks & Spencer, gin and limes and new inks from Shirley-Anne's studio. 'Look - go down to the billiard room and put your feet up. Take The Telegraph. I'll get a few glasses - oh, for Heaven's sake, what's the matter?'

Steven was hunched like a sick hen; preoccupied. 'I don't like it - do you smell that? Dry rot - spores get into your lungs - sure you weren't followed?' He felt his way to the billiard room seeing menace everywhere. It hadn't been easy. The storm stopped the trains for a day and a half - trees on the line - and Steven had been alone and just like back at Tom's studio, he didn't do well with being alone. He was convinced Tom would say something - without knowing what he was doing, he'd give Steven up. Richmond's murderer was nearer than Tom realised.

Steven did have choices but none of them good. He could tell Tom the truth - that he was a plant - put into their lives to rob Shirley-Anne. If he did that, would Tom pity him - help him to escape say, over to France? Probably not. More likely, he'd turn against him - give him up to the police or Vic or both? Or, Steven could tell another truth - that Tom was a fool who trusted too easily and life just isn't like that.

Then there was a third. Do nothing - let life sort itself out. Tom called from the kitchen '- idiot - you left the fucking ring on - have you any idea -?' The place was a rabbit warren with old wiring, drafts and a propensity for fire that alarmed even Tom.

The picnic on the billiard table was a pleasant affair. Tom poured triples and in the glint, saw himself shaking hands with the Metropolitan Commissioner of Police - maybe, standing outside Buckingham Palace with his morning suit and OBE - photographer of the year, services to art, etc.

'Only a matter of time -'

'What?'

'- before it sinks.' Steven could hear the wind clattering through the roof.

Tom poured another. 'Bombay Sapphire - aah, nectar of the gods. Here. Eat something - it's not all wet. Try this. Olive bread. Not bad - chewy, but on the whole -' he dropped in a curl of lime '- not bad - cheers.'

The bad weather was around like a rowdy guest. 'Hear that?' said Steven.

'Old houses creak,' said Tom. A hammering sound came from the upper landing.

'The landing door - catches the full force of the wind coming off the cliffs -'

Steven paced and the hammering got louder '- someone's out there.'

Tom licked his lips, now pleasantly numb. 'You know, a greater part of the brain is devoted to the lips and the tongue

190

than legs and arms and everything in between. Imagine that.'
His heart skipped a beat and he took a swig from the bottle then
it all went hazy, in a droopy but pleasant kind of a way.

The storm went on for two days. When it ended, Steven
was still asleep on the couch in the Billiard Room. 'Sea gulls
wake you?' He didn't answer. 'Lovely day. Breakfast on the
walkway. Calm as a mill pond - who'd have thought?'

Steven moved, then winced. He'd been in and out of a
fever. 'I left you - you know, yesterday. Sleep well? Here,
found this -' Tom gave him his cashmere dressing gown.
Steven didn't speak. He moved slow. Tom opened a shutter and
looked out to sea. 'Look at that. Not a cloud in the sky. Hope
the delivery didn't wake you? Got in a few bits. Times or
Telegraph? Oh yes, Racing Post. Buck up. Caught a bit of a
chill but you're over it now -' Tom took Steven's arm and
helped him to the billiard table. He was light, like a cat. Tom
talked about the weather, cricket, salmon fishing, foreigners,
the fucking French, anything to send away the silence of the
last two days, because being alone with his thoughts, Tom
started to doubt. Steven was afraid of the wind, of everything -
shouldn't Tom let him go - shouldn't he just let him go?

'Sit there. I've put the kettle on; bring up a bowl of warm
water. You're going to love it here - just wait.' He emptied
buckets out of the window.

'…leaks…beams…generator   back   on…nice   view…
falling to bits…'

Steven coughed into his hand.

'Eh?'

'Why keep it?' A hoarse whisper. 'This place? Why? I
mean, why?'

'Oh, a few broken bits - nothing a few nails won't put
right.' Tom shook Steven's shoulder. Steven was awake and
OK and the day was bright and Tom was happy. So damned
happy. 'How was the couch; seemed a bit restless? Here, sorry
- bit creased. I want the crossword.'

'Oh? Sorry - did I disturb you?'

'No -' Tom lied '- place like this, bloody noises everywhere. I remember Veronica used to say -'

'Veronica?' Steven caught Tom's glance at a painting. Large, half hidden on the end wall. A nude with a Boa Constrictor.

'Yes, her. One of the old crowd. Nice girl. Excitable. Well, cocaine will do that - anyway -'

'Her?'

'Will you look at that? Not a cloud in the sky. I've rustled up some breakfast.' Tom tensed.

'Is that a snake?'

'We could go for a walk down there, when the tide's out.' Tom stood at the window looking out. 'Glorious - and there are coves further along and - '

'A leftover, was she? From one of those famous weekends?' Steven gestured to Tom to help him over to the portrait. He stretched his neck and sniffed. 'Damp - bit of mold. Who painted it?'

'The old girl, if you must know. She painted it. They were friends. Dead now, of course - Veronica that is.'

Steven tapped the canvas. 'Damp and loose -' he lifted the bottom of the frame and ran his fingers along the inside. Tom shrugged. 'Spirited crowd - most dead now. Dead or mad - look, if you can limp, there's a bathroom just down there; worth a look. Pink marble from Italy - same as the Vatican. I've got sausages on the go, on the walkway - lovely view - lovely day - better get back to the Primas.' He wanted to go, before Steven's curiosity pulled them both too far. 'Here, hand me the torch.' Steven tried to look behind the frame. 'Can't see much in this light. Canvas needs stretching - if you can get to the wedges - and push -'

Tom turned away.

'Says here: Vernie. Did they forget it when they took the others? They left quite a few, does she know that - Shirley-Anne? Can you help me lift it?'

'Oh, leave it.'

'I think I've found the wedges - yes, can feel -' Steven ran his fingers blindly along the back of the frame again '- don't want it to loosen any more - if these things slip -' slithers of wood moved '- there's nothing holding it -' then he felt something different. Paper. Folded. 'Complete amateurs - look what they've stuck -' he looked round.

Tom was gone.

****

It was noon and the two men sat by a primas on the upper walkway, roasting sausages. The day smiled. 'Hardly a breath.'

'Another?'

'Too early for me.'

'Don't be polite - there's another bottle in the kitchen.' Tom half-filled the tumbler and dropped in a curl of lime. Steven closed his eyes. 'Sure you're alright? There's coffee in the flask, if you're desperate?' Steven cried in his sleep. He looked over his shoulder. He trembled for no reason. 'You were asking about Veronica?'

'None of my business. Sorry.'

Tom felt something - like a patch of sunlight.

He liked Steven - in another life, he'd still like him. He put a blanket round Steven's shoulders and opened another bottle of Bombay Sapphire. He told stories about Sea View - all funny, all true and especially the ones about Veronica. 'Things were different then,' said Tom. 'It was all about fun.'

Steven tested a pork pie. 'Strictly speaking, I'm vegan - didn't mean to pry.'

'Veronica. It's hard you know - when it's on offer. A man has needs - younger then, of course.'

'Is that chutney Fair Trade?'

The way Tom saw it those days were golden. Shirley-Anne had her painting and her ways. An open marriage. Veronica was a lively thing; funny, clever, full of spirit. Shirley-Anne knew - well of course, she did. And what did it matter? It was all about fun. 'Hard to say no. Bit of a fling. No harm done.'

'No harm done?' said a voice. 'You bastard.'
'Pass the salt.'

****

They stayed most of the day up there on the walkway, Tom reading the newspaper, Steven dozing under the blanket, the broken walkway door squeaking in the breeze. The sun was setting. 'You look dreadful.'

'Thanks.'

'No, I mean it. You've hardly touched a thing. There's chicken, ham, odds and ends - I'd steer clear of the stuffed vine leaves.'

'Can't believe you let it run down like this,' said Steven. 'How long have you had it? This place -?'

Tom explained with pride that Sea View was nothing to do with him. It was Shirley-Anne's. That is to say, it was all that was left of the Brille family. Tom wanted to amuse him with more bits of family history - all funny - but annoyingly, Steven kept cutting across with questions about visibility from the road and access to the nearest hospital. He pulled at the blanket and Tom saw welts across his side; grey, old.

'- am I talking to myself?'

'No. No. Go ahead. I'm listening. Bored, but listening.'

Steven didn't like the place. 'Everything. Decay. The watercolours - have you been up to the bedrooms? ...fading around the edges...no time to lose...have you any idea how unstable ...am I talking - no really, am I talking to myself?'

'You know, for my money, nothing beats lime. Knew a girl once, made a very respectable chicken soup with limes. Arab or was it Italian? No. A Kurd - small, but beautifully put together.'

'I can't stay - obviously I can't stay. I can't help you - what was I thinking? I'll go tomorrow. Yes. It's been nice - but - yes, time to move on.' A glint flashed from the cliff behind, orange and sharp.

'Yes. Yes. It'll be fine. You put the old girl's picture things in order - it'll work out.'

Steven screamed. 'I'm not putting anything in order - the house is open and it's falling to bits, don't you understand - those drawings of Shirley-Anne's, upstairs - they'll bleach if the sun hits them - they'll be nothing - you need restorers not me. I can't help you. I'm fucked - just in case you hadn't noticed.'

'Yes. Yes - all true - and by the way, might have a buyer for your own drawings - did I mention that?' A gust came up from the sea.

'I'm dead remember?'

'Yes - but not forever.' Tom groped his way to the railings. The sea breathed - that thing - out there - making all of this so small. Steven came over and stood beside him, the way Eve used to. 'If you come up here at dawn you'll see the birds. Seagulls. They come up from nowhere; sailors thought they were angels.'

'Sounds like you spent a lot of time up here?'

'Used to. Someone I knew liked it - the sea and stuff.'

'Knew her well?'

'No -' Tom fought to think of other things - things that still mattered. Money. Women. Gin. Running. Fucking. More money - and - 'sometimes I'd come up and find her here, by herself. Looking out. Over there to - I don't know - whatever it is - out there.

Died of cancer.'

'I'm sorry.'

'Don't be.'

'I am though.'

'You didn't know her. It's getting cold, we should go in.'

'I'm still sorry.'

'Lung cancer. She came up here. I had no idea. She didn't say until it was too late - but that was her.'

'They say the end comes quick.'

Tom remembered Clapham Common. The clinic. The wait. The fun fair.

'No' he said. 'No, it doesn't.'

* * * *

It was evening and time for Tom to go. Steven was calmer now but still intent on leaving if not tomorrow then certainly soon. 'Tell me - eight years? Bit of a stretch?' They were at the top of the steps, listening to the night.

'Manslaughter. Not that it matters.'

'Oh?'

Traffic was light and headlights were coming along the coast road. Tom patted his pocket. Ticket. Money. Phone. 'What's it like -?'

'What is what like?'

'- to kill - someone?'

Steven shrugged. Then Tom - 'They say, when you kill, a part of you dies too - rubbish, right?'

'Hear that? Why does the sea sound louder at night?'

'How did it happen? Was it an accident? Isn't that what manslaughter is, an accident? Doesn't mean you'd do it again - I mean, anyone can make a mistake? Maybe you were drunk?'

'What do you want from me, Mr Amis?' The wind was gathering and they both knew the answer to that. Tom wanted Steven to save him from the police and from himself. 'Just tell them what you saw.' It wasn't a lot to ask. If Steven didn't give evidence to the police, Tom's life was over. If he did - Steven's life was over. Tom wanted Steven to die, so he could live - underneath all the nice talk that's what it was.

'Your shivering,' said Steven 'we should go inside. The taxi will hoot.'

They stood looking over the coast road and Steven told how he ended up in gaol. He wanted to make it light - in the wrong place at the wrong time, he said. 'I was doing a stint in a lab. ProFo Chemicals, know them? Cosmetics.'

'Yes. Nice work. Up there, with Cornice.'

'Yes. Nice. We were lining up for an Autumn campaign. Mouth Wash. I was on the team for the general press; needed some research slides.' Steven watched the past come back along the coast road. Locked doors. Cages. Dogs and cats pinned on metal tables - alive - and in their eyes, trust.

'You alright? Not going to faint -?'

'Fine. Low blood sugar. Anyway - my last day there, I took a wrong turning, it was night and raining and the joke is - I was trying to get out.' Steven was back in that lab. He remembered running, reversing his car. He remembered a lot of people, a lot of noise, a lot of rain and bumping into things. He got as far as the motorway - then he stopped. 'Police. They took my keys. Then my life.'

'You clipped someone? It was dark, raining, you didn't know what you were doing - they can't put you away for that?'

Steven shook his head. 'One of the company Directors. Died the next day. They thought I was with the people outside - protesters - animal rights - it was a nightmare - I had no idea - I just let it happen.'

'Never mind. It's over now. Young man like you - everything to look forward to -'

3.6

La Petite took the tablets without interest. Calcium and Vitamin C were given with the best of intentions, but that's not how she saw it. She was getting what she deserved, that's how she saw it. She let two lives drop over the edge and now it was her turn. That's how she saw it.

Meanwhile, Vic put on an apron and for an hour a day helped in the pantry. He mentioned Steven Witt - he'd met him he said, at that very nice arty party back in Chelsea - and he looked for a reaction either from Tom or Shirley-Anne, but got none. He was watering the indoor geraniums now and listening to a rising crescendo from the drawing room upstairs. Shirley-Anne had a visitor.

'How dare you. How dare you. Get out this instant.' The drawing room bell rang. Shirley-Anne sat rigid. The visitor - a woman - had large teeth and it looked like she used them. This was Betty Reece Rae. Richmond's death hit her hard and now she was back. 'Darling, oh Victor, an ashtray s'il t'plait. Pour - pour -' Shirley-Anne waved her hand in the direction of Rae.

'It's going to come out,' said Rae, unmoved. 'Only a matter of time, you know that.' She lit up again. Skinny legs, black lace stockings. Heavy jewellery. Ash.

'I'm sorry Miss - er - you'll have to forgive us. I'm really not sure what more -?'

'Why did she die?'

Silence.

Old ground. Shirley-Anne pretended boredom, inside she boiled. 'It was all so long ago. The records are there. You are the journalist, if you find something new, perhaps you'd let us all know? Now, if you'll excuse -'

'Open verdict?'

'Yes. We read the newspapers too.'

'You were on the brink - you had a following - already showing in the Guggenheim, the Hayward and then -' she threw up her hands '- poof. Gone.

Why?'

Shirley Anne could feel Gilmore in the room. They will ask questions, he said. They only want what they can get from you. No escape. He said that too.

'Give me the story and you can control it. I can make it work for you. You need publicity - without it, you're nothing.'

Shirley-Anne shuddered. 'I have no idea what you are talking about.'

'I think you have. You were there.'

'Veronica Lakey's death was a tragic accident,' said Shirley-Anne, gasping.

'So they say.'

'We took it hard, of course. Thomas, Mr Amis, my husband - they were close. We all took it hard. She meant the world. She was a nobody. We took her under our wing. She had the sweetest nature. To drag this up now - really -'

Shirley-Anne whined. Rae had the scent of something. This is why she sent Richmond down to Sea View - she knew there was a story down there somewhere. It was common knowledge at the time, that the Amis marriage was a sham. Lakey and Tom were lovers and made no secret of it. Shirley-Anne was violent, unpredictable, then - Lakey was gone. No witnesses. The house closed up. Sealed like a box. 'One dead nobody - and you disappear.'

'My dear, the death of a loved one - we were all so close.'

'Touching - and then there's poor Penelope Richmond. Your husband was having an affair with her too and oh dear - dead too. What a co-incidence.'

Shirley-Anne trembled. She wanted to sink her teeth into this creature's eyeballs. She wanted to suck their glutinous mass - every last drop.

'You've seen the papers? Yes, of course you have. Makes good copy, don't you think - recluse emerges - first exhibition in decades. Then a girl jumps. Twenty years ago the same thing: Shirley-Anne Brille. A New Vision - then, a girl jumps. Two dead women. Both women having an affair with your husband - well?' Rae had brought the week's papers with her. There was a double-spread interview with Steiner; there were spin offs and pictures in the throwaways.

'What happened to Penelope Richmond? What happened to Veronica Lakey? What happened to you?'

'I won't diminish myself -' Shirley-Anne stared into space. Rae's words were missiles - but where were they coming from? Shirley-Anne lived an invisible life. She left no trace. How was any of this possible?

'Get real, Amis. Once you're out, you're out: people can say what they like - doesn't have to be true. You need me - control this before it controls you.' Rae hesitated. 'Then - there's your brother. Severin Brille. Strange. He contacts you out of the blue - a year later guess what - dead. And now that we're on the subject - what about Mrs Amis? The first Mrs Amis? Young woman on the mend from surgery until you arrive then - oh, whoops - dead. Don't get me wrong Mrs Amis, I'm genuinely sympathetic - really, I am - but you can see - doesn't take much to make something out of this and it doesn't have to be true. It never has to be true. Am I repeating myself?'

Three minutes later, Vic closed the door on Rae. Shirley-Anne remained in the drawing room with the live stub of a cigarette, watching the fibres curl.

****

Shirley-Anne waited. A day went by, then another. Nothing bad happened. Harry Steiner and Butters were still fluttering and the sun still shone. Rae's threats were empty.

Down in the garden studio, she drew a line of colour. She was talking to Gordon, the Charity accountant. 'No, you're right, Gordon. I have been using the charity's money like it was my own. Stupid. Stupid. I'll give it back, of course - once my exhibition is up. Think of it as a loan.' She told Gordon that in order to keep Steiner interested in Shirley-Anne, The Artist, she had insisted on covering all up front costs herself: packing, shipping, storage, restoration, publicity - yes, in a way that was dark and funny, it was actually Shirley-Anne who was funding Betty Rae and her nonsense. She needed to prove to Steiner that she would not be a burden. And Harry Steiner being Harry Steiner, let her.

What she didn't tell Gordon was that she had also re-mortgaged St James' Gardens. Not Sea View - although she tried, but no one would take it. She'd taken out a loan using the house in St James Gardens and the self-portrait of Mother, as security. Gordon was a good listener but still an Accountant. 'It's June' he said. 'Nearly eighty thousand has gone missing, since January. All cash.

Do you think I was born yesterday? What have you been doing?'

It was a bit sticky. After Gordon left, Shirley-Anne went quiet. In the day she stayed in the garden studio, at night she walked round the square. Tom saw this and kept away. He persuaded Steven to stay a bit longer at Sea View and he spent more time down there with him. He told himself he was doing it for Steven, but he wasn't. A man has to live.

He bought a newspaper outside Queensway station. Solly had news and wanted to meet. Tom was early so he sat in Kensington Gardens. It was a nice day for good news. Solly would tell him the team wanted him back. They were paying him, right? It had to mean something. These and other comfortable thoughts floated by in the sunshine.

Solly waved his spoon as Tom came in. He pointed to the envelope under the saucer. 'Check it' he said. 'Cheesecake's fresh.' Cash. Money for two, again. Four thousand quid. Nice. Solly called over for cognac and they toasted. He was in high spirits. Tom gave him the update - he said he was working alone most of the time, down at Sea View. Painting and drawing didn't come easy. He told him about Denise. He wasn't a good storyteller like Solly, but Solly listened. Solly asked about the police and Richmond. 'Bloody mystery' he said, pouring cognac into his coffee. 'Sure you don't know? You must know something - you were shagging her?'

'Anyway,' said Tom, 'good to be back in the swing of things - back on the team. Worth more to me than anything.'

Solly smiled. He wanted to know more about Richmond but a wiser part pulled him back. He said the agency liked the watercolours. 'In fact - and this is a hoot - they liked them so much they binned the shots. Yes. How funny is that? So the great photographer falls. You have to laugh. Another?'

'Not the photos?'

'I know. Bloody French. Still - why should you care - fucking anything that moves -'

Solly rarely drank. Drank - that is - like Tom. 'Yep. Pen and ink baby, pen and - fucking ink.'

'So? Settled then? Sure about that?'

'Seems that way.'

'And if they're not taking photos, do I still get paid - you know, twice?'

Tom waited. He needed that money. 'I've made commitments.'

'Oh, yes?'

'Yes. Extended the lease on the studio. Another year. Dear God, how they can charge those rents - I remember when no sane person would work in Clerkenwell. Unbelievable. Anyway, time we agreed a few figures - more than running costs, I mean. Not that I'm not grateful - four grand a month is something, but -' Denise was expensive. He knew he should give her up but he couldn't '- like I said, I've had to lay out. How much did you say they were putting up front?'

'Don't recall.' Solly was slurring now.

'I can give you invoices.'

Solly nodded. Then - 'thing is, they've got someone else on the pictorials. Yup. Not just me. See?'

'What? Someone else pitching? But you said you were in charge - if I'd have known -'

'What? Exactly what - if you'd've known?' A bit of that hatred splashed out.

'I'd have done it differently, that's all.'

'You mean you wouldn't have blown it all on that little tart?'

Tom coughed. 'No, you're right -'

'Look - sorry, Badger. Of course you need up fronts. Thing is - this new bloke comes at a bad time. No one saw it coming. Getting a bit tricky. He's looking at expenses; have to rein it in a bit, that's all.'

'What's happening?'

'Going down the toilet - sorry, thought I said?'

'Ah?'

'Oh, don't worry - not you. Nothing ever touches you. We - I mean, we of the normal 9 to 5 castrated males who don't get it handed to us on a plate. We're the ones going down the toilet.'

'Sorry.'

'Yes. Well. At least you've got four grand there. Make it last. You will get paid - just not as much and not so often. Cash flow I think it's called.' Solly's gaze wandered.

****

When Shirley-Anne went into the Chancel Clinic, the maid's future looked sealed. A nice Care Home with good views of the South Downs, but that changed on the night when she let herself be seen by Shirley-Anne and the man.

Now, when Shirley-Anne looked at the maid, mistrust looked back.

Shirley-Anne told herself that the maid deserved better than a Care Home talking to strangers. She needed Shirley-Anne. It was the very least she deserved. It made for tension.

It also precipitated a conversation with Tom, which baffled him but which calmed Shirley-Anne. She confessed - in a light-hearted kind of a way - that she had known about his re-acquaintance with Mr Solomon for some time. In fact - and how extraordinary was this - she bumped into him recently on one of her evening walks round the square - poor Petite was out, taking the air at the same time - imagine that. She said Mr Solomon told her about the tourist campaign and she was pleased to know things were going so well for Tom. She said she understood, when this extra work kept him out, sometimes all night.

'Thomas?'

'Best tofu I ever had. Curried you say - and that white stuff? From a goat?'

'Was it a terrible journey?' They were in the downstairs drawing room.

Dinner was quiet. 'Thomas?' Tom was back later than expected. He told Shirley-Anne that he'd been on the Kent coast taking shots for Solly's campaign and the train was delayed coming back. 'You know what those lines are like - power cut somewhere round Rochester. How's Frenchie - still under the weather? I should look in on her.' He wasn't in the mood for talking. He'd been at the Clapham flat all day - waiting for Denise and she didn't show up. She didn't show up yesterday or the day before. He spent the day, sitting by the window trying not to think of who she was with and what they were doing.

'I don't know why we have a rail service in this country, we'd all be better off walking.'

Silence.

'You seem tired, Angel. You've had to shoulder a lot recently, what with poor Penelope and darling Steven. By the way, I thought we might organise a small remembrance; they were so dear? Victor has very kindly been in touch with those people Penelope lived with in Shepherd's Bush - you know, she didn't have any family and we're having great trouble locating any friends? She was a private girl in her way - did she happen to say anything to you? I mean, a small service with her closest - it's the least we could do?'

Tom took a glass of pressed apple juice, obediently. Shirley-Anne was not a fool. Was this her way of giving him a way out? Let the past bury itself?

Her eyes were full of trust. 'And then, poor Steven. You know, the strangest thing - we can't locate him. I'm sorry, darling - that came out wrong. What I mean is, it seemed fitting to include him in our little service. Victor has called all the hospitals - no sign of him - did he speak of any family?'

Tom shuddered. She was so open and he was so closed. Could he not tell her Steven was alive - give her that comfort, at least? He hated himself for his silence.

She smiled at him, knowing and forgiving. He took her hand and kissed it, thinking of Denise.

3.7

The warm winds of June were up and the sky and the clouds and the seagulls sang. The universe sang. Steven spread his arms to take it all in - it was like he'd woken up and life was good. La. La.

Back in London, Tom squirmed. He was behind with the rent, Solly was nowhere and the police were everywhere. 'I wouldn't worry Mr Amis. These things happen. Sure I can't get you a glass of something - fizzy or still? Going to be another hot day.' Tom was in Phipps' office. 'Sorry' he said. 'Don't know what happened. My secretary's been away; got a temp - this isn't the only thing she's cocked up. Sorry.'

Phipps nodded and counted the rent money. 'Cash. Did you want to do next month as well - save coming in? Or, there's BACS?'

'Yes. Yes, of course. I'll see about that standing order - I travel a lot.' Tom took out another roll of notes and counted them. Solly's steady stream of money wasn't happening like he promised and Tom needed to pay Steven something. Back at the flat, Tom opened the front window and drew back the curtains. He'd taken a few things from St James Gardens -

Galle lamps, some small pictures, a few ornaments and the place was looking less empty.

Love Nest. Next week he'd buy a new bed, maybe ask Phipps about redecorating - he liked the idea of pink and yellow. The feminine touch. It was stupid expecting a girl like Denise to be happy in a place full of junk. She deserved better. She was a good girl, in her way. He pulled a cork with his teeth and spat it across the room. Denise promised she'd be here and soon, so he pulled a chair to the window and waited. Forgive and forget. Forgive and forget.

He woke just before dawn, numb. Where was she? What the fuck was happening? He locked up. He should have dumped her months ago. The chagrin was short though. After all, there was more to life than a tart. Tom decided to go down to Sea View, maybe stay a day or two. This time of year with the wide blue sky, nothing was better. 'Fuck her.'

****

Tom took the early train down. It was nice watching the mist lifting off the fields. Somewhere to go. Someone to see. Strange how it turned out with Steven and maybe even Tom could flog his work off to other agencies, no really - this could turn out good. Tom was mentally calculating the tax advantages of running Steven as an off shore company, when he tripped over the laundry basket by the front door. 'Woahh.'

'Caught the first train up.'

Steven was hanging out sheets.

'Knew you'd be up. Not in the way?' Tom ducked under the impromptu clothesline and went in. 'Spring cleaning? Sea air obviously agreeing with you.' Sea View had a clean lived-in feel to it with the light from the sea bouncing in. The last of Shirley-Anne's works were packed and stacked at the end of the hall and it really did look like a place where a person lived.

'Yes, thanks. Busy. Here - this way, mind those -' Steven pushed a pile of dusters and tins of polish against the hall wall. He'd re-hung the shutters and was quite pleased with himself.

All the windows were open. Everything looked bigger, brighter. 'Fresh air and - and - is that lavender? No. I like it. I like it.' The fragrance was something. 'Is it polish or a woman?' Tom laughed. 'Like what you did by the way, on the steps coming up. That rope. Remember the way you slipped that time? Glad to see you walking straight.'

Steven had fixed a rope rail to both sides of the steps coming up. If Tom looked closer he would have seen that the stone steps were also swept and washed and that there were other footprints. 'Yes. Up and about. As a matter of fact, I make a point of walking up and down one flight of those damned steps every day. I'm getting there - I really am getting there.' Steven looked bigger. Just bigger.

Tom walked the length of the hall. Light blossomed like the glow of grace. 'Anyway, here -' he gave Steven a package '- go ahead. Open it. It's yours and plenty more where that came from.' Steven took the package slowly, questioning. 'I'm sorry.'

'What for?'

'Is this to do with me not working fast enough? I've got a few sketches on the go, I can show you? Is that why you're here?' Then - 'God, Tom? This is wonderful. Are you sure? I mean - for me? Are you sure? It will make a difference, I can start all over again - oh, Tom, I can't thank you enough, but - here - let me take your coat. Where are my manners? Good journey up? You must have taken the first train - it's barely nine o'clock. Wish you'd given me some warning I could have made up one of the beds. Staying the night? Nothing is ironed - place is a mess.'

'Could do with a drink. A Pink gin, I think. Any bitters?' It felt like a celebration. Steven was recovered and more than recovered. There was something new about him.

Tom was happy for him - for them both. 'Yes, my boy - couple of grand and it's just the beginning. Once you talk to the police, you can take flight - anywhere in the world. Do anything. Be anyone.' Up on the walkway there were two deckchairs, both angled towards the sun. An empty crisp packet fluttered off; there was an unfinished gin on the table. This was happiness. Tom leaned on the railing and breathed deep. He could see now why Evelyn loved it here.

Below in the kitchen, Steven moved quickly. He chipped ice with a screwdriver, mentally checking for anything out of place. When he came up with the tray, Tom was sitting comfortably, his face to the sun. 'Solitary drinking' he said, waving towards the table. 'Start like you mean to go on, eh? Ice? No bitters?' Steven poured. He said that most days he sat up here, looking out to sea sketching. He couldn't remember being happier. He'd even learned to like gin. Tom was glad. It made it easier.

'You know I'll do right by you. You do know that? And besides, once Richmond's killer is put away, you'll never have another worry. Money and a new life - how good is that? Confession is good for the soul.'

They stretched in the early sun, drinking and talking and the bitterness of Denise and the fear of the police turned into something better '...and you'll never guess what's happened. No? Well, just when it looked like things were over for me - guess what turned up?'

Steven shrugged.

'Another calendar' Tom was carried - an idea - an inspiration - it came out of nowhere.

'Oh? Not that bloke over in -?'

'Amsterdam. Yes. I was thinking of showing him a few of your drawings - that is, if you're interested? So - more money - more reason to get this thing with the police done and dusted. The future is ours - yours.'

'Oh. God. Oh. God.'

'I know. How lucky. Use those inks. Whip up a picture a day - you'll be on your way in no time.' Tom poured another. Bombay Sapphire - sea air - it didn't get much better. Seagulls circled and his eyes grew heavy. Sounds drifted - the breeze, the crunch of a car on the gravel below, the call of the far away. They spent the day drinking - not heavy, but steady - and now, in the dark, on the walkway, it was hard to tell the difference between being drunk and being lost. Tom called a cab and they stood looking down, waiting. Something in Tom wanted to stay.

'Billy.'

'What?'

'You used to ask after Billy - remember?'

'The cat? Oh? How is it?'

Tom laughed. 'There you go again.'

'Just being polite. You never shut up about that damned thing and its ailments.'

'Well, its rheumatism now, the vet thinks. Doesn't move. Spends his life asleep on the record player. Still snores. What you need is a pet.'

'Yes, if you say so - but I have the birds. I look at them - I sometimes wonder what it must be like to lift with the air - to be up there -'

Tom swayed. They'd been talking about a lot of things but mainly about Shirley-Anne. Steven made Tom promise on his life not to tell Shirley-Anne anything about the accident or about him being here at Sea View. He didn't want to worry her, he said. Steven wasn't Solly but sometimes his questions were odd - inquisitive in a way, hard to understand. He asked Tom about his feelings for Shirley-Anne. Did she matter to him? Did she *really* matter?

Tom answered yes, without thinking. 'I am nothing without her.'

They talked about Veronica too. 'Just a fling,' said Tom, now. 'We were ending it the night she died.' It was almost the truth. Tom at least was ending it - although Vernonica had other ideas. It would never be over, she said - drunk, of course. She'd written a letter that would put Shirley-Anne behind bars for the rest of her life - she'd use that letter if Tom left her.

'If that were true -,' said Steven, now '- if such a letter did exist - would you destroy it to save Shirley-Anne?' Tom nodded. He wanted to say if he could go back and do things differently - keep his hands to himself - he would. But he didn't. He just nodded because it was easier.

3.8

Shirley-Anne and Dr Gilmore were taking a spin and this was new.

Gilmore wanted to build up her strength, he said.

'Robin, you really are too good. The way you watch over me.'

'I know when I am beaten.' Gilmore laughed and slightly - just slightly - touched her knee the way a man does when a woman repels him. 'If you are intent on doing this damned exhibition thing, we must make you as strong as we can.' That's what it looked like, but Gilmore's real intention was to show to them both that Shirley-Anne was nowhere near ready for life on the outside. She was still vulnerable and the problem of the letter remained.

They were on their way back from a boat ride on the Serpentine. Shirley-Anne recalled her rowing days at university. 'On the swimming team, too.' It was her way of fighting back.

'I enjoy our little outings - we should go up to Box Hill sometime. That is when you're up to it?'

'Straight down from Marble Arch, sir?'

Gilmore lifted a finger, enough for a servant to read. She disliked this in him - the way he displayed his power; so working class. Gilmore pointed to the police station as they passed the junction at Ladbroke Grove. 'Heard anything?'

'No. Should I?'

'And, Tom?'

'You mean, have they arrested him yet?' He didn't answer. She wanted to say, how can you pick on someone so helpless? But she knew that he could - and he did.

'And his nerves? Standing up?'

'I must ask him. He's been so busy, of course you know that - helping me organise my paintings. Tower of strength.'

'Just as you say.'

In a corner of her mind, she saw two large birds sitting side by side on a rooftop; one pecking at the other. She wanted to say: 'I'm not alone. I have a husband - someone who will take me away from this - from you.' Instead, she said: 'Darling, Robin. Always at my side. I ask so much - sometimes I think, too much?'

Gilmore folded his hands tightly beneath his armpits. 'I have tickets for the Royal Academy -' his voice strained '- we could go next week?' She felt a stab of embarrassment. Royal Academy? The son of a postman? Would people stare? They drew up outside the house. Gordon the accountant, was looking out of the drawing room window. No doubt, more bad news. Why did she agree to set up Pilgrim House in the first place - it wasn't her idea. Nothing was ever her idea.

Harry Steiner would be coming round later. The picture restorer kept calling with new problems. Butters' detective was asking about that fucking missing picture and the snake of a journalist was on the phone every day. 'It used to be so simple.'

And then there was the problem of Steven Witt - she could control the problems in front of her but waiting for Witt to surface was different - you can't fight something you can't see. Gilmore opened the car door and stood on the pavement until she went in and as usual, she turned and smiled and thanked him for a nice day out.

****

Down in the pantry, Tom stirred the maid's tea. He was fond of her and he hated to see her like this. He was telling her - in ways she'd understand - that he was going down to The House (as they called it in the old days). Sea View. Time to bring the old place back to life. La Petite sighed the sigh of the inconsolable. He patted her hand and promised to take her down to see the sea. 'You liked it once -' She knew what he was saying and it was true, she did like it once - feeding the seagulls, watching the stars, turning a blind eye. But that all changed the night Tom and Veronica Lakey fought. In the mess of it all, no one saw La Petite, small and quick up on the walkway trying to get away - and she did get away, but not before Veronica Lakey was tipped over the railing and not before Tom slipped and passed out. La Petite saw it all. She thought in time she'd forget. She thought in time, it wouldn't matter.

'Well, I'll be off then' Tom patted his pockets. He'd taken an old bottle of Angostura which La Petite kept behind the olive oil. He was going to teach Steven how to mix gin and bitters. They'd have a picnic - roast sausages, gossip, walk along the ridge. He'd stay down for a day or two - glad of the peace and quiet.

Solly was waiting for him in Addison Avenue. He flashed his lights and Tom got in. 'Nice car. Leather seats? New?' Tom slid back. 'Didn't know you could drive - you know you've got a dent on the side?'

'Bloody sidelight got crunched - well, that's Bayswater for you.'

'Anyway - can't stop. On my way up to the old girl's place; want to catch the sunset over the cliffs.' He watched Solly smile. Eager. 'So? Any news? I'm on the payroll, yes?'

Solly gave him an envelope. 'Count it.' Tom ran his fingers over the notes. 'No need.'

'Count it.'

It was all there. 'Well,' said Solly, 'what have you got for me?' He waited. Then, 'you know, this is getting embarrassing.'

'Photographs are easy but drawing takes time. I'm not an artist, you know that.' Tom felt the wad in his pocket. Two thousand quid. Nice, but the paydays were changing. 'And like I said, I'm on my way now. Look - why don't I come in - to the agency? I could explain - there'd be no trouble, really. I mean, meeting like this -' his voice trailed off. What was going on? Last month it was four thousand quid and a lot of promises, now two thousand and Solly tight-lipped. What was going on?

'I need to show them something,' said Solly. 'Or -' he brightened '- the deal's off.'

Tom got the four-fifteen train and settled back in pleasant anticipation - ah, the good life. 'Bracing. Bracing.' Being with people. For Tom, that's what it was all about. Being with the right people. He'd happily jack it all in - he and Steven could set up on one of the Greek islands - tourist stuff - an easy life. Gin and bitters on the terrace, scrambled egg and salmon, watching the lights from the ships. Tomorrow the beach; the coves were a miracle of colour. Steven painting, Tom building a fire. Sausages on sticks. Gin and bitters. Gin and bitters gin and bitters gin and the years fell away. The train got in late. The evening was mild and Tom walked. He took the coast road. A sea mist was rolling in like an old friend. He took the steps up at an even pace. The soft air turned playful after the first landing and higher up it got stronger. He laughed. This wind.

'Hallooo. Anyone home?' The front door was open. He took off his shoes and followed a dim light coming from the Billiard Room. He'd surprise Steven - 'Steve? You there?' He laughed. 'The hour of your deliverance is at hand - bitters, anyone?' He laughed as he pushed the door. In the half-light something on the floor moved. It was Steven naked and asleep. Next to him, Denise.

3.9

Tom disappeared.

'What happened?' Solly waited three weeks. In the worst of his drinking days, Tom never went quiet like this. 'I liked it better when you were drunk.' They were back in the café. Tom was haggard. He'd been doing a lot of thinking.

'I said - where the fuck have you been? You look like death.'

'Shut up.'

Solly was always one step ahead and it unnerved him when things happened he didn't expect. Tom threw an envelope across the table. 'What's this?' Solly recognised it. Money. Tom was giving it back. He'd been a fool.

Solly fingered the envelope. 'Ah?' For Solly it could mean only one thing.

'Look, I know what you're thinking -' But no - for once, Solly didn't know what Tom was thinking.

'It's over,' said Tom, his eyes fixed on the street.

Solly - 'listen to me.'

'Fuck off.'

Solly waved the waitress away and slid the envelope back to Tom. 'Don't do this' he whispered. 'It's not what you think - I can explain.'

'I'm tired. Tired of being lied to - tired of being treated like a fucking joke.'

The mess was back and Tom was angry - his eyes still on the street.

'What is it? What's out there? Badger?'

Tom didn't hear. In his mind he was fighting with everyone - with Shirley-Anne for squandering her fortune, with Solly and Steven for giving hope and most of all, with himself, for believing. 'There's a man over there -' he said '- see him? Other side of the street - reading a newspaper. He's following me.'

Solly called over two cognacs. They drank in silence. Tom softened.

'He's been spying on me, just like you. Only, for a bit - I did actually trust you. What was it? Shirley-Anne paying you to find out about my not so secret, secret life? You disappoint me, I thought even you'd have better things to do. Anyway, the joke's on me.'

Solly laid his hand on Tom's arm. 'It's not what you think, Badger.'

The man across the street folded his newspaper and hailed a taxi, but he'd be back. Tom had seen him before, and yes, he would be back. Tom was a man without hope and his wife employed spies to keep him from finding that out because if he did - well, what did he expect? 'No. Look -' said Solly '- OK. You're right - in a way.' It was true. Last year - out of the blue, Shirley-Anne contacted Solly and told him she was coming back into the public eye. She knew Tom was drinking and all the rest and she didn't much care except for one thing. Penelope Richmond. She wanted Solly to make enquiries, that's all. Was Tom having an affair with Richmond and did it matter? Shirley-Anne didn't want to be dragged down by him a second time.

'I don't believe you.'

'I don't blame you.' Solly liked Tom. He'd always liked him. They had their disagreements but they also had good times - and you can't fake that. 'Do you remember - that day up in Burlington Arcade - last summer?' That was no chance meeting. 'You want the truth?' said Solly.

'From you? No.'

Solly took out his phone. He told him to call God, ask what he liked - and, said Solly - you'll be surprised to learn that we are doing a tourist thing for the Government, that most of the visuals are subbed out and that you are on the payroll as T. Amis - and that they really do like those fucking painteey-drawingeey things. 'Go ahead. Be my guest and say Goodbye for me while you're at it, because when God knows T. Amis is actually you and that I was the one who put you on the payroll - you won't be the only one looking for a job. Go a fucking-head. Tosser.'

A crumb to a starving man.

'Don't lie to me.'

Solly dialled. 'McVie & Co,' said a voice. He put the phone in Tom's hand 'Go ahead - don't be shy.'

'Hello. McVie & Co - McVie -' Tom closed the phone. 'How much did she pay you? Why didn't you tell me?' Solly was a greedy man and Shirley-Anne was paying him a thousand quid a week and all she wanted to know was the thing about Richmond.

'I don't believe you.'

'I'm flattered,' said Solly. 'Most people think I'll do anything for money.' Solly did tell Shirley-Anne about Tom and Penelope Richmond. He also told her that he had a thing going with Richmond - met her on one of those grim dawn runs round Shepherd's Bush Green. They met up a couple of times after that and that she was a boring little tramp who talked a lot about herself. Solly just wanted to know what he was paid to know i.e. was the little tart fucking around with Tom and did it mean anything - that's all. Solly wanted to keep the peace, he said. He told Shirley-Anne that Richmond meant nothing and that Tom was starting to work for the agency again. He even visited her in that Chancel Clinic place. Oil on troubled waters, he said - oil on troubled waters. And all of this was true, as far as it went. 'You misjudge me.'

What Solly didn't say - because he couldn't - was that the magic that was Penelope Richmond, rubbed off on him, too. What he didn't say, was that it burned to see Tom Amis playing with her. She was young and fresh and she needed someone real. It burned because it brought back all the other times women threw themselves at Tom and Solly picked up the pieces. Solly, the bag carrier. Solly, the eunuch. It burned then and it burned now.

Solly and Tom sat side by side in silence, looking out on the street. The envelope was still on the table.

****

Solly's money was the devil. It made Tom agree to go on giving the agency pictures he didn't have and now it pushed him into a betting shop to forget.

Tom used to gamble. He stopped after Veronica died. He made a promise to Shirley-Anne when he was lying in a hospital bed with nothing left but her. He vowed to mend his ways; stop gambling and everything, and he kept his word about gambling, until now. The voice on the wire called him over '… and the going's soft to good…' Tom put down a few hundred each way on the favourite and for as long as the race lasted, there was no mess. One by one, Tom threw the stubs into the gutter. Each a near miss. His phone rang and he answered without checking. It was Denise. Her spidery voice lifted his skin - 'Tom Tom? Yeah, it m…' He clipped it shut.

'Cunt.'

It was early for her; she wasn't what you'd call a morning person. He went across to the newsagents for cigarettes and to buy time. She rang again. 'Yes?'

'It's me.' Pause. 'Oh, don't be like that. Tom Tom. Just letting you know not to be late. I'll be waiting.' She giggled. He wanted to tear her throat out but something deeper held him.

She was a prostitute. What did he expect? Really, what did he expect? 'I'm glad you got my message' he said. In those three weeks of silence it dawned on him slowly, that he was the problem. Not Steven Witt. Not Denise. Not anyone - just him. He tricked himself. He wanted to believe this half-life could be more. Better. But now, thanks to Steven Witt and Solomon Solomon, he could stop believing. Despair brings its own relief.

'Had some kind of virus - been out of action - did you miss me?' He would use Denise the way she deserved and the thought of having sex with her now had a kind of zest. He could do what he fucking liked. 'Sorry - going into a tunnel - call - later - what's the -?' He turned the phone off.

'Citanes.' He paid and went back to the betting shop. Bessy's Boy was running in the four-thirty. Long odds and risky. Most of his cash was gone, but if Bessy's Boy came in, he'd recover. He tried to picture the horses lining up but he saw only naked bodies, young, strong - happy '…lining up now…'

He fought to stay with the race but Steven and Denise were everywhere.

He saw himself waiting in Clapham like a fool - he saw her that day in Clerkenwell - they must have been together then '…yellow flag…starter's orders…' The voice on the wire pulled him back to a better place '…two hundred each way on Sand of the Desert…'

'- and they're off -' Gate up. Too late. Too late. Too late. It's too late and it doesn't matter. It was always too late -

'…and it's Lucky Chance rounding the first…coming up Admiral's Man, it's Admiral's Man Lucky Chance Adm…' he was running and it was the greatest feeling '…two furlongs and it's…Sand of the Desert…Sand of the …home straight and oh coming up on the inside Bleaker's Bounty…' he ran and ran and for less than a second it looked like hope.

'…Sand of the Desert Sand and Bleaker's Bounty neck and neck and Sand of the Desert Sand of the…Sand of…and it's Lucky Chance by a head…Ooh the favourite.

Lucky chance.'

****

Tom sucked on a peppermint. He was down a grand, his indigestion was back and his jaw ached. Solly came clean and things that made no sense before, made sense now. So, he'd been played for a fool - get over it. So, he took Solly's money - get over it. He'd string Steven Witt along for a bit longer, make him know what it's like to be nothing - yeah - that was something.

He stopped off for a few drinks at The Castle in Holland Park Avenue and then went down to Clapham. He took his time. Denise could see things were different. It worried her. He liked that. 'What kept you? I was waiting -' she ran at him and flung up her arms. He pushed her away. 'Easy, now. Get me a drink, there's a good girl' he pushed and he pushed her again, for the hell of it.

'What? Is it the coat? They said it was mink. Going cheap. Oh, come on Tom Toms. No one can see.' And it was true. The coat was mink. The laurels were high and no one could see - no one but him. He stroked the side of her neck with his index finger and thought of Richmond twitching.

'How did it go?'

'Oh?'

'- you know - the meeting? Thought you'd be back sooner.' It was seven o'clock. She was naked beneath the coat and shivering. She had the smell of cheap nail varnish and fear. 'You're laughing. Why you laughing?'

'Just glad to see you, my dear - here, like this.' He hated her.

'I need a credit card.' She leaned back against the fridge and let the coat drop, without effort. He watched, without interest. 'Nice. Get one.'

'No, silly. I thought - you know - you could give me one. Only, we've been together a while; seems only right.'

'Oh? Yes. Yes, why not.' He went through the post, another reminder about the rent. Another bit of Shirley-Anne's jewellery that didn't sell. He thought again of the horses and shook his head in disbelief.

'What's that big boy?' The sickly taste of cannabis caught in his throat.

'Oh, just doing some sums; so much money - hard to keep track.'

'So how about it? The Card, I mean. Saw some nice rings in Harrods - I want to look pretty for you?'

He unwrapped another peppermint and sucked on it and thought of Richmond - here one minute, gone the next. So easy.

'Oh, Tom Toms - there you go, laughing, again.'

****

Alan Tree was surprised to get a handwritten note from Shirley-Anne inviting him to tea. It said little except that she had a small problem and hoped he might help.

'So good of you. No, really - at such short notice and how is Mrs Tree? Sugar? To tell the truth, I thought we'd lost you?' A rhetorical question because Shirley-Anne was only too aware of Alan Tree and his questions. She gave him a small cup and saucer and her hands hovered, waiting. Dulled by the conversation so far, Tree's eye caught the china. He held the cup with unusual grace, given the size of his hand. 'Meissen?'

'But Mr Tree, how clever - you are a collector?' They drank mostly in silence, stopping now and then to comment on the weather and the health of the maid - still poor. This skirting about was not unusual in conversations destined to be murky. Tree already knew that Shirley-Anne kept a tight rein on her husband via his one-time friend, Solomon Solomon. He assumed he was not here because she wanted to know more.

The clink of the china filled the room. The doctor's driver passed by in the hall. Shirley-Anne followed him with her eyes. She didn't speak again until he was gone. 'Well, as you know -' she whispered, 'I have a small - how can one put it - problem?'

'Problem?'

'Yes. Of course, ordinarily one would overlook this sort of thing, one's Christian duty - but then - and you come so highly recommended, my sister still talks about the way you recovered that violin and I gather you've made great strides tracking my poor painting?'

Tree said nothing.

'One trusts, do you see? That's what makes it so difficult.'

'I don't follow.'

'No. How could you?' She lowered her voice, again. 'The simple truth is, I've been robbed.'

'Robbed?

'Yes. I thought perhaps you might be able to shed some light on it? It's all so distressing. One trusts, so - oh, I've said that.'

'Robbed - or blackmail?'

'Blackmail? No. No? Why - what a preposterous - why? - why would you say that? I've got nothing to hide.' Alan Tree shifted, uneasy. He was a big man and sitting in an 18th century drawing room chair wasn't easy.

'Entre nous, of course - I rescued him. I tried - well, we all tried - and then, for this to happen. I'm sure you understand?'

'No, I don't think I do. Are you telling me you know the thief?'

'Witt. Mr Steven Witt. I used to visit him in prison. Took him under my wing. He was so young, do you see? I thought for him, at least, there was hope.'

Tree sipped. What could he say? He wanted to tell her she was right, Steven Witt was not what he seemed and yes - he was dangerous. How much did she know? 'To tell you the truth, Mrs Amis, I've had my doubts about this man - when he got out of prison, he was close to your brother - it always struck me as strange -'

'More tea?'

'Thank you.'

Shirley-Anne handed him a slice of cake. 'I made it myself. Cherry and almond, anyway, where was I?'

'You were telling me you were afraid -'

'No. Not afraid.' She laughed and a blush ran over her face. 'Why, no - no, Mr Tree, I am moved - by pity. Is that so hard to understand?'

'Ah.'

'I would like you to find poor Steven ...'

Tree nodded. He could see she was afraid.

'...these people have so little. Anyway, he's back to his old tricks. Light fingered.'

'What has he taken?' Tree knew Tom sold things on the quiet - the price of booze and women. 'How do you know it's him?'

'Another slice? I ground the almonds myself.'

Tree raised his palm politely. 'Did you ever find who stole your picture?'

'Does it matter?'

'Professional curiosity.'

'No - although, well - one has to suspect it was poor Steven Witt - that night at Harry Steiner's, everything was fine until he arrived - well, there it is -' she raised her hands, helpless.

'Why don't you just call the police? They're a lot cheaper.'

'The police are hopeless and anyway, call me a fool but I would still like to save him - prison is a dreadful place. Dreadful. I thought you could make a few enquiries. Discrete. He's disappeared - he could be lying injured somewhere, or dead -' she waved her hand, to stop Tree speaking '- I just want you to find him - I feel responsible. Find him. More tea?' Shirley-Anne said a small vase disappeared from the mantelpiece last summer. Dresden. An unusual design with Hollyhocks. Valuable. She saw Steven Witt put it in his pocket - 'I felt pity, do you see? These people have so little.' She hoped he would return it, so she waited. But now he was gone, without a word - just disappeared. 'I'm not angry - just, hurt.' She wanted to meet him. Talk to him. 'I still have hope -' It was his sudden disappearance more than anything that hurt.

'You want me to find a missing person - not a missing vase?'

'Well, now that you put it like that. Yes. Yes, I suppose I do. Discretion, do you see? You'll know from my darling sister, that - well, how can I put it? - we are hopeful that very soon I will be something.' She laughed, embarrassed. 'What I mean is, somewhat in the spotlight. It really wouldn't help, do you see? - A whiff of scandal - people have such evil minds. I am in your hands.'

It was almost true.

3.10

Back in January, the day after Penelope Richmond died - Steven Witt was picked up by the bin men. He stayed still and said nothing. Lying in hospital, he drifted in and out of consciousness with the look of a man who deserved what he got. With no identification, he was patched up and discharged with four weeks' meds. The police were not notified. He couldn't believe his luck.

His memory of that night was still muddled but he knew enough to know that he was not safe and he needed to get out of London, as soon as he could walk. Lulled by painkillers and by the strange exhilaration of having cheated death, he lay in bed planning his escape. Then came Tom.

Tom was in a bad place and Steven owed him. That's how Steven saw it.

So he stayed. But after nearly a week alone in an airless studio in Clerkenwell, Steven's worries got the better of him and by day six, he couldn't go on. He still had enough meds to drift off and not come back. Tom would understand - he'd probably be relieved. Steven was a burden. The police would find Penelope Richmond's killer - they'd see it wasn't Tom. He'd be OK. It would work out.

He lined up the tablets and chewed them without thinking and he didn't know why, but he started to cry. Was this it? Was this all he amounted to - a frightened little man in a room with no window? His hands shook and he dropped the Zopiclone. He took a handful of Tramadol but coughed, then choked and that's when there was a knock on the studio door. It was a girl. She was passing, she said. Was he alright? Could she help? Her name was Denise.

Little did Tom know - two hours later, when he bumped into Denise rounding the corner of Bowling Green Lane that it was too late to move Steven to another hiding place. Way too late.

****

It was nine months since *'Poppies in a Jar'* went missing. The next tax bill was coming and Harry Steiner's grip on Shirley-Anne was tightening. Butters needed something and a call from DS Rainbow was what she got. She assumed it was about the stolen painting. She assumed there was something in it for her. She was wrong.

This was about Betty Rae and the story that was slipping.

Rae had half a story and unless she could trigger some police activity, she wouldn't have that. So, she paid Rainbow a visit. Penelope Richmond worked for her as a runner, she said. Richmond found evidence linking her employer, Mrs Shirley-Anne Amis, to the deaths of Severin Brille, Evelyn Amis and Veronica Lakey. Richmond knew someone was trying to kill her - well, worth a try.

Evidence? Yes. A letter. Richmond found a letter - she was going to give it to Rae. No. Rae hadn't exactly seen the letter - but it did exist -

In another world, Rae would have been just a journalist fishing, but there was something in what she said about Severin Brille that caught Rainbow. This is why Butters was sitting in

Interview Room 4 now and why Shirley-Anne was sitting in another interview room further down.

Severin Brille was looking like a closed case - unexplained death with no leads - but Rainbow didn't see it that way and he was willing to chase a new lead, if one existed. He interviewed Butters first. The investigation into the death of Mr Severin Brille had raised a few questions, he said - a few loose ends. He looked for flickers of recognition - did the death of Mr Brille come as a surprise to Butters - given that she had him followed in that last year of his life? Yes? A surprise? Why? Butters knew, surely, from Alan Tree, that Mr Brille was going off the rails? 'He started meeting up with Shirley-Anne and she gave him money. Cash. Strange, don't you think? Why would she do that?'

Butters blanked. What was this man saying? She stopped reading Tree's reports months before Severin died.

'Why did you have your brother followed? Tell me,' said Rainbow 'your sister - Mrs Amis - leads a quiet life?' This is what interested Rainbow. 'Don't you find it strange that she would meet up with your brother, like that - I mean, bit out of character?'

Butters was stung. She had no idea that Severin made contact with Shirley-Anne and that Shirley-Anne was giving him money. And sitting here in a grey room with a grey man, only one explanation was possible - they were planning to rob her. Yes. The Brille Trust. They were going to cut her out. Butters reeled. 'Oh, she's not all she seems, I can tell you.' Her grip loosened. 'Quiet life? Quiet? Oh, please.'

'But,' said Rainbow 'she's been housebound for years - doing the odd bit of charity work - visited only by her doctor?'

Without knowing or caring what lay behind Rainbow's questions, Butters gave herself up to lust - the ravenous lust of letting go. 'Don't be an idiot. It's a pretence - surely, you've worked that out?' Shirley-Anne's breakdown was a myth. Butters laughed 'til she cried. 'No one believes it. We all know - we all know -'

'What?'

'The stupid bitch murdered one of her husband's lovers - cheap slut - pushed her off a cliff - hushed up - but we knew - we all knew.'

'Any witnesses?'

'None came forward. Too scared -' ideas long dormant, shot up. Shirley-Anne was dangerous - calculating - oh, please - it was only a matter of time - nothing stays hidden forever. Butters watched the ship of her dreams slip over the horizon. 'I might have known - the way he turned up with that box -' she saw in Severin all the things she feared in herself '- calculating little fucker - the box was a sign - they were planning to cut me out even before his birthday - what a fool I've been.'

'What box?'

'That fucking box back at that tea at the Ritz, Severin planned it all -'

'What box?'

'Oh do shut up - it wasn't the box - it was what was in it.'

Butters left the station an hour later, numb and no wiser and Rainbow heard Rae singing in his head - Severin knew something and Shirley-Anne knew it too. Was he blackmailing her? Did she kill him?

****

As Butters stumbled into a taxi, Shirley-Anne sat quietly in Interview Room 9, listening to DS Rainbow telling her what Betty Rae told him. She did not flicker.

****

Back in the gallery, Butters went into orbit. 'To think - the help I offered - and all along they were planning to rob me. You knew - you must have known?' She was screaming at Tree. 'She was giving him money - no doubt bribing him to cut me out. Why didn't you tell me?' But Tree did tell her. He told about Shirley-Anne and Severin meeting, the way they argued and how she knocked him to the ground on the same towpath where he died a week later. It was all in the monthly reports that Butters never read.

There was a small porcelain box on the desk. The one Butters took back from the Ritz. Severin's happy family box. Shared memories. The box contained tiny china figures, wrapped in tissue paper. When he placed them on the table - back there at the Ritz - Shirley-Anne went pale. Butters took little notice at the time, keen to keep focused on the subject of money. It was only now that she looked at these things more closely.

'Why would a man keep these?' said Tree.

Butters picked up the pieces one by one. A small china doll - presumably once, Shirley-Anne's. Its hair and dress singed. Trees. Other small figures for a toy garden - a white picket fence, flowers in flower pots, a patch of green grass and a tiny rope with a loop at one end which Tree assumed was for pulling a donkey, although there was no donkey.

'It was a game they played - Severin and her - they took that box everywhere.' After G.F. Brille died, no one wanted the children. They were split up and ferried between boarding schools and nannies. 'It went on for years - whenever we met up - school holidays - this lot would come out. To think I'd forgotten.'

'What was it - this game?'

Butters sighed and poured herself a whiskey. 'Who knows? Who cares?'

'It must have meant something. You said Shirley-Anne went pale when she saw it?'

'Yes, well - maybe embarrassed. Didn't want to be reminded.'

'Reminded?'

'Hanging that doll from one of those tree things. Always the same. The doll got caught in the rope, Severin and Shirley-Anne took it in turns to come to the rescue and they all lived happily ever after. I think that's how it went.'

****

When Shirley-Anne left DS Rainbow later that day, she was as confused as Butters. Trying later to recall the interview, all she remembered was an empty room and telling a man that Severin was alone in this world. He reached out to her for help - what was she to do? He devoted his life to helping unfortunates - of course, she gave him money; she wanted to help. He had the sweetest nature.

Back at his desk, Rainbow opened a file and looked again at prints taken before Severin Brille was cut down. Smooth sand. What kind of person would watch a man die like that - watch him kick and then smooth the sand? And the area CCTV prints - they showed nothing but shadows.

Rainbow recalled when he first interviewed Shirley-Anne Amis just after Severin died - it was at the house in St James' Gardens. He remembered silver framed photographs on a low table, one of a girl - young - standing beside an upright skiff and smiling. That girl was Shirley-Anne. She knew how to row a boat.

****

Alan Tree closed the box in Butters' gallery and he went for a walk on the towpath to the blue bridge where Severin's body was found. He was thinking about Shirley-Anne too.

A game of rescue? A game where it all turned out right in the end - so, why did she go pale? Shirley-Anne wasn't embarrassed. She was afraid.

Tree looked into the water. In the eddies, he saw what Butters told him of their early lives - how mother died in an accident and the empty years that followed. The box kept them together but was it also a reminder of bad times? Shirley-Anne played the game when she was a child but did she want to be reminded of it now? Shirley-Anne was a timid person. She avoided the world because for her it was dangerous. Severin was inviting back into a place she thought she'd left behind - she couldn't go back. That's how Tree saw it. Severin was impoverished and Shirley-Anne met him to buy him off. She wanted the past gone. All of it - including, Severin.

3.11

Shirley-Anne stood in her surgeon's whites and Harry Steiner kept still. This was survival and it wasn't nice. 'Darling, Shirley-Anne - when I told Emily, she was so proud -' he lifted his chin '- this OK?'

Shirley-Anne was painting his portrait. A kind of 'thank you' for everything. 'That's it - hold it just there.'

'When can I see it?'

'Soon -' then '- Harry, you know, I was thinking - that journalist - Betty Rae - is she absolutely necessary?' The mood between them was relaxed and after four days of painting, talk was easy. Shirley-Anne complained that Rae was intrusive. 'What was she thinking - going to the police? Does she want to ruin us?' Shirley-Anne hoped Steiner would see it her way. 'I mean, publicity is one thing, but scandal - and lies? Lies - Harry.' Steiner stifled a yawn. He knew what Rae was doing. 'I really wouldn't worry - when I think of your dear mother - ah, the scandal -'

Steiner arrived for the final sitting at ten o'clock the following day. He was in a good mood and joked that Shirley-Anne should include this portrait in her exhibition. But Shirley-

Anne was worried. Everything was on hold until the damn letter was found and destroyed. But. But. But. Alan Tree didn't come cheap. The roof over their heads was on loan from the bank. She needed money and she needed it now. 'Harry, time isn't on my side.'

Steiner was a comfort. He understood, he said. Coming back into the world wasn't easy. 'Trust me' he said. 'Rae is a journalist - smoke and mirrors - we'll give her the odd bit of nonsense - she'll jump through hoops for us.' And if Rae or others took shots at the past, so what. He was here. What's the worst that could happen? 'You are not alone,' he said.

'Harry, darling. You must think me a fool.' The clock in the square struck twelve and the packers would be here soon to take the next batch of canvases. He walked to the window and noticed with relief that today it was only two.

They stood facing the wall. Shirley-Anne was painting every day and sometimes through the night. He didn't approve. 'Listen. Why don't we take the rest of the day off? Come to lunch - my treat? Do you remember how we used to stroll through Hyde Park - how about it - play truant? It's a lovely day - do a twirl on the Serpentine?'

Shirley-Anne smiled and tapped her watch. He shrugged and went back to the chair. As he sat, he nodded to the open door across the hall. 'That portrait in there - could do with a clean.'

'Oh? Mother? Yes, she was always rather grubby.' They laughed. Steiner made no secret of his liking for G.F. Brille's self-portrait; it was a rare thing. Shirley-Anne recalled that Stringler said the same.

'A remarkable person.'

'Was she?'

'Like mother like daughter, eh?'

'No, Harry. Different. Very different, I'm pleased to say. Now sit still will you.' Shirley-Anne held the point of her brush over the canvas and then stopped. 'Harry? You mentioned putting her in my show - were you serious?'

'Foolish idea. Forget it. You're right: two different artists, two different people. Let's get on; the packers will be here.'

'No, really Harry. If you think it would help - I don't mind - it's a business, after all?'

Steiner shrugged and raised his hands like a man whose secret was out.

'Well. If you push me, I can't deny it would help. It's a bad world we live in, where the dead mean more than the living - sorry, that came out wrong. Sorry. Look, look, back in pose. Off we go. How's this?'

Shirley-Anne wiped the brush and put it down. 'No. It's OK. I understand.' In the silence that followed, something sweet stirred. 'She - that journalist - desperate to do something on me. Keeps ringing. Yes, I know, flattering. Anyway, says people want to know about me - whatever that means. It's a new generation, she says. Want to know where I came from? You know, the old crowd - the art, the mad things we got up to. I suppose it can only help?' Steiner said nothing. Shirley-Anne felt it again - that sweet thing. 'Oh, well look -' she grabbed Steiner's hand and pulled him to her bedroom '- tell me honestly, how on earth can this help me now?' She pushed him up close to the portrait of Mother but he resisted. 'Oh, Harry - look. Look, will you?' That thing coiled and tightened. Sweet. Tight. Money. 'Personally, I've got no problem including her - why not? Two for the price of one -'

Half an hour later, Shirley-Anne poured coffee and Steiner stood by the window. The packers didn't come - just a man and a van. 'Seems in a hurry,' said Shirley-Anne, distracted, turning over papers on a side table. 'Do you think Mr Grobstein's place will be big enough? I must say, it seemed a bit cramped.'

'Quite so. Quite so.'

'I'm not complaining - there are a few in the garden studio - about six.

Yes. Ah, here it is' she gave Steiner a list of her paintings, old and new. He put it in his pocket. 'Yes. Cramped.' His mind was elsewhere. Shirley-Anne watched, suddenly anxious.

'Actually, no,' he said. 'You're quite right. There isn't much space down at Grobstein's place. What I thought -'

He was torn - then she realised - 'but, Harry - you're going to take them?' Relief swept over her soft and blind. 'Oh, Harry -' she threw her arms around him '- you're taking them back to your gallery? I knew it. I knew it. You're taking my pictures to sell them, before the exhibition - God knows, we could use the money. Oh, Harry, you sly dog.' She squeezed his neck with childlike faith.

'There, there. You worry too much.' He was touched. 'Leave the worrying to me.'

'You're right. You're right - well of course - sorry. Stupid. I thought with mother's work, well - I thought I might be left out in the cold again - stupid, stupid - oh, why do you put up with me?'

The man came up the basement steps with the works from the studio under his arm.

'Harry, they're hardly dry.' Was she imagining it? 'Harry - shouldn't you wrap them, first?' Steiner put his hands on her shoulders. 'Now what did I say? Leave the worrying to me.'

'They'll scratch. The surface darling - put some glassine paper between them, at least.'

'Now, now. Easy.' He turned her from the window. 'We've been doing this for a long time - if you want to go down and tell him how it's done, you can' Steiner waved and blew a kiss. He left, a happy man.

****

Maybe Shirley-Anne was tired, maybe the police upset her more than she thought, but Harry Steiner skipping down the steps like that - was not right. She spent the rest of the day pacing and drinking until about five o'clock that evening when she fell into a deep sleep.

She dreamed it was a fine day and the world was coming to an end. It was a pleasant dream in its way; the sun was shining, the sky was blue and out there - on the horizon - a wind was gathering. It looked like nothing, but it wasn't. In the dream, most of the people had gone. The few who remained were tending their gardens. They smiled and waved behind white picket fences. The grass was green. The lawns were neat. They had no idea.

3.12

The alarm went up after midnight. Harry Steiner took the call. It was now three in the morning and he was standing in Shirley-Anne's bedroom with Dr Gilmore. 'I've told you, already -,' said Steiner '- she sounded strange.'

'What do you mean - strange?'

'Drunk. She sounded drunk.'

The call from Shirley-Anne unnerved Steiner. He came round immediately. The front door was open and all the house lights on; he called but no one answered. He followed the sound of tapping upstairs - an open window and a broken blind. Shirley-Anne's bedroom door was open and the words - 'No No No' - were scrawled large in red lipstick on the dressing table mirror. 'What does it mean?' he said now.

Gilmore shrugged. 'We'd better clear this up.' The window pane was shattered like something heavy was thrown against it. Bits of torn paper shivered on the walls. A chair lay at its side, broken. Steiner shuddered. He noticed Gilmore slide something into his pocket. 'Can you do that? I mean, what if something's happened - shouldn't we leave it for the police?'

Gilmore smiled. He put his arm around Steiner's shoulder. Casual. 'What you need is a stiff drink old chap. Doctor's orders.' He eased Steiner towards the door. 'We see this kind of thing all the time. A tired mind.' But Steiner tensed. He was a risk taker but this frightened him. 'I told her to slow down -' he kicked over an empty Vodka bottle. An A3 sheet covered in faces, slid from the bed to the floor. Faces were daubed on the back of the door. 'Look -' this wasn't his fault '- look -' he ran his hand over the wall - faces everywhere - human, animal, cartoon. Leering. Savage. Gilmore ignored him. 'She wouldn't listen.'

'She's ill. You knew that - yet you kept pushing.'

'Pushing?'

'Day after day. A picture a day, she said. Sometimes, more. I really think you should wait downstairs, this isn't for you. My driver will take you home.'

'Don't be absurd. I didn't push her.' Steiner screwed the paper into a ball and threw it. 'I didn't push her - anything, but.'

'I saw them - what were you thinking? Please leave. This is a medical matter - you have no place -'

Steiner laughed, appalled. 'Sorry. Sorry.' He made an effort to stay calm, to think straight. 'Look at these. No really, look -' he lifted sheets torn from a sketch pad '-scribble.'

'Yes?'

'Rubbish. Complete rubbish.'

Gilmore looked away.

'We were easing her back - or trying to. A little at a time, I said. I was hoping to sell one or two smaller pieces, privately. You know - test the market.' He sighed; it looked like he was going to cry. 'Just look - rubbish - complete bloody nonsense.'

'You forced her. She told me.'

'No, I didn't. Think, man - why would I do that? Have you any idea what it costs to promote a nobody?' Steiner's hands dropped to his sides. He looked up at the portrait above the fireplace, the only thing undamaged.

'Are you telling me the exhibition wasn't your idea? Are you telling me Mrs Amis pushed you into it?'

'No. It was my idea - but not this -' he waved wildly '- not this.'

'Where have you put her paintings?'

'Oh, they're perfectly safe. A little place we have down in Docklands. A lock up.'

'Not at your gallery? Not in Bond Street? But she told me -'

Steiner shook his head. 'We were trying to help, that's all. We've known the family for years. It was a tragedy the way she lost her brother - life hasn't been good to her, well - Emily, my wife, persuaded me - she felt sorry for her. Anyway, we did what we could - you know, the usual - got a tame journalist on board - bought a small work - early trivia - thought we'd kick start some interest - made it a mystery buy. Our journalist contacted that young assistant - I forget her name -

'Richmond? Penelope Richmond?'

'- if you say so - anyway, we didn't want it to look like charity - Shirley-Anne can be sensitive. We paid Reece Rae - the journalist - a small fee. Sift out a story - just a few column inches. Nothing more. We meant no harm. A favour to a friend, nothing more -' his voice trailed off; it sounded so trite, now. 'Anyway - showed a couple of her newer works in a small view we had back in August and look how she loved it. She really came out of herself that night - and one of the pictures actually sold. Remember? You were there?'

Gilmore was going through a folder of correspondence.

'We had no idea - it's not as if -' Steiner broke off.

'- not as if -?'

'- it mattered.'

Gilmore went into the bathroom and checked the cabinet. He came out with his bag clipped and ran downstairs. Moments later he was back, breathless. 'Where's Amis?'

'God knows.'

'Who was last with her?'

'I don't know.'

'You say she called you?'

'I think so.'

'Think? Either she did or she didn't?'

'Yes. Yes, she called - just - sounded odd.'

'What did she say? Think. Did she say where she was going or if she was going to do something - stupid - or anything - think?'

'I told you, she said - "it's not here." That's it. Then she hung up. I came right over - that's when I called you.'

'Did she take anything? Keys? Clothes?'

'Look around - she's just walked out -' Steiner looked up, bleak. 'What's happened? You think it's suicide? You do, don't you? Call the police.'

'No -' Gilmore coughed. He put his hand over Steiner's phone. 'No - that is, not yet.' He forced a smile. 'It's not the first time. I probably shouldn't be telling you - but under the circumstances - anyhow, she's gone for one of her walks. Imagine how she'd feel if the police were called - imagine, what a journalist would make of that.'

Steiner looked blank. 'But she could be in trouble. Where's the maid? Let me speak to her -'

'Maid's ill. Flu. I've just checked on her. She's fine; sleeping. Hasn't been herself; no point making this bigger -' Gilmore's eyes scanned as he spoke. '- she'll be back. Trust me. Done it before.' His voice was light, like he was tripping through daisies.

'What did she mean then -,' said Steiner 'when she said "it's not here"?'

****

It was just after dawn when Tom heard. He was walking down Holland Park Avenue on his way back from the flat in Clapham. He recognised Gilmore's car and stopped when he saw the driver's window wind down at the traffic lights. It was Vic who told him. Gilmore sat in the back looking the other way. Vic's story wasn't quite accurate but it suited both Tom and Gilmore not to speak to each other.

Vic said Shirley-Anne had been drinking. She was missing, probably gone for a walk to clear her head. He said Steiner knew where she was and so there was no point involving the police. The traffic lights changed and the car moved on before Tom could reply. He didn't go home. He went instead to Steiner's house in Chelsea, where he found Shirley-Anne sitting alone in the pool house. Her feet were bare and cut. Steiner was also there, in the library; speechless with anger.

'It's a bit like a grotto,' said Shirley-Anne. Her voice calm.

'Yes.' Tom smiled. 'Yes, I suppose it is.' They sat side by side, looking into the pool.

'Mother always wanted an underground swimming pool -' it rippled dreamlike.

'Peaceful.'

'Yes.'

'We could drift away.' Steiner had closed that part of the property. He told the servants that there was a problem with the water filters.

Tom held Shirley-Anne's hand. He wanted to say it was alright; that everything was alright. He knew about her interview at Ladbroke Grove station - he imagined their scorn and the hurt.

'I'm sorry, Thomas.'

'For what?'

'Everything.'

'Now. Now. You're tired.'

She shook her head and cried silently. This was his fault. All of it. 'Tell me about that swimming pool - mother's you say? Underground? Imagine the insurance.'

'Don't humour me Thomas, I'm not a child.'

What could he say? The shattered glass at the end of the pool house - how did she do it? Where did that violence come from? 'No. I'm interested. Really. We've been together - how long?'

'A million years.'

'- and sometimes I think I hardly know you.'

241

She squeezed his hand. Their gaze stayed with the water. 'I don't think Harry would thank me for taking a dip in this state' she rubbed at the dirt and dried blood on her feet. 'She had plans drawn up, I remember.'

'Oh?'

'Mother. Pool. Took it into her head to have a glass wall set into the rock, so you could swim and think you were in the sea.'

'Good idea.'

'Father didn't think so -'

'- you've never really spoken about him.'

'He left. Don't remember much. I know he didn't like mother's friends. I suppose he was afraid of what mother's pool parties might do. In a way, I think mother was afraid too -' her voice trailed.

'Damned expensive. Putting a pool in that place - imagine the damp?'

'Yes, dearest. Practical as usual.' Then, an odd thought came to her - 'How did you find me?'

'I guessed' he lied. He didn't want to say that he knew - they all knew - she had nowhere else to go.

'Dear Harry. Such a friend. What must he think of me? Do you think they'll get them out?' She pointed her foot at soft dark things lying like turtles, at the bottom of the pool. 'I didn't mean it. You believe me, don't you Thomas? Harry knows that, doesn't he?' Steiner's sculptures. All but one, at the bottom of the pool. At the end of the pool house something lay on the floor like a large bird with a broken wing.

Tom took out his handkerchief and wiped the dirt off her face. He wanted to say - sorry. Sorry for bringing her to this place. Sorry.

'I don't know what happened,' said Shirley-Anne. 'I don't even know how I got here. I was asleep, then I woke up - and there were all these faces looking at me, judging me.'

Tom stayed with the water.

'They said such terrible things. Robin thinks if we find the letter that will be the end of it - but it won't. Those faces won't go away - like crows - they'll keep pecking.'

Tom took her hands and held them in his. He had no idea what she was saying. 'Have them out in a jiffy.' He said. 'Didn't Harry say just the other day, about time he had this place cleaned out? You don't remember?'

'No. I don't think I do. He said that?'

'Yes.'

'So, it's not all bad then?'

'No. Not all bad.'

The water lipped and murmured and told Tom what he feared most - that this was love and it wasn't nice.

Book Four

4.1

'Darling, don't ask me to make a speech.' Shirley-Anne's voice carried like a bird. It was August again, a surprise again.

'One more. Smile. This way. This way.' Click. Click. Click. A late group arrived. More cheering. More friends. 'Over here - last one -' A private club near Camden Lock. Steiner wagged his finger at a photographer. 'Now, make sure it's a double. I don't want to be stuck in a corner, like last time.' He shrugged and laughed. 'Talking to myself.'

'These young people - were we ever like that?'

'Butters!'

Fingertips and half-filled glasses moved above heads. More people arrived. In the crush, Tom let himself be edged towards the door. Outside, the night was clear. He loosened his tie - this is what it was about - the wide sky, the crescent moon and getting what you want. A strand of smoke curled under a street light. 'Harry -?'

Steiner turned into view. 'You, too?' He opened a silver cigarette case.

'Tempting - but no. Given up.'

'Sensible. Filthy habit.' Fat cigarettes. Handmade. 'Emily won't have it in the house. I'm an outcast.' He laughed. 'I sometimes think, I'm the only one left. Hear you've given up the wild life?'

'It was never that wild -'

Steiner smiled.

'- no more running around for me -' said Tom, pointing back to the door '- deadlines. Who needs it?'

'Who, indeed?' Shirley-Anne's "blip" - now two months ago - never happened. When Steiner's pool was drained and the sculptures lifted, nothing more was said. Shirley-Anne went back to painting - this time with Tom close and Steiner closer.

'Back to basics is fine by me - bag carrier - nothing more strenuous than a G&T and an early night.' They stood looking up at the stars.

'Nice night.'

'Yes.'

'Stars.'

'Yes.'

'Clear.'

'Yes.'

These days Tom and Steiner talked a lot about the weather.

'No rain then?'

'No. Chilly though - later on.'

'Yes. Chilly.'

Steiner was hard to understand. There was talk, of course - jealous talk - that he led people on, promised things he couldn't deliver - but, he was doing so much for Shirley-Anne, it had to mean something - 'I never did thank you -'

'Wonderful isn't it? Steiner touched Tom's shoulder. 'Seeing her - blossom, like this?'

'Oh? Yes.'

'I knew she'd do it. Nothing stands in her way.'

'Women.'

'Yes. Women.'

Tom hesitated. 'Tells me you've sold a few? That right? Really?'

'Testers.' Steiner shrugged. 'Smaller auctions - you know - pacing it. We bought one ourselves, in fact. Emily - great fan.' There was an edge to Steiner which was new. Maybe he was secretly angry or maybe just plain embarrassed - hard to know. But what was beyond doubt - once Shirley-Anne returned to her senses - was that Steiner was everywhere. He blamed himself, he said - for not realising sooner how hard things had been. He wanted to make amends, he said and he started to lend Shirley-Anne money. Not wanting to offend, she accepted.

Steiner took over her debts - all of them - and maybe that was the edge.

'Anyway,' said Tom 'she appreciates - well, we both appreciate - everything.'

Steiner drew long on his cigarette - it bloomed like a peach. 'Turkish?'

'Yes. Get them made up - little place, off Piccadilly.' A beautiful aroma.

Money. Not a man to take chances.

'Can't be easy - taking on a new artist. I don't know when I've seen her so - happy.' What Tom really wanted to say was: why? Why are you doing this? Nobody wants her - not really - so, why?

Steiner crushed the butt with his heel. 'They'll be missing us.'

'I just wanted -'

'Yes?'

'- nothing.'

'Dear Shirley-Anne, we'd do anything for her - when I think of those parties by the sea - showing my age, now.' Steiner patted Tom's shoulder, again. Inside, a piano started up. 'Shall we?'

Tonight was what Steiner called 'a little gathering.' Shirley-Anne confided in him that she still didn't feel ready for an exhibition - nerves, she said. She hoped he'd understand - and surprisingly, he did. So, no exhibition date was set and it didn't seem to matter. Instead, Steiner organised these little gatherings, just enough to keep Shirley-Anne in the public eye,

249

but nothing more. It puzzled Tom. Steiner's patience puzzled Tom.

Laughter rolled out when the club door opened. Tables were being cleared. Shirley-Anne was waltzing slowly by herself, with the fixed smile of a drunk. Tom turned and as he did, he caught the flash of a man in the street looking directly in at him. Back at the table, he called for water. The music was too loud and Shirley-Anne was swaying in a way that made people look away. He wondered if he should rescue her - make it look like he cared - then a chair scraped behind him. 'Sorry I'm late. Was it good?'

'Steven? Yes - why? - I mean, how?'

'Your wife. She didn't tell you? That drink taken? Cheers.'

'Tell me? Tell me, what?'

'Yes -' Steven downed the drink and signalled for another '- she didn't say? No? Insisted. Nice to be remembered. You told her then - where I was - let the dogs loose?' His eyes darted. He picked over the remains of the food.

Tom hadn't seen Steven for months. Not since Sea View. Denise was around and more than around, but not Steven. He just evaporated. What Tom didn't know was that soon after he walked in on Steven and Denise at Sea View, so did Alan Tree and so did Vic and all that.

Vic was pleased to be of help while the maid was still convalescing and pleased also to see the signs of new money starting to trickle in. It did a lot to ease his mind and there were hours, almost days, when he forgot Penelope Richmond. Vic was so grateful for those islands of relief that when he caught up with Steven at Sea View, he was more than willing to give him another chance.

As far as Vic was concerned, Severin Brille's money was real and waiting.

This was his focus now.

Steven was gaunt. 'Good of you to stop by,' said Tom. 'Been busy?'

'I know what you're thinking - I will give evidence to the police - I know you need that - it's just, I've had things -'

Tom yawned. He wanted nothing from this man - but it did amuse him to think he - Tom - was still having sex with Denise. Steven had no clue and that really was funny. 'Another drink?'

'Thanks.' Again, Steven downed it in one. 'So? Another party? What about the exhibition - postponed? Wants it bigger? Great isn't it - the way it all worked out?' He spoke quickly, scanning the room.

'Yes. Big plans. Big plans.'

'Must be pleased? That bread taken?'

Tom waved to the waiter again. Shirley-Anne waived back - and yes, she was pleased. Harry Steiner had faith in her. Steven raised his empty glass and did a mock bow. 'You know, I trusted you - I really thought -' his breathing was heavy, misty.

'Oh?' Tom wanted to keep this funny but Steven and Denise together and happy, twisted in his mind and something in him wanted to hurt and hurt and go on hurting.

'Tell me,' said Steven. 'I don't care, just tell me - why?'

Tom dabbed his mouth. 'Believe what you like. You forget, I have - or, had - a good reason for keeping you safe. So, on the run again - anyone I know?'

Steven spat - 'yes - someone you know -' Alan Tree was Shirley-Anne's eyes and ears and when he walked in to Sea View, Steven knew his freedom was over. 'Look, Tom. Sorry - so much has happened - you disappeared - I didn't know what to think. I tried calling -'

Tom laughed. 'Yes - bit of an accident.'

'Oh? Nothing bad?'

'No - messy, but not bad.' This was nice - playing. 'Anyway, things have changed - no doubt, Mrs Amis told you? I've closed up shop - working for her now.' And it was true. After that night in Steiner's pool house, Tom finished with Solly. He called him up, cancelled everything, said he was back on the bottle but that they could still be friends. Solly took it surprisingly well, considering. 'So, been tied up. Should have let you know sooner - sorry.'

'No - it's me - I should say sorry. It just ended so quickly - after all the help you gave me - all the money - that helped - more than helped. Thank you.' Then - 'actually, it's why I'm here.'

'Oh?'

'I went to your studio -' Steven was returning to his old self, now. Friendly, gullible. Was this going to be an apology for stealing Denise? Tom said nothing. 'I waited -' He took off his glasses and cleaned them, the way he did when he was nervous.

'Leave it.'

'No. I can't. There is something -' Tom shrugged and poured them both another drink. 'Look. Like I said, water under the bridge. Sorry, no ice.' His hand was shaking.

'You're angry. I know you are - I let you down. We had an arrangement - I promised artwork - I know, I know -'

'What do you want?' said Tom. Steven was nothing to him and he wanted him to know that. 'Better I think, without ice - don't you? Straight? My, my. Single malt - something to do with the peat.'

'I want to explain -' said Steven '- I had to get away - I had no choice -'

Tom yawned and looked at his watch. 'People mix it with ginger - hard to believe.'

'I am still a witness. I can still help you.' He wanted to say more. He wanted to say that Tom was in danger. Tom sighed loudly. 'Nice of you to offer but I believe they have other leads - the police, I mean.'

'I wanted -'

'But you're not a whiskey man, are you? Or do you take anything on offer - even, when it's not on offer?'

'I was desperate.'

'Ah -' Tom poured another whiskey for himself. His hand was still shaking and it splashed.

'Yes, you're right. Not thinking straight - don't need me - OK, OK, I get it.'

Steven looked over his shoulder to the door, then back to Tom 'Look, can we talk - outside?'

'I like it here.' Tom turned to the dance floor, it was an effort.

Steven scraped his chair closer. 'Things have changed. I can't keep running. I've got commitments -' he hissed '- you're in danger - no, forget that. Thing is, I have someone -'

Tom nodded. He was numb but smiling.

'- a wonderful person. She's changed my life. I see things differently now.'

'Oh?'

'She speaks about you. I know - you two knew each other, once -'

'Well, it's been lovely - now, if you'll excuse me -' he tapped his empty glass '- I have a life.' Steven spat under his breath. 'You're a dead man - you need me -'

'Do stop by again and bring a few friends - you seem to have so many.' Tom was drunk now but not so drunk that he didn't feel something in Steven turn. 'I want money.'

Tom coughed into his drink. Heads turned. Someone raised a glass and Shirley-Anne waved again. From across the room, it looked like they were two friends, sharing a dirty joke. 'Look. I didn't want to do it this way - come outside -'

'Get away from me you little shit' Tom could spit, too. He knew he should walk away. 'So, how is dear Denise? Knitting socks by the fireside, as we speak?'

'She's a free spirit - speaks well of you.'

'Oh, yes?'

'I respect that.'

'You would.'

'We don't live in each other's pockets.'

'Ah? Gets about a bit?'

'I didn't say that. We see each other when we can - not easy, you know - with things -' the veins on Steven's neck were standing out. Tom smiled. 'So you say. Tell me - what has Denise told you about herself? All good, I hope?' Sex with her now, was better than ever - he was fucking Steven, fucking Steven the way Steven fucked him.

'I know what you're thinking,' said Steven.

'I doubt it.' Denise was Hell, but she was Tom's Hell - not another man's.

'You're thinking, I don't deserve her.'

Tom nodded. 'Actually, yes - that was what I was thinking.' The room was beginning to spin. He knew he should get up and go but he needed to hurt - he needed Steven to know what it felt like.

'I agree. She could do better. I know that. I'm as surprised as you -'

'Touching.'

'Don't patronise me - Denise and I, well - you might as well know, we're going to get married -'

Tom looked up, instantly sober.

'Yes. Yes - a room in a boarding house, it's no place to start a family…can't keep running…'

Tom's mouth opened.

'… need a job - just a start - worked well together once, remember - you, me? So, I was thinking, you know, maybe…I'd pay you back, don't get me wrong - she looks up to you …' Steven pressed a flat package into Tom's hand.

Cheers went up as a chocolate fountain was wheeled in. Shirley-Anne beamed.

Without thinking, Tom opened the package. 'Fucking Hell - that's -'

'Yes. A few sketches. What do you think? She makes a good model.

Patient - has a feel for art.'

Tom was lost. '- but - this - it's make believe - a joke?' He turned each sketch over. 'They're identical to -'

'- Veronica? I'm glad you see the likeness.' Steven was going in and out of focus. 'I knew you'd understand. I know I am nothing to you but you are something to me, Tom - I think you know that.'

'What -?'

'Here, take this -' Steven poured something into a glass - water - 'remember a real drinker paces himself - you taught me that.'

Tom drank without thinking. 'What do you want from me?'

Steven poured another. 'She - Denise - always believed that you and I were business partners. I don't know why. Suppose I was flattered - you know, her thinking we were the same.'

Tom gripped the glass.

'I'm not much, I know that - a broken thing, off the street - oh, don't worry - I know -' his voice trailed off.

'Fuck off.'

'Please. Listen. There isn't much time -'

Tom's head nodded forward, he wasn't sure if he was awake or dreaming.

Steven's phone buzzed.

'Leave and don't look back,' said Tom.

'You don't understand.'

'Oh yes, I do.'

'Denise. I can't.'

'Can't? Can't? What do you mean, "Can't"?'

'I can't let go.'

'Oh, for God's sake.' Tom held his head in his hands.

'She seemed so alone - don't laugh. Once it started - I can't explain - I meant no harm. I said I was doing work for that man - remember? I said soon I'd get paid and we could go away together; have our own place by the sea. I meant no harm.'

'What?'

'She's pregnant.'

'What?'

'It doesn't change things; in fact, it makes it easier. We have to marry. No choice. I want to do the right thing.'

'What?'

Tom felt disjointed. He wanted to say there is a choice - in a clean world, there is always a choice. 'Look. Tell her it's fallen through - this, this thing. Tell her you've got no money. Tell her to fuck off; your lies will catch up with you.'

'But it's not a lie. He did buy my work. You know that.'

'Leave it.'

'All I'm asking, is a helping hand - then I'll go. I'll go forever.'

'Get rid of her. She's trouble.'

'Tell me who he is.'

'Who?'

'The man from Amsterdam.'

'He doesn't exist.'

'It's alright, you won't be involved. He knows my work. He liked it. If I could show him these and I've done some colour work - landscapes -'

'Haven't you heard?' Tom stood and swayed. He felt sick - the kind of sickness that knows it's too late.

'I'm begging you. Tom. Please. You helped me once.'

'No. I didn't. I helped myself.'

'He's your contact, I know. I respect that. All I need is -'

'Get rid of her.'

'I can't.'

'Don't be a fool. You don't know her. She's not what you think.'

'Please - I'm not asking for the world.' But he was and he knew it. They both knew it.

****

When Tom left, he could walk but only just. There was a mist coming up from the lock. The Club door slapped. 'Steven? That you?' Footsteps followed him. He kept to the centre of the road. You're in danger - Steven was an idiot. Did he really think he could frighten him? Tom heard his name called, then feet running.

The night bus stopped at the top of the road and Tom got on. He didn't look back. He left Alan Tree standing on the corner, breathless. Outside the restaurant, Steven sat in a car with Vic. They were talking.

4.2

Tom stretched across the bed in the afternoon sun. 'Oh, Thomas, look at you - purring like that flea-bitten mutt of yours.' Billy didn't purr anymore. He was a bag of bones now. He was upstairs, the maid was downstairs, both beyond caring.

'Being here, like this -' Tom couldn't remember when they last made love '- been a while.'

'I know -'

It was still 'her' room and he was still a visitor, but he was at least - here - and there were real clothes in the wardrobe - grown up clothes. Things a man could want. 'Saw Steven last night - Steven - what's his name? He's not dead - oh, yes - you know that. Glad to see you two have patched things up?' Tom tipped an empty off the bed with his foot. Shirley-Anne arched her back and giggled. He reached down for his bathrobe, oddly embarrassed at his nakedness. 'Any Alka-Seltzer?' He went into the bathroom, looking for something to take away a bitter taste. 'Shall I get that?' The landline was ringing. It switched to the answering machine - Alan Tree, again.

'Oh, come back,' said Shirley-Anne 'you were up most of the night.'

'Sorry - did I wake you?'

'No - I heard you on the stairs - another bad night? Oh, never mind Tree - he'll call back.'

He came out of the bathroom and tapped his head. 'Migraine - rose champagne - and by the way, he's changed. Been in an accident apparently.'

'Pardon?'

'Steven. Steven Witt. Remember? We thought he'd died?' In a wiser part of his mind, Tom knew he should keep Steven away from Shirley-Anne although he wasn't sure why.

'Oh?' said Shirley-Anne, trying to remember. 'Yes. That'll be why Mr Tree is calling - wasn't it wonderful? Dear Steven came to our little party - there and then gone -' she turned on her stomach and slid a finger through the raspberry compote '- any idea where he's staying? I'd like to keep in touch.' Tom wanted to say, who told you he was dead? What made you think that? You couldn't wait to get rid of him - and now you want him back? But in these days of ease - and ease it was, with Steiner's money coming in - questions like this didn't last. 'I'll take this lot downstairs' he said, lifting the tray. 'You stay. I'll get tea.'

Steiner phoned earlier to say that he'd wired through another twenty-five thousand pounds to Shirley-Anne's account. He'd sold a few water colours on-line. Promising, he said - and he went on feeding money to Shirley-Anne. 'The fighting fund' he said, and he was right. 'I am so indebted' she said, and she was right, too.

****

Back in her gallery with bills she couldn't pay, Butters had other ideas.

'He's after mother -' Steiner incensed her '- the stupid bitch, can't she see it?' Butters wanted the Portrait of G.F. Brille and she saw rivals everywhere. Tree held his peace. Butters was becoming hard to manage since the interview at the police station.

'It's been hard -'

'Hard? Hard? Moron - you have no idea - hard? What the fuck have you done? You didn't keep that stupid bastard alive - you lost me a fortune. You still haven't found that stolen painting - what exactly am I paying you for?'

Tree had plans. He was going to put Steven Witt into the hands of the police - certain that Witt would crumble and take Vic and the silent others with him. Tree saw what no one else saw, but he needed time. 'You're wrong - at least about Mrs Amis. She's in trouble - there is a way out of this, but you must trust me.' He told Butters how Severin Brille boasted about the Brille Family Trust and how he was shadowed in the last months of his life by criminals. These criminals were now shadowing Shirley-Anne - even Harry Steiner suspected something and that's why he wouldn't chase the theft. Harry Steiner was scared - Tree saw that, too. What Tree didn't see was his own fear. The warm spread down the leg, the panic, the being an old man - a no one. He needed to nail Steven Witt. He needed to show that they couldn't write him off, yet.

'But they met - and secretly -' she screamed '- they were hiding something from me - that bitch -'

'No -' said Tree '- Shirley-Anne met Severin but it wasn't hidden. They argued - out on the street in daylight - she even hit him - on the tow path where he was found dead a week later - sorry -' Tree believed Shirley-Anne was trying to get rid of Severin - buy him off. She was giving him money to prove she didn't need or want anything from him. She didn't want him. Then

'Tell me - that box? Strange? I mean, Severin - grown man - box of toys - odd?'

Butters shrugged.

'Why did he just leave it on the table and walk away?'

'He didn't walk away, as you put it -' she said '- he gave it to Shirley-Anne, she's the one that left it.'

'Why did you take it, then?'

This was the tea at The Ritz. Butters wanted no falling out, no friction, no problems. If that meant taking a box of trinkets home, she would do that.

'And you say, Shirley-Anne went pale when she saw it?'

'So, what?'

There were any number of reasons why this box might have touched a nerve in Shirley-Anne, but Tree saw only one. Severin was moved. He and his sisters lost their mother, their lives, themselves - and with her birthday card, Butters was reaching out. They were stunted people. Severin was in the gutter, Shirley-Anne was a recluse, Butter was sinking. Severin wanted to say 'yes - you are right. We are more than this.' Severin was ready for a better life. That's what it looked like. But Shirley-Anne saw it differently - Severin was a bad past - an open grave.

Shirley-Anne argued with Severin and he argued with her - it made sense.

They both wanted different things. Severin - stupidly - thought he could buy Shirley-Anne so, of course, she gave him money. He had nothing she wanted. She was not for sale.

Tree was there the hour Severin died. He didn't see it happen but he saw enough.

Shirley-Anne arrived, out of breath - she ran to the blue bridge where a man was waiting. That man was Steven Witt. He'd seen Severin and Witt meeting here before. It had to be Witt - it's the place he'd come to.

Witt murdered Severin.

There were a few gaps. It was dawn, the light was bad, Severin was singing and for a second, Tree looked away. When he looked back, Shirley-Anne was gone. It had to be that she recognised Witt from Belmarsh. She must have run - leaving Witt there.

It fitted. Steven Witt killed Severin. Shirley-Anne knew but was too afraid to do anything - a timid woman, easily frightened - who knows what Witt threatened? Then he walked back into her life at that Private View the following August.

She was trapped and she knew it. Of course she wanted Witt found.

Found and arrested. She wanted her life back.

That's how Tree saw it. He also saw Vic and a trap around Shirley-Anne that was tightening. He left Butters and took a taxi to Clerkenwell. He wanted to reach Shirley-Anne but Vic was in the way, so he did the next best thing - he found Tom Amis and put a gun in his mouth.

****

They were in Tom's studio. 'Thank you for coming, Mr Amis.' Tree clicked the safety. Tom gagged. The gun stayed. 'You know you're not hard to find, Mr Amis - not hard at all.'

Tom recognised Tree and in a strange way, he was relieved. 'I know - you've been following me for years -' Tom thought he'd got a text from Steven, wanting to meet at the studio. He arrived to find the door open and this man waiting. Sitting here now, he half expected curtains would open and there'd be an audience out there, laughing. 'I know - I've always known - you don't frighten me -'

Tree unloaded the gun. He pointed to the bullets - 'real.'

Tom started to cry.

'I want to help -' Tree was calm. He told Tom about Steven Witt. 'A career criminal -' and to someone who didn't know different, Tree was persuasive. Tom was used - it happened slow. Tom and Shirley-Anne were targets. 'He made it look like you were making those things happen - bringing him in to your life - but none of it was you.' Severin. His fortune. Shirley-Anne meeting up with Witt in prison - and then at Steiner's show - 'these things don't happen by chance.'

'So? What? It's money?'

'In a way.'

'You've haunted me - and it's nothing to do with me? You want to catch a thief?'

'Yes.'

261

'Then fucking catch him and leave me alone -' inside his head Tom was back holding a bottle of Angustura - thinking Steven Witt was a friend, then the curtain opens and the audience is out there, laughing.

'Don't be angry -'

'Fuck off.'

Tree tried to explain. It never is about 'one' man, one crime. He told Tom about Butters - how she paid him to follow Severin Brille in the last year of his life, keep him out of trouble - and how he'd seen Brille shadowed by Steven Witt. Everyone at the Soup Kitchen knew Shirley-Anne would inherit a fortune and they planned to get it - and if it took years, they would wait. They use. They kill. They move on.

'Tell me, Mr Amis - your brother in law - Severin Brille. Suicide? And Penelope Richmond - accident?'

It dawned on Tom slowly that he wasn't the one in trouble - it was someone else.

'I trusted him -' sweet relief - honest and just, swelled through him '- I trusted him -'

'Yes.'

'- and it was all a lie? A game? Everything - the car accident - hiding him at Sea View - helping him - none of it real?'

Tree didn't answer.

'And when he said he knew who killed Penelope Richmond - another lie?'

'No -,' said Tree '- that was true. He did know. It was him.' Balm. Balm to the soul. Other people's problems, other people's crimes. Not him.

'So - it's about money - then what?'

'They kill you.'

'They?'

'He's working with a man call Vic - know him? Driver? Maybe this will help -?' Tree showed Tom phone shots from the club. Witt was sitting at a table talking to Tom. Vic was there too, on the edge of the room. 'Look at this -' a close up, Steven giving Tom something to drink. 'You remember? No?

You left soon after - you got away that time, but there will be a next time and -'

'- no -' Tom lifted his hand. 'Make it end.'

Tree put the phone down. 'Trap him,' he said. 'He trusts you.'

****

DS Rainbow stood outside Pilgrim House looking up. Betty Reece Rae was with him. 'I'm doing your job for you' she said. She had leads. Three women - all in relationships with Tom Amis - all dead. 'She's a killer -' Rae wanted access to Richmond's flat '- I can show you - it's up there - evidence.' Rae was certain Severin Brille knew and he was blackmailing her - she killed him 'it's staring you in the face.'

The flat was sealed but Rainbow was tempted. He wasn't part of the Richmond investigation but things had stalled on Severin Brille and any lead was better than no lead.

'Penelope Richmond knew -' Rae's agitation held him. 'Get that letter -' she said '- it's up there -' they stood on the pavement. Rae was spinning half-stories - all she needed was a quote, a reaction - anything. 'Severin Brille - his life was a mess - he'd lost everything - why wouldn't he go after easy money - they hated each other.'

Severin Brille was a person of interest for a time. He looked like a banker on the slide but after months of surveillance, all that showed was a man on the slide and that was no crime. Brille was about to be closed when he died. The circumstances of his death kept him on Rainbow's desk - open and going nowhere - and that is why Rainbow was here now. He wanted him gone.

Back at the station, he went through the CCTV stills again. They didn't show much. 04.48. Black. 05.58. Shadows - foxes, a badger, anything. 06.00. Shapes, now. Someone on the towpath walking towards the bridge. Then another.

06.05. Severin Brille shows up on the tow path. He stops. Looks around. Lifts his arms.

263

The other two go under the bridge together. Severin follows. Then nothing. Rainbow looked again at shadows on the water. Mist and bad light and a hungry mind could turn it into anything - a small boat crossing to the other side - a person swimming - a trick of the light - anything.

It could be that two people waited under the bridge and killed Severin Brille - one being Shirley-Anne Amis. It could be that they left by water. A dingy.

It could be - but could be, was not enough.

Rae and her half stories were not the only things on Rainbow's mind. Alan Tree had something to say. He'd been following Severin Brille for nearly a year. He was there when he died - he saw a man waiting by the bridge. He saw Shirley-Anne arrive soon after. No, he didn't see everything. Yes, he was distracted by Severin singing, but only for an instant. Shirley-Anne didn't stay - she ran. No, Tree didn't see her run and did that matter? He certainly saw Witt - he'd know those glasses anywhere. He did it.

Brille had served his purpose and so Witt killed him. Shirley-Anne would be killed too - in time. That's how Tree saw it.

Tree wanted arrests and for this, he needed Rainbow. Shirley-Anne was afraid - too afraid to talk to the police, but she trusted Tree. She told him Witt was stealing from her - it was her way of telling him that Witt was dangerous and that she was trapped.

There'd been problems between Vic and Witt - Witt stealing from Shirley-Anne made him a liability and he was going to be killed. Tree knew where and when. Break the network, was the message here - 'one swoop and you've got it.' Tree was giving it to Rainbow, free.

'Be there -'

It was grubby.

****

Rae saw blackmail. Tree saw theft. Both saw Shirley-Anne.

Later that day, Rainbow picked up a yellowing bundle of papers - Coroner's report: 0951/EA/003b. Amis, Mrs Evelyn. Cardiac arrest - information incomplete - open verdict. Below the interview buzzer went.

'Thank you for coming in sir, just a few things then we'll be done this way -'

Gilmore followed the custody sergeant into interview room 1.

'Really, Officer, I don't see -'

'Take a chair sir, won't take long.'

'I have a choice?' Gilmore expected this. He was a precise man. Tidy. It made for few surprises. Yes, he did work at the Clapham Convalescent Home - a long time ago. Yes, he did recall a Mrs Evelyn Amis although not well - and - did she die? If you say so - it was a long time ago - read the notes. Yes, he was physician to Mrs Shirley-Anne Amis and no it didn't strike him as strange that she was a friend of the late Mrs Amis. Life is full of co-incidence. 'Is that it?'

It was pleasant, as interviews go - and shorter than expected. It ended when DS Rainbow asked about a letter and a night spent at the Ritz with Penelope Richmond - "before she died", obviously. Dr Gilmore left, shaken. On his way out he passed Shirley-Anne on her way in.

The way Rainbow saw it, Shirley-Anne Amis had holes in her life - not in itself a crime - but still holes. 'Thank you for coming in Mrs Amis, just a few loose ends.'

'You said that last time.'

Rainbow asked what she knew about Dr Robin Gilmore. 'I mean - you two go back? It seemed curious he said, that Dr Gilmore should meet Shirley-Anne and in a matter of weeks, go from being a poor man to being really quite a rich man? 'I was sorry, by the way, about Mrs Evelyn Amis - dying like that - unexpected - good friend of yours?'

Shirley-Anne looked up, her face open and innocent.

'And you married Evelyn's husband - what? - three weeks later?'

When she spoke it was soft. Evelyn - the kindest person - her passing was so sudden. 'We were distraught,' she said. 'Helpless.'

Sitting here in this room, Rainbow wanted Rae to be wrong. He wanted what he saw in Shirley-Anne to be real. He wanted the world to be a place where good and bad are not the same. 'Your assistant - Penelope Richmond -' but Rae persisted inside his head. Penelope Richmond spied on the Amis household - she took things - personal - she sold them to a journalist - surely, Mrs Amis knew?

'Tell me Mrs Amis, why would a journalist be looking into your life? Why were you giving Severin money? Was he blackmailing you - did you kill him?' Rainbow showed the CCTV stills of Severin's last movements along the canal path. Did Shirley-Anne recognise anything? Was she there? Shirley-Anne heard none of this or, at least, none of it registered. She was very sorry not to be more help and DS Rainbow and Mrs Rainbow were welcome to take tea with her at St James' Gardens anytime, really, any time. She would have left the interview unmarked, were it not for something that Rainbow said at the end, almost to himself -

'The box? What was in it?'

****

Rae was back at St James' Gardens and the story was sinking. Shirley-Anne and Gilmore stood like granite, in the middle of the drawing room. 'Time is not on your side,' said Rae. 'The police are looking - tell your side - no one cares - say something -' Rae snorted '- say something or this thing will write itself -'

Shirley-Anne believed she said something clever about the gutter press, her personal dignity and a lot more. Gilmore said nothing. When Rae left, Shirley-Anne walked to the window and waved her wave and after that, the world cut out.

When she opened her eyes, it felt like years had passed. She was lying on the floor, breathing in small eddies of dust. What she didn't know then - or later - was the sharp crack. 'You fell,' said Gilmore, now. He was sitting in a low armchair by the window. 'Nothing serious.' Her head was heavy. There was a decanter lying on the floor and a tumbler on its side. 'We had a few drinks. You fell. You've been asleep.' He helped her to the couch. He said he thought it best to let her rest - it had been a trying day what with the police and all. They'd had a few drinks and argued, he said - did she remember any of that?

No, she didn't remember.

She'd called him a parasite - a working class parasite - and he agreed. Did she remember that? She'd slapped his face and screamed. 'You owe me - you twisted little fuck.' She'd said that too - but at that point she was making no sense, not even to herself. 'Darling, I must have blacked out?' she said now.

'Yes.'

Gilmore waited. Would it come back to her - would she remember the bit where he picked up the decanter and hit and hard because - because - he'd been waiting a lifetime?

The room yawned.

'It's got to stop -' she said, without knowing why.

****

Steven was still running from Vic and from the two people he knew killed Penelope Richmond.

Vic was doing all he could to think of Shirley-Anne's money and nothing else and it made him gullible. Steven sensed this. He told Vic that the Brille Trust was starting to pay out. He said Tom Amis had a lot to hide and now that his wife was a rich woman, he was only too keen to pay Steven off. It made sense, at least for now.

Steven was buying time. He was on the mud flats now at West Silvertown, watching Tom Amis approach. Vic was in a car, waiting.

'There must be twenty cafes and you want to meet here - in a fucking - fucking - what is this place?'

Steven pushed Tom through an iron gate into a compound. There were a lot of seagulls. 'Recycling. We're OK here - careful where you walk.'

'Well, this is nice.'

'Shut up - where is it?'

Steven was all about money now, just like Vic. It helped him not to think about the things that mattered. Just like Vic. For Steven it was all about buying a new life with Denise.

'You said I was in danger - back there, at the club. What did you mean?'

'Yes - I want to help -'

Tom snorted. 'Help? How?'

'- money first -' Steven wanted £100,000.00. He'd told Tom it would be a one-off and he'd never see him again. Steven planned to give half to Vic and then run. Vic wouldn't come looking for about 48 hours - enough time to make the ferry at Portsmouth. That was Steven's plan: him, Denise, the ferry and running.

Tom pushed Steven's outstretched hand away. 'Fuck off. I know you killed Severin Brille - you killed Richmond and - you think I'm going to give you my wife's money - you think she's come into a fortune well, I've got news for you - '

'No.'

'- It's not going to happen -'

'No - Tom listen - there is a theft - it hasn't happened yet - I had no choice - but now I do -' Steven didn't want trouble. He thought Tom would pay anything to get rid of him. What he didn't expect was this. The look. The hurt. 'I can explain -'

Tom screamed '- you lied - you lied about everything - what kind of a friend do you call yourself?' From a distance, it looked like they were arguing. It looked like Tom was panicking and this pleased Vic. Close up however, it was different.

Under his skin, Steven was caught. He wanted a clean break. He wanted to despise Tom Amis but he could see now, it wasn't that simple. Tom was torn - Steven let him down, he promised things he couldn't deliver. He played Tom for a fool yet Tom was here, still trying to help him. 'Look, Tom - none of this is what I wanted - you have to believe me -' what was it? This thing? This thing that pulled him back?

Tom could hear Alan Tree - the tempter. 'Go on - he trusts you.'

Tom smiled. 'Look. Sorry. You're right - I know - or, I know enough - thing is, yes, we were friends - that doesn't have to change. I will help - I don't have the money now but I will get it - cash? Yes. Why, not? For old time's sake?' The words were stones in his throat.

'You mean it?' - and in the eternity between one stone and the next, Steven was his. 'You really mean it?'

There was more.

Tom explained his reason for meeting up with Steven today. The man from Amsterdam was here. 'How lucky is that?' Tom was taking him up to Sea View, the day after tomorrow. He told Steven to be there - 'this is your future' he said.

'Thank you,' said Steven 'with all my heart.' They shook hands and the sea howled.

4.3

Dr Gilmore trod lightly.

'Epilepsy, you say?'

He was dressing Shirley-Anne's head wound in his rooms in Wimpole Street and speaking softly. He put himself in Shirley-Anne's hands, he said. They were talking about Penelope Richmond. 'I confess - I was worried. I wasn't sure if she knew -' Gilmore listed the symptoms of epilepsy: Penelope "swooned" and time passed and things happened around her that she couldn't explain. 'She was a nervous person and obviously, I didn't want to alarm her. I was going to say something, suggest seeing a specialist - but then, the place flooded. I couldn't just leave her there. I felt responsible, do you see? I put her up at the Ritz for the night - nearest place with a halfway decent room.' He accepted, he said, that it might look odd to someone who didn't know - like the police.

Shirley-Anne turned to him 'I know you didn't kill the little cunt if that's what this is about?' It was eleven in the morning. She was on her third double.

'Ah.'

'I know she was having an affair with Tom - do you think I'm stupid?'

'Ah.'

'Yes, she could have had a fit and fallen under that train - but she didn't. She was pushed and no - it wasn't Tom. Happy, now - or would you like me to tell you who did it and make you an accessory?' Since the crack on the head, Shirley-Anne changed, like a bit of her stopped working. It made her blunt. Gilmore dabbed more antiseptic. Shirley-Anne winced and raised her hand. The wound was small but still open. 'No. Leave it - you don't give a fuck about me, so let's stop pretending.' Gilmore smiled. 'Just as you please. Tell me about this yacht - Cordelia, you say? Finally, that long awaited break? You certainly deserve it - you both certainly deserve it.' The relationship so carefully crafted over years between Shirley-Anne and Robin Gilmore, was in bits.

'Robin, you poisoned the maid? Was that your way of getting that ape in to spy on me?

Gilmore poured another whiskey. Deep down, he knew this day would come. They drank in silence. 'It's not about Vic - or that silly little bitch - it's us - and you're right, time to stop pretending.'

'I'm tired of playing the imbecile.' Shirley-Anne threw her drink against the wall. The stain spread like a long face laughing. Gilmore coughed. He was alone in this. 'So long as we keep our stories straight -' he said; and there were stories to keep straight. Veronica Lakey. Evelyn Amis. Severin Brille.

'Oh, you and your stories - let it go.' Gilmore's timidity crept like a disease.

'Right - as ever' he said. But she wasn't right. She wasn't the one who took risks - it wasn't her hand on the needle, it wasn't her signature on the medical record. Without him, Shirley-Anne Amis would still be the spinster nobody wanted. That's how he saw it.

Shirley-Anne saw it differently. She was an innocent but she wasn't blind. 'You've been trying to protect me for too long - and - well, the truth is - I never needed your protection. I put up with it - with, you.' Veronica Lakey died because Shirley-Anne - drunk at the time - pushed her over the edge at Sea View and she fell to her death. This in itself was never a problem. What worried Gilmore and even worried Shirley-Anne for a time, was what Lakey did before she died and that was the reason Robin Gilmore and Shirley-Anne Amis were stuck.

Lakey blew in to their lives like a spirit from the desert, taunting and carefree. When she first showed up at one of those weekends, Tom was straying and Shirley-Anne was withering. She made Shirley-Anne come alive - she flattered her, made her feel like she was someone. They had an affair and in the thrill of it all, Shirley-Anne told Lakey things she shouldn't and so Lakey knew all about how Shirley-Anne snared Tom. Maybe it was anger or maybe Shirley-Anne just wanted to make herself more interesting but whatever the reason, it was also stupid.

When Lakey tired of Shirley-Anne the way everyone tired of Shirley-Anne and when she turned her attentions to Shirley-Anne's straying husband - Tom - she would remember.

Tom and Lakey had an on/off affair over a few years. It was open, tawdry and occasionally violent. Tom tried to walk away and finally on that night, Veronica Lakey gave him an ultimatum. She had information about Tom's wives - yes, both of them - and about Shirley-Anne's faithful doctor. She would use it if Tom left her. She put it in a letter and threw it at Tom. A few hours later, she was dead.

'Twenty years is a long time - I'm sorry Robin - about what I said just now. You know it was just me, being me?' Gilmore smiled. He'd spent a lifetime waiting for the next mistake. A life. His life. 'You know, Penelope Richmond was going to give me that letter? We were going to get it the night she died - what happened? Did you push her?'

'No.'

'But you know who did?'

Dr Gilmore had Vic. Vic was his eyes and ears and there was nothing in Shirley-Anne's life that didn't reach Gilmore. 'Don't ask,' she said.

Neither mentioned Severin. They didn't have to. They both knew what happened to him.

****

Tree admired Vic. It took discipline - 'no, really; I mean, turning up four days a week to do the washing up.'

'Don't know nothing,' said Vic now, polishing the kitchen silver. They were in the pantry at St James' Gardens. Tree was curious, he said, about that nice girl - what was her name - Prudence? Primrose?

Vic had a strange jealousy. Back in December, Tree watched him sit outside Pilgrim House sometimes all night. Vic saw men coming and going.

What did he think? 'I met her once - pretty, as I recall?' said Tree, now. 'Popular.'

Vic went on polishing. He nodded as Tree spoke. 'Wish I could help.' Vic was in love with Penelope Richmond - she was dead and he was trying hard to forget and Tree needed to find a way in to that.

'You're very trusting' Tree said. 'I admire that - I mean, being here, helping out when everyone else gets rich -' he saw a flicker. Vic assumed Tree was looking for information about the missing painting, he realised now he wasn't.

'Don't get me wrong, I mean there's nothing shameful in it - helping out - too many people see that as a weakness, but I don't. After all, Mrs Amis lost so much in - you know, her secretary - she trusted her, that's what makes it so hard. 'Anyway -' Tree turned to leave '- you're busy.'

'I didn't know her,' Vic blurted. 'Penelope. Didn't know nothing.'

'No. I know. It's just - well, she was stealing from Mrs Amis, that's why I'm here. That's the real reason. Kept it hidden, of course. Well, she was scared. We think she was forced into it by a man - 'John Smith? Mean anything?' Tree saw the roses and the note left by a John Smith. He guessed - rightly - Vic would have seen them, too. 'Hard to think anyone

273

would want to hurt such a lovely young girl - her whole life ahead of her - could have made another man very happy.' But no - John Smith got to her first. He made her steal from her employer '- and of course, John Smith is not his real name - his real name is Steven Witt.'

Vic dropped a spoon.

Tree shared his burden. 'Money,' he said. 'What some people will do for money.' Poor Mrs Amis came into a bit of an inheritance - actually, between you and me, a fortune. Witt knew about this. He was using Penelope to siphon it off. You know, he fooled a lot of people - clever, I'll give him that. Meek, timid on the outside - poor Penelope took pity on him. He reeled her in -' Tree coughed '- raped her.' Tree waited. 'She was never the same. Imagine that?'

Tree wanted what he wanted. He saw Steven Witt behind the deaths of Severin Brille and Penelope Richmond and he wanted to be right. 'She was trying to escape that night - he pushed her under that train - but of course, the police won't catch him - too clever - too clever - and the worst thing is that he is doing the same to another young woman - he's still stealing money from Mrs Amis. Poor Penelope - dead for nothing. How can people be so bad?'

Tree left, satisfied. The spoons in the pantry got finished. They were all laid in neat rows in the drawer. All facing the same direction.

****

Two men in a car stopped Solly and gave him a fright. They invited him back to Ladbroke Grove police station and then gave him a cup of coffee. One talked about the weather and the other talked about perverting the course of justice. It was all very civilised.

Rainbow sat at the screen watching. The CCTV stills in front of him - enlarged, enhanced, redefined and one still in particular, interested him now.

06.00 a.m. - something - a flash - a glint. Alan Tree insisted he saw Steven Witt at the bridge and the glint that Rainbow saw now could be glasses. Witt wore glasses but he wasn't the only one.

'So, Mr Solomon -' the interviewing officers were interested in Tom Amis they said and Solly warmed to the task. Yes, he knew Tom Amis and yes, he'd known him for a few years on and off. Yes - bit of a character, bit of a drinker - fond of a pretty face. Bit aggressive - well, violent. It was nice to tell his side of the story.

Solly told them Shirley-Anne contacted him a year or so ago. She needed his help. She was afraid for Tom's safety and she wanted Solly to keep an eye on him. Tom Amis was a buffoon - there was talk that he pushed a woman to her death; years ago. His wife feared he was going off the rails again - 'you know, people don't change - do they? I mean a killer is a killer, right?'

When they asked him about the night Penelope Richmond died, Solly was only too pleased to help. 'Saw him the night whatshername died - the coffee shop - el Saoud, know it? No? Anyway - snow storm, nothing moving, he came in like - well, I don't know - like he'd seen a ghost. I don't think he killed Penelope Richmond - they were having an affair - she ended it - probably found a man she really wanted - but no, he wouldn't push her under a train for that, would he?'

Rainbow listened. He looked from the CCTV stills to Solly and back again and the more he looked the bigger it got. The glint.

'We think the same person who killed Severin Brille killed Penelope Richmond,' said one officer. Solly smiled '- OK, if you want the truth, he was obsessed with her - couldn't let go. There - you got it out of me. He knew she was seeing other - you know, men. Hard to know what goes on in a mind like that.'

They thanked him. He'd been helpful. More than helpful. What they didn't say was that they knew he - Solomon Solomon - spent a lot of time watching Penelope Richmond.

They knew she phoned him every day back in October and then in November, she stopped. They didn't ask why he watched her window at Pilgrim House and bought her flowers and why she didn't answer the door when he knocked. They knew that already.

****

Shirley-Anne sat smoking a cheroot, her silk dressing gown open. 'You know, we don't do this enough. Cheers.'

'Yes. Cheers. Nice place -,' said Solly. 'I was a bit surprised - didn't think I'd hear from you?' To tell the truth, Shirley-Anne was a bit surprised herself. She thought she was done with Solomon Solomon. 'Help yourself - single malt - probably wasted on you - Jew boys don't drink, right?' She was drunk and didn't care, she said that too. Solly had been a good servant; she appreciated that. She really, appreciated it and for a gut churning moment, he thought she was offering to have sex with him.

'My - Mr Solomon - you've gone very pale. Are you alright?'

The soft running of feet down the stairs precipitated a head round the door '- all done - if you'll just sign, here -' it was the last of the packers. He came in and handed Shirley-Anne a pen and I-Pad.

Solly took the moment. 'OK. Yes. Well. I'll be off then -' he was quick but not quick enough. 'Sit the fuck down,' said Shirley-Anne, slurring. 'You're going nowhere.'

Mother was gone. Steiner's packers came this morning with wood, Styrofoam, balance sensors, floating paper. They cleared the library and constructed a packing case and a case within that case and into this they placed Mother. She - the G.F. Brille Self-Portrait - left St James' Gardens at precisely 12.32 pm, secured, insured and signed for.

Shirley-Anne leered. 'Good for publicity. That's what the little Jew boy says - know him? Harry Steiner? Gave me a great deal - willing to write off all I owe him if I give him the portrait

- and they wonder why we put them in ovens - sure I can't tempt you?' She raised her glass.

Solly squirmed. A better man would have walked. 'I'm assuming I'm here for a reason and no - thank you -' he declined the drink. She was unsteady but her gaze was fixed. 'Tom tells me you've been speaking to the police?'

Solly nodded. He was the sole of discretion - there was nothing to fear. But Shirley-Anne was of a different mind. 'Get that letter. Get it or you'll be the next one up the fucking chimney.'

4.4

Tom was back at the café in Bayswater. He was early and sat reading the newspaper. Tree was right, he owed Steven Witt nothing.

'I've ordered - you want cheesecake?' Solly pulled up a chair. 'Yes, thank you, I did have a pleasant journey. Circle Line with signal failure; crushed like sardines - Myrtle sends her best.' Solly was unusually brusque. 'So? Don't tell me - money? Well, there's a surprise.'

'Look, sorry - I have no right - I know - it's just for a few days -' Tom rang the Agency. He needed cash for Tree's plan. 'What possessed you? Telling them 'emergency'? Called me out of a pitch - only bite in 3 months. Hundred thousand quid? It had better be good -'

'Sorry -' Tom guessed rightly, Solly could lay his hands on this amount.

Enough to look convincing, said Tree.

'- here.' Solly threw a package on the table.

'Thanks.'

'Count it.'

'I'll pay you back - it's just a blip -'

'Blip?' Solly turned sharply. He was breathing heavy. 'Check it. I don't have all day.'

'What's going on? Why didn't you answer my calls?'

Solly tried hard to stay calm but Shirley-Anne's words cut deep. 'This - is - advertising. It - worked - for - a -while. You - walked. I - walked. Are we really having this conversation?'

'I know.'

'Well? Well?' Solly was quick. Tom faltered. 'Sorry. I valued our friendship. The old girl and I are going away for a bit. On her sister's boat. Maybe we could meet up, when we get back? Once a week - here - bit of a tradition?' He didn't want to lose Solly. He could see now that he was the only friend he had.

Solly poked at the package. 'Another little tart? Ever stop to think where it will end -' at the back of his mind smoke curled out of chimneys and into the sky '- you didn't matter then' said the smoke - 'you don't matter now.'

'What?'

'I mean that bitch, Richmond. Clever but obviously not clever enough.

You know the police are still looking for her killer? They told me she had a letter - it got her killed. What did she say to you?'

'Nothing. I hardly knew her.'

'You were shagging her.'

'Yes. I hardly knew her, anyway - they've got her killer - same man that killed Severin Brille, can you believe it?' Tom wanted to part friends, so it was a small thing, under the circumstances, to tell Solly what he knew.

****

Tom and Solly did part friends, which was a relief. Solly went off with a skip in his step and Tom went back to the flat in Clapham. Denise was waiting for him, nervy. 'You sure about this?' she said, taking Solly's money. 'Why not give it to him yourself?'

'Better coming from you - you know, nice surprise.'

'So? True then? That bloke bought those pictures of me? I'm going to be famous?'

'That's right - he liked your look - you and Steven, great team.' The joke was beginning to pall. 'Ain't seen that much of him but he did reply - did as you said -' Tom knew Denise and Steven communicated by text - one of the many useful things she told him. '- suppose you're right - he'll do - for now.'

'Yes,' said Tom 'he'll do, for now.' He could hear the audience out there, clapping. 'He trusts you. Oh, what a joke.' Then

'What's wrong with you -?' Tom pushed Denise into a corner, his fingers deep into that velvet forgetting. I admire you, Tom - it said - I think you've always known that. Denise slid to the floor, her legs and her life open - all comers welcome. Tom reached deeper to the coast road, the car lights - the sea - that thing out there.

It didn't take long and he rolled back, wet with hate. Denise lit two cigarettes. 'Your hand's shaking - silly boy -' She inhaled deep and held Tom's hand and her eyes said to his eyes - are you really going to do this?

This time tomorrow she'd be dead. Steven would be dead. Vic would be in custody with Solly's money. All of them gone. Tree was certain - 'and the beauty of it all is - none of it touches you.' Tom laughed like a hyena.

'Dear God.' An iridescent ripple came in from Steiner's pool. Denise squealed. Tom tried to get up and go but his watch buckle got caught on lace or ribbon or something and the more he tried to free himself the tighter it got. 'Oh, you've torn it -

- you've fucking torn it - oh, fuck off.' The room spun bright like an exploding star. Tom and Denise rolled and rolled like they were having the finest time.

****

Next day, Tom took the first train down to Sea View. The trap was set.

Tree told him to stay away - but he couldn't. He needed to see for himself.

His indigestion was back and the wind on the steps made it hard to breathe. He remembered Steven here, frightened of slipping and Tom pushing him against the rock to keep him steady. 'Bag of bones - like a sick cat - frightened of everything -' the wind got punchy towards the top. Thieves fall out, said Tree. It was bound to happen, if not today then one day - a man like Steven Witt - a Judas -

A stone bounced down. Solly's face flashed into Tom's mind - Solly - dependable Solomon Solomon - bag carrier. Faithful. There. Always there.

Another stone. Someone was up on the walkway. Tom could hear Tree in his head. You owe this man nothing. That girl, Denise will deliver the money - Vic will see it - trust me, he will be there. He will kill them both. Thieves see thieves everywhere. The police are waiting. Tom was near the top and sweating. Indigestion squeezed like a hand. He took another peppermint and pulled himself up the rest of the way by the ivy, commenting out loud on the weather, the views, the good times that waited. Steven's words whirled in the wind 'you're in danger.'

If he was going to kill Tom, why would he warn him?

If he was part of a criminal network, who tried to kill him? Why didn't he run when he could? Tom sucked in the cool vapours but the pain in his chest got worse. Tree's voice steadied him. The voice of Reason. Tom and Shirley-Anne lived like fools. Sitting ducks. 'It's him or you. Him. Or, you.'

Tom got to the top and a puff of smoke hit him, bitter like burning rubber. Broken sounds came up from the road - car doors, voices, running. The front door was open and at the end of the hallway, Tom could see bright light jumping in the kitchen. Flames. He closed the front door and waited. He could hear snoring from the Billiard Room. Steven must have left the pan on again and fallen asleep. Steven Witt, the fornicator. Steven Witt the drunk, the liar, the man sleeping while the house burned.

Tom felt his way along the hall and the snoring got louder. Hard.

Choking. Shameless.

'Fucker.'

****

It was dark from smoke. Hard to make anything out. Tom saw a gaping hole where the portrait of Veronica used to hang. There was a rolled carpet on the floor. Tom kicked it. Dread and heat burned. 'Run,' said Tom's head.

The carpet moved.

'Fucker -' he kicked again and the carpet rolled over and Steven fell out, hog tied. Nylon rope cut into his neck and every time he breathed, it pulled tighter. The blood in his throat was choking him.

Steven opened his eyes. He knew it was Tom - there - like he promised.

It was OK. It was all OK now.

****

The coast road was cut off by the fire engines. Nothing got through - not police, not men with plans or girls with money, nothing. Two hours later, two ambulances pulled away. When the site was secured and the fire extinguished, a man with a bag walked down the steps of Sea View, unnoticed. He got what he came for.

4.5

The days of your life know you. You think they don't, but they do. It was a year since the fire at Sea View and Tom was in a side room watching, even though he tried not to.

Back then, in the fire, a beautiful blank overtook him and he didn't know a thing when the fire crew got in. Heart attack. On the operating table the going was good until a vein in his brain burst. Big vein. Big burst. Now he lay here, watching. This was Fuschia Ward, bright and airy. The voice of the nursing assistant flew like a sparrow down the corridor. 'Can you hear me, Mr Hamish? Press my hand if you can hear me.'

****

La Petite spent her days looking out of the back window at the birds and at things in the sky no one else could see. It was a long time coming, but when Shirley-Anne saw her that night on one of her walks around the square, what plans she had to move the maid into a nursing home stopped. La Petite seldom spoke although it looked like she had plenty to say. Shirley-Anne told herself that she was devoted to the maid and nothing on earth would part them. The maid could say what she liked. No one was listening.

Vic was still around, which helped. He was sorry he didn't see John Smith at the end because deep down it still mattered. The money he sensed a year ago didn't materialise but instead of walking away, it made him keener. He believed he could and would get Shirley-Anne's fortune and when that happened, the ache would go. So he stayed and lifted things and opened things and on good days he talked to Penelope and she talked back. He told her he understood, although he didn't. He told her that soon she'd see that no one got the better of him. He said that often.

Meanwhile, La Petite's fingers wandered. They flitted and picked and found their way into a paper bag in the dustbin full of bits of porcelain. To her, it looked like a broken plate and while she watched the birds and things in the sky, her fingers set about putting the bits together. Already there was a house and a picket fence and a piece of string with a loop on the end.

****

Upstairs, the mood was good. The investigation into the death of Steven Witt ended with a simple statement from the coroner - an old house, an electrical fault, an unfortunate accident. Tom was in a nursing home. The police were gone.

'What time?'

Shirley-Anne and Dr Gilmore were together in the library, watching the clock. They'd been talking about Steven Witt and his funeral, attended by Shirley-Anne and one other. Shirley-Anne paid for it and she went to some trouble with the flowers. The other person at the funeral was DS Rainbow. Outside the church, Rainbow stopped Shirley-Anne. 'Alan Tree -' he said '- he believed Witt killed your brother. Did he tell you that? He believed Witt was going to kill you - and here you are, the only mourner at his funeral?' Shirley-Anne placed her hand on Rainbow's arm and smiled. She knew and he knew there was no case to answer. Fire will do that. All that remained was a story - it didn't need to be true, it just needed to fit and fire will do that, too. 'But Inspector' she said 'I was devoted to him. I wanted only to forgive.'

The Coroner's story was a good one. The Amises took Steven Witt in. Tom argued with him over a woman. There was a fire, wind, a struggle, they were overcome by smoke. A tragedy. Death by misadventure.

The Severin Brille case was closed - lack of evidence. The Richmond case was closed - a snowstorm, black ice, a slip - no crime to answer. Betty Reece Rae and Alan Tree were both gone. It was just Rainbow the man that remained. Here. Looking.

When the fire crew gained access, they found Steven Witt lying on top of Tom. Witt was burned and near dead. It looked like a struggle - Tom being older and weaker, fell first. It looked like he dragged Steven Witt down with him. Steven fell and his body took the flames. That's what it looked like. That's not how it was.

Rainbow was not a body man but instinct told him that the end is never that neat. Witt's body looked like it was wrapped over Tom Amis - like a deliberate thing. Did somebody do that? Was there another person there - all the time? Was it Shirley-Anne? Rainbow knew there was more but that light touch on the arm, that smile told him - he could think what he liked, it didn't matter. 'Our hearts are full of gratitude' she said 'for everything.' Rainbow watched her walk away without a scratch and in that moment he hated - he hated the way things happen and it doesn't matter - it never fucking matters. Then 'the box -' he called after her '- what was in the box?'

The day after Steven Witt's funeral, Shirley-Anne paid a visit to Butters. An olive branch, she said. Butters didn't believe her but she did give Shirley-Anne the box - something to remember poor Severin by, she said. Back in St James' Gardens, Shirley-Anne smashed the box and the porcelain figures inside. She put the pieces in a paper bag and put the bag in the dustbin outside the pantry window for the bin men. It never got to them.

Back in the library now, Shirley-Anne pressed her fingertips to the window and watched. Gilmore paced. 'I said, what time?'

'Nearly eleven' she said. This was the last thing -

'What makes you think he'll come?'

'Why wouldn't he?'

'You've got the money?'

'Yes.'

'Can you afford it?'

Steiner was gone. The parties, the crowd, mother - all gone. The market had fallen - and none of that mattered because the thing that kept Gilmore and Shirley-Anne stuck, would soon be theirs and they would be free. The letter. Veronica Lakey's letter was found at Sea View the day Steven Witt died. He didn't give it up easily, but he did give it up. A sigh of relief breathed in St James' Gardens with the news, but Gilmore counselled prudence. The fire attracted attention so he and Shirley-Anne stayed still and endured for one more year.

That year was now up. 'Yes, I can afford it - of course I can fucking afford it.'

The wound on her head healed but nothing else did.

'And it's the last payment, right?'

Outside, the clock in the square struck 11. They both looked up. Vic - a man of habit - pulled up outside. 'You don't need to be here, Robin. I can do this.'

'Two heads are better than one.'

Shirley-Anne ran to the door before the bell rang. The delivery was prompt and wordless. This was the man who'd done her bidding and been paid well: he waited under the bridge for Shirley-Anne and with her, watched Severin Brille die. He smoothed the sand. They left by boat. He pushed Penelope Richmond and he killed and more than killed Steven Witt. He had the letter.

Shirley-Anne handed him an envelope. A Banker's Draft. The agreed amount. He gave one back. She closed the door.

'Oh.' Gilmore swooped from behind and took the letter. 'Upstairs -' he said, running back to the library '- there's more light.' But Shirley-Anne lingered. Something wasn't right. When she came up, Gilmore was standing close to the window. He held each page up and a slow hardening came over him. 'It's faded.'

'I know.'

'This is it?' Gilmore whispered - 'this - is - it?'

Shirley-Anne stammered. In her adult mind she saw immediately that the letter had been exposed to sunlight - there could have been any number of reasons: '- it's been left out - Penelope exposed it to the sun when she was reading it - cheap paper - bleached - after years of being sealed - time - climate - '

'You said it was hidden -' Gilmore screamed '- hidden behind that fucking picture - that's what he told you? Isn't it? Isn't it?' Shirley-Anne was back to being small again and being nothing again and something fierce ignited inside again.

Butters was right. Severin's box of toys did touch Shirley-Anne but it was no game. Both Shirley-Anne and Severin felt something about mother's death that wasn't right and wouldn't let go and when they were still young enough to believe in magic, these small figures helped. They eased their fears. They helped them to believe that they were stronger than the monster within.

It was all about G.F Brille and how she died. G.F. Brille was not cut out to be a mother although at first she tried. The children bored her and she lived in hope that one day they'd go. Cordelia - being the first born - had a certain novelty value and for the first 18 months of her life, mother made an effort. The infant Cordelia saw in mother's eyes, some sign of life - enough to tell her that she was something. Enough to make her feel safe. But Shirley-Anne was different. When she was born, mother had nothing left. She looked at Shirley-Anne with blank eyes and where there should have been a happy child, a monster grew instead. When mother reached out to Shirley-Anne in the last minutes of her life - the monster came back. Mother choked and Shirley-Anne walked away. It felt right at the time.

But there was more.

Shirley-Anne grew afraid of this thing inside. Herself.

Severin - 4 years her junior - saw mother die. He knew. He watched Shirley-Anne from beneath the hall table and although it looked like he was too young to understand, he did. And it marked him, too. Did he do that? Would he get punished? Would it come back? Then came the game and the game eased their worries because no one was bad and everyone got rescued. It worked for a while.

Then came the birthday card. Severin was 49 years old, exhausted and half mad. There was nothing left to sacrifice and then the promise of a fortune landed. No longer making sense, he saw the hand of fate. This was the final test. He would divest himself of this inheritance - save his invalid sister - and his troubles would be over forever. Inside his head, it made sense.

But inside Shirley-Anne's head, it made no sense at all. Tea at the Ritz was a nightmare. Severin told her of his plans to make her happy and in short stride, he asked what she knew of their childhood. She was appalled.

Out of nowhere, Severin found a voice. How did mother die - I mean, really die? Shirley-Anne realised too late, the gift of the money was nothing compared to what Severin wanted in return. Things she'd thought were gone, were back. Empty eyes that said 'You are nothing' and deep down, the monster stirred. 'I am not nothing' it said back. 'I was never nothing.'

In the last year of his life, Severin was a desperate man. He put on a brave face - he told the Soup Kitchen about his grand plans - but Shirley-Anne's resistance made it hard and fear rippled. Did mother die because of him? Did he do something bad? What did he need to do to make it go away? Really, go away. Shirley-Anne feigned indifference. She told him she had no answers and finally she drew a knife and threatened to rip his throat out if he didn't leave her alone and that's when a beautiful clarity dawned.

There on the tow path, a week before he died - it came to her. She told Severin that if he really did want to know what happened to mother, she would show him. Yes, he said. Yes, he did - and after that he would leave her alone forever.

Gilmore screamed now. 'You're day dreaming - look at you -' he shook Shirley-Anne by the shoulders '- how did the light get to it?' and this was the moment when he should have kept quiet. But the scream and the flat eyes did it. He screamed 'you stupid little fool - you're nothing - nothing -' and she didn't need to hear that. She already knew that.

Shirley-Anne spun and sunk her nails into Gilmore's face. She bit. She kicked - this fierce thing inside would live. Gilmore stumbled back, pale. An age passed. When the ticking of the clock brought them back, Shirley-Anne was half lying on the couch. 'You came over faint, again.' Gilmore took her pulse. 'Robin, darling - your face - it's bleeding -'

He kept a measured tone. He picked up the pages again and walked to the window - 'can you trust him?' He looked across the square and saw no way out. He was in a room with a woman that frightened him and really there was no way out. 'How do you know this is it? How do you know he hasn't kept the real one, how do you know in a year or ten he won't be back?'

Shirley-Anne sat upright and quiet. She was a creature of the here and now, wasn't she? Isn't that all that mattered? Here? Now?

The clock ticked, time passed and neither knew what to do next. 'Time heals' she whispered. 'People forget.'

****

Out in Holland Park Avenue, Solomon Solomon hailed a taxi. He sat back with a bump and swayed with the traffic. He thought good thoughts about money and tax avoidance. It was something he did to pass the time. He was a rich man now and he had time.

He rested his hand on a small overnight bag on the seat beside him. It was white and empty except for memory. He kept it because you never know when you might need to carry something. That's what he told himself.

****

A mist came up and surrounded Tom. He was hot and it was cold.

'Open up Hamish.' It was 12.15 pm on Fuchsia and Wednesday and macaroni cheese, as usual. 'Open up for me - here it come. Nice yunch - wheeee.' He ached.

He was pinned down and going nowhere.

A voice - not his - called out from the mist and he called back 'who's there? Who are you?' The clatter of Fuchsia went on. Hard, sharp metal sounds and the ache in the mist went on. 'Come on naughty boy - you no eat you no get better. You want get better - you want go home, lovely boy.'

Home?

Christ.

'Here. Here. No cough. Swallow. Yah -' delicate fingers clamped his jaw shut.

The mist lifted. It was August again and Tom was back on Clapham Common with the fair and the horses running. Shirley-Anne was there on a chair with a knotted plastic bag full of blood.

'Eat up, lovely boy. Yah. No. No cough.'

The fair and the good times melted into the el Saoud and Tom looking out at the mist looking in. 'I know you. I know you' he screamed. 'You don't fool me. You've been following me for years.' Tom saw Sea View and Steven hog tied and choking. This was the last conscious memory Tom had of what happened - what really happened - before it ended.

Steven was a mess - back there in the fire. The smoke was black and poisonous and Tom's lungs burned. He dragged Steven and for a skinny man Steven was not light. Tom wanted to run but he didn't and he didn't know why. He still didn't know why. When he fell, Steven crawled back. He covered Tom with his body. It was all he had left.

Back on Fuchsia, the bright clatter went on and a bit of macaroni got stuck in Tom's throat. 'Yah. No. Leave him. He sleep it off. He going nowhere. Ha. Ha.' Tom was weak and the macaroni stayed and he stopped breathing. With oxygen draining, wild things flew up. It's not over yet, they sang - in a clean world there is a choice - there is always a choice. Come back. Come back. Shirley-Anne waved that wide wave above her head and Tom waved back - I am nothing without you he said, as if it mattered. The sun is still shining, she said - come back.

'I am nothing, without You.'

Then it faded. Someone was trying to breathe but couldn't. Someone was trying to move but couldn't.

'Who are You? Why are You following me - I am nothing - don't you get it? Nothing.'

'- nothing,' said the mist and the weight got heavier. Run, said the great far away - run to where the sun still shines - run - run to us - we are bright, right, light - run while you still can.

The mist was choking - 'Steven? Steve?'

'Run. It's a trap - don't - don't -'

What was it? What was it Tom felt?

'Steven -? I am here - reach out - show me your hand -' he reached into the mist and the mist reached into him.

'It's alright. I've got you,' he said and he grasped the hand of a broken man.

No time. No time at all, passed and the mist was gone.

Lifted.

Gone back to the Sea, like it never left.

At last.

The running was over.

End